Grea'nock

Grea'nock

The Tree of Two Worlds
and
The Shadows of Elvendom

The first book of the Grea'nock saga

James Ramey

Illustrations By
Ensign Dante' Marshall
Chief Petty Officer Krizgeorge Gonzales

iUniverse, Inc.
Bloomington

Grea'nock
The Tree of Two Worlds

iUniverse books may be ordered through booksellers or by contacting:

iUniverse
1663 Liberty Drive
Bloomington, IN 47403
www.iuniverse.com
1-800-Authors (1-800-288-4677)

Because of the dynamic nature of the Internet, any web addresses or links contained in this book may have changed since publication and may no longer be valid. The views expressed in this work are solely those of the author and do not necessarily reflect the views of the publisher, and the publisher hereby disclaims any responsibility for them.

Any people depicted in stock imagery provided by Thinkstock are models, and such images are being used for illustrative purposes only.

Certain stock imagery © Thinkstock.

ISBN: 978-1-4620-5948-5 (sc)
ISBN: 978-1-4620-5949-2 (hc)
ISBN: 978-1-4620-5950-8 (e)

Library of Congress Control Number: 2011918533

Printed in the United States of America

iUniverse rev. date: 11/18/2011

To Commander James Paul Lowell

For second chances when even gunners need a hero.

To my wife and beautiful children

You are my every reason for doing anything in this world.

To FC1 (SW) Kevin Lagreca

You are the true savior of Hillsborough.

Special thanks to Jeannine Ramey (EPM),

YN2 Madison Jonas,

and GM3 Landon Yazzie "Wind Talker"

If you feel that you can no longer make a difference in the world, then make a different world.

Prologue

❖ ❖ ❖

Grea'nock. The word used to mean green rock and was the word for the way the world was. Those were the beginning days of the world. Those were the days when the first evil, called Dagoth, and his servants arrived in the world. Those were the days when the four houses of immortals came to war with Dagoth. Those were the days when the warrior smith, a mortal man called Kingsteel, defeated Dagoth. Those days have gone.

Kingsteel grew old and passed away. The might of his blood became lost in the long years that followed. The four houses grew small and secretive and showed their might no more in the world. The cities of men and dwarfs grew into vast empires and turned against each other with greed.

The great fortress cities of old were then torn down, and civilization began to balance on the edge of ruin. Then there came those who paved new roads out of the rubble to new places. They began to make cities away from the war and greed that had ruined the last place. There they live today on the edge of the wild in a world reborn from ashes.

Grea'nock—the word used to mean green rock and the way the world was. Now it means time lost and the way the world will never be again.

Table of Contents

Part 1

◆ ◆ ◆

Tree of Two Worlds

Chapter 1

❖ ❖ ❖

Hillsborough

The mountains—there was something about them that comforted the people who lived nearby, though the range had become as quiet as the grave due to the lack of dwarven industry, and haunting voices echoed from peak to peak amid the winter storms. Still, those living near their base saw them as a lasting structure of security. Unlike the fortress cities of old, the mountains were pure and indestructible. "No army will ever pull those walls down," many of the old-timers would say.

Here at the base of the Northridge Mountains lay the gentle foothills of the township of Hillsborough. The wealth of the foothills of Northridge was in the trees, from the evergreens of the higher slopes to the municipal orchards that lay south of the town. The town of Hillsborough grew as rich in people as it did in lumber- and fruit-bearing trees in the several generations following its founding.

The men of the mountains, or Mountainfolk, were the first to live here. Giant-like and incredibly strong, these hardy folk were among the very few capable of living among the giant yews of the highest northern slopes. The smaller yet more ferocious Hillmen who lived and hunted throughout the barren hills to the east also came to trade among the townsfolk of Hillsborough.

Then there were the Vanguard. They were the descendants of the people who populated the great fortress cities that used to dot the land. They were the largest in number in the town yet were smaller and weaker than their wild cousins. However, among men they possessed the greatest knowledge of industry and considered themselves the upper crust of society.

But it was the dwarfs of this region who were considered by most to be the real high society. Although few and far between, dwarfs who lived among the peoples of Hillsborough had become synonymous with convenience and innovation.

The most mysterious of all were those descendants of immortals and men who still walked openly in the world. These half-elves and Quadrian elves lived and traded quietly among the people of Hillsborough.

The town itself, sitting on top of the broadest foothill of Northridge, was walled in by a large square of blue granite. Each home of Hillsborough was made of the same granite as the protecting wall, and the streets were paved in the same.

The farming folk of Hillsborough worked the orchards to the south yet still enjoyed the protection of the walled town, staying safe from the wild. There were, of course, those who lived among the wilds of the green world. These people only ever came to Hillsborough to trade. This sort was never well liked or trusted within the walls of the town. This sort never really cared for the trust of the sheltered folk and never will.

Chapter 2

◇ ◇ ◇

An Unlikely Meeting

A wide gravel path begins out the south side of Hillsborough through the wall's only gate. This path leads south down the hill and through the first of many municipal orchards. When the gravel gives way to dirt, this is called the Green Path.

Lumbering up the Green Path on a late afternoon day in early autumn, there came a large man of the Mountainfolk. "Boy" would be more accurate, being as he was only sixteen years of age. He was a man in size alone. His movement was aided by a large iron rod, nearly as tall as he was, that he took everywhere with him. He was limping from a childhood injury that had never quite healed and was dressed in soot-covered clothes. He was wearing gray torn work clothes under a brown apprentice tabard. Wearing a tabard was an outdated tradition, but his employer, Kreg, insisted he wear it. Kreg had taken him in after his parents had died.

His name was Erik. Because of the giant walking stick, he was called Erik the Rod, or just Rod for short. Due to his injury and a healthy appetite, coupled with the fact that he was of the Mountainfolk, Erik was enormous. Not only was he very tall and muscular, but he also had a large belly and a round face that made his eyes squint.

On this day, the blossoming apple and peach trees were shedding their petals and giving off a sweet scent. The petals painted the deep green path with wisps of pastel colors that shifted slightly with each breeze.

Erik was red in the face, huffing and puffing his way up the green path toward Hillsborough. He was carefully cradling a wreath of blue plum blossoms, the rarest and finest flowers known in that region. He was to present the gift to the girl of his dreams, Gayle Fletcher. She was a raven-headed Vanguard who lived in town. Only a year older than Erik, she was already regarded as one of Hillsborough's finest archers. Erik knew blue was her favorite color and thought the wreath of flowers would make a good present before he asked her to the harvest dance in the town hall later that year. With considerable effort, he made it to the south gate only to be greeted by the unkind voice of his employer, the smith, Kreg.

"There you are, you miserable heap! Where have you been? Not gathering wood for the smithy, I see. Instead you're out picking flowers?" Said Kreg as he came stomping from around the other side of the gate.

"We have plenty of wood for weeks of work, especially now that there is another smith in town," replied Erik.

Kreg's face contorted into an enraged mask. Erik knew that he did not like being reminded that there was a new smith in town—let alone a dwarven family.

"Do I need the word of an apprentice to tell me how to run my forge?" bellowed Kreg at Erik.

Kreg was also of the Mountainfolk, although not nearly as large or strong as Erik. He was instead cruel and strong-willed. He was a sight of frightening measure when he was angry, and he had beaten Erik in public many times. Now he was very angry. His black hair was dirty and matted, and a beard streaked his murderous face. He was wearing only his smithing apron atop his trousers and black, steel shank boots. His hammer in the hand, he drew back, but he was halted.

"Hold, Kreg! You are to move this argument out of the gateway, or I'll clap you in the stocks for my own amusement!" said a stern voice.

It was the captain of the gate guard, Dregor, a Hillman by birth, but raised a Vanguard family. Dregor was much smaller and of slighter build than Kreg. His bronze hair was pulled back into a ponytail, revealing a weathered but thoughtful face of tanned, almost leathery skin. His beard was braided and beaded in the dwarven fashion, and his piercing blue eyes gave him a fierce appearance. Clad in dwarven forged mail from spaulders to boots, with a long sword at his side, he gave anyone who looked his way the feeling that he meant business.

"My apologies, Lord Dregor," Kreg responded. "Where would we be without you here to protect us from apple thieves?"

Erik smiled at Dregor and had turned to continue toward the Fletchers' place when Kreg's foot caught him at the ankles, and over he fell, crushing the wreath beneath him. His iron prop clamored loudly on the cobblestones and rolled away.

"Serves you right, you worthless heap," said Kreg. "If you want to spend the day picking flowers, then you can earn your keep selling them in the square for copper because I'll not have you!" Dregor came forward, fingering the pommel of his blade. Seeing Dregor's approach, Kreg withdrew and headed off toward the Grey Ram, the town's only pub.

Erik picked himself up slowly, not believing what had just happened until he drew his left hand out from underneath him. The wreath he produced was a mess of crushed flowers and broken limbs as he rocked back to his knees. It was all he could do to keep from screaming at the top of his lungs. His face went red, and he started to shake. Kneeling on the side of the street, as the ox-drawn carts left through the south gate, Erik slung his apprentice tabard to the ground with a roar. He was picking himself up and looking for his staff when Dregor took him by the arm and lifted him the rest of the way to his feet. With his other hand, Dregor returned Erik's staff.

"On your feet, boy. Don't let that dung-heap of a smith burden you a day longer. I am tired of watching him abuse you," said Dregor.

"How will I make a living? Where will I live? Gayle won't want to dance or even speak with a fat, homeless cripple!" replied Erik while turning his head from side to side.

"You, who can barely walk, risked life and limb in the wilds to find a truly rare gift, just for a girl, when you could have sold these for a week's worth of wages. This girl would appreciate that if she had any sense," answered Dregor.

"What of the rest of it then, captain? I would be a thoughtful but homeless and fat cripple," stated Erik.

"I can take care of that!" said Dregor as he produced a key and a large coin purse from a satchel on his belt. He handed them to Erik.

Erik took them, unsure of the meaning of this gesture.

"The key," said Dregor, "is to the southeast corner guard's post. There you can stay as long as you like. It is not much, but fine for a bachelor's life. The purse is a gift of sorts. It should be enough for you to eat and drink on for months. Should you need more, you should head to the Grey Ram this evening. Many of the tradesmen spend supper there and talk amongst each other for extra help. You may not find another master to apprentice under, but at least there may be some odd jobs for honest coin."

Erik's eyes widened in disbelief. "I can do a few things with ordinary arms but I can not mend stone or even your fancy armor," said Erik.

"I guess I will go to your competition for that—and I don't mean Kreg. He is finished in this town, especially with what he is charging for his labor. The dwarf will have all his business within the month," replied Dregor.

Erik smiled. "I can't believe something good is actually happening to me."

Dregor laughed and said firmly, "It's been overdue and I am sure you have questions as to why I have done this but I will explain later Go enjoy your moment. I recommend the Grey Ram." Looking thoughtfully at the crushed wreath on the ground, Dregor bent down and plucked an uncrushed flower from the wreckage and handed it to Erik. "But first," he continued, "take what is left of that wreath to the Apothecary. Be sure not to let the blossoms fall. They are still quite valuable even in this state."

Erik, still trying to wrap his mind around what had just happened, stooped down, grabbed the wreath, and hobbled off. Dregor, smiling, shook his head and resumed his duties.

- - -

THERE WAS A LOUD CLANG at the doorway of the Apothecary as Erik entered, smacking his staff against the doorframe accidentally.

Kristia looked up from a well-portioned pile of various ingredients she had just chopped to see a very large, rather confused Mountainfolk stumbling through her door. Kristia was a kindly silver-haired widow. She still ran the shop in her husband's absence. It was her charge to daily prepare all medicines needed for use at the hospital, as well as any other remedy any paying customers might need.

"Hello, Erik," she said, genuinely surprised to see him. Erik just stood there blinking for a second. Then he held up the crushed wreath. Kristia hurried forward with a joyful squeak. She quickly grabbed the wreath and began to clip the crushed blossoms off into a large mortar. "You're a fine young man to bring this here for medicine and not waste it on some foolish girl. You will be paid a fine price," said Kristia as she hurried to a nearby drawer. She grasped a small stack of gold and silver coins and thrust them into Erik's hand. "Now be off, young man! This infusion will take complete concentration on my part." Erik nodded and left without question.

— — —

ERIK WONDERED WHAT HIS LIFE would be like on his own, free from that tyrant Kreg. He would have a hard time filling his own days with back-breaking labor.

He was now nearing the Grey Ram as the sun was setting. The last light of day painted the blue granite red. Above the double doors of the Grey Ram, which stayed propped open at night to attract patronage, the granite blocks were carved in the image of a ram thrusting a mug of ale from left to right across the doorway. Erik always found this image amusing.

The doors opened as Erik approached. It was the barkeep, Jared, and his brother, John, propping the doors open for the night. After wedging the door open, Jared looked up and in a pleasant, yet businesslike tone, greeted Erik. "Hello, big fellow, come on in—have a roasted ram shank and sit a while!" Erik smiled and hobbled in with the sound of his staff beating the pavement.

Not two seconds after Erik walked in, Kreg arose from a table in the corner and approached, shouting, "Shouldn't you be selling flowers, you ungrateful heap of—" Before he could finish, he was effortlessly knocked to the ground by Erik's outstretched left arm. Kreg hit the ground with a groan and rocked back on his arms to see Erik towering above him.

"I no longer work for you, Kreg. Should you come near me again, I will put you down," Erik threatened in his most menacing tone. Seeing that his threat had little effect on Kreg, who was naturally skeptical as to whether Erik had the capability to finish him or the money to pay for the burial (which is the law), Erik then smashed the table Kreg was lying beside to splinters with one heavy stroke of his rod. Kreg's eyes widened as he skittered backward and away from his former ward.

Jared yelped, "Erik! Tables are made from trees, but do not grow on them. You will have to pay for that!" Erik turned and approached the bar at the back of the lamp-lit tavern and slapped down a stack of gold that would pay for the table many times over. Jared understood his meaning and said aloud for everyone to hear, "That is far too much. This amount would pay for a proper burial."

Erik looked back at Kreg and said, "Well, since I do not want to offend the towns guards, especially since Kreg has been overcharging them for his services, make it a round for these who serve and a ram shank for supper."

The half-dozen or so guardsmen let out a cheer to help goad Kreg, whose eyes now glinted with rage as he took his hammer from his belt.

"You're not going to use that in your condition, are you?" said a youthful voice from what seemed to be a smaller man in the doorway.

No eye in the tavern had beheld him before now. Dressed in a sleeveless leather jerkin over a gray wool sweater that came halfway down his arms, he additionally wore a large knotted hide belt, off which hung two beautifully decorated scabbards for the elvish-style short swords resting in them. His light brown trousers were tucked into finely crafted boots of land drake hide. This person was obviously a professional adventurer, or else a rich man looking to get robbed or murdered. His locks of dark brown hair were flecked with silver and tucked back behind long pointed ears. The luminous star fire in his dazzling blue eyes left no doubt that he was an elf.

"Elfling, are you old enough to be here or even away from your mother?" jeered Kreg.

The man answered plainly. "Your eyes deceive you, child. I am much older than any hag you could have crawled out of."

Kreg spun into an immediate rage and with a leap forward swung the hammer meant for Erik at the strange man. The man quickly ducked under the blow, tumbling into the middle of the room. He sprang up to his feet with blades drawn. He then asked aloud, "Is this man a public servant?"

One of the nearby guards replied, "No. He is a member of questionable standing with the trades guild. Will you duel, or shall we intervene?" The stranger watched Kreg approach, preparing another swing with his large smithing hammer.

As soon as Kreg came close enough to strike, Jase smiled and said coldly, "Duel."

What happened next was almost too quick for the eye to manage, and those who saw it were left dumb and blinking for some time before Stephan, the senior guard present, said, "I'll get Dregor."

In two blinding motions, the stranger had severed Kreg's arm that was wielding his hammer, while at the same time decapitating him with the other blade. He then plunged both blades into Kreg's quivering torso before his legs gave way. Kreg fell over in his favorite word—a heap.

With his blades still sticking out of Kreg's corpse, the stranger leaped over the body and proceeded to the bar. He took a stool next to where Erik was standing, as the latter man's mouth hung open in amazement. The patrons of the tavern, all now terrified with the exception of the guards, began leaving. Duels were not illegal but were still rare with in the walls, and only seldom did they ever end in a death.

John was doing his best to clean up the mess now that the guards had taken the pieces of Kreg outside. John looked pale and ill, but for some reason, Erik could not take his eyes off the blood. Jared was furious. "You can't expect to be welcome here after killing one patron and frightening off the others!" screamed Jared, who was standing right across the bar from the stranger.

Erik snapped out of his trance and said, "That's enough, Jared. I will pay for your lost business tonight, and besides, the guards will want to drink and talk about this one tonight!"

The stranger raised his right pointer finger and said, "Indeed, but no need. Keep your gold. I have some of my own fine metal," From underneath this jerkin he produced a small bar of smooth white metal and laid it on the table. "There you are. That will, of course, cover a healthy tab as well."

Jared picked it up and looked at it skeptically. "Way too heavy to be silver. What is this well-polished steel?"

The stranger shook his head in disbelief and said, "Has dwarven industry become only legend? That's platinum you're holding."

"What in green hell is plate'em?" barked Jared.

"True silver," said a rough voice from behind. They all turned their attention to the middle of the room to see Dregor standing there frowning, and the town's new dwarven blacksmith smiling next to him.

The blacksmith was dressed in brown leather work clothes and was covered in soot. His wetted and braided beard was tucked under his smithing apron. "Grimhold is my name," said the smith as he handed the stranger back his beautiful and freshly cleaned single-edged swords.

"Jase is mine," the stranger replied as he sheathed his swords. He then produced a finely cut jewel from his trouser pocket and handed it to the dwarf.

Grimhold examined it half a moment and gave out a hoot. "I'm at your service, Mister Jase!"

"And I yours, Esquire Grimhold," said Jase.

"What the green hell is true silver there, Grim?" blurted Jared.

Grimhold took Jared aside and explained while Dregor approached Jase looking genuinely angry. "You had better have more riches for fines and burials, or you'll be in the stocks, boy!" said Dregor.

Jase's eyes narrowed. He did not like being called a boy, being that he was several times Dregor's age, for sure. He restrained himself and answered, "I do, and more, Good Captain," Jase held out his hand and dropped three large gems into Dregor's hand. There brilliance was dazzling even in the dim lantern light. The stones made the area around the men dance with spectral lights.

Dregor's eye widened. "Treasures of an ancient world," he said softly. After a moment, Dregor came to his senses, and beckoning Grimhold, he asked, "Good dwarf, are these glass?"

Grimhold and Jase laughed in unison.

"Perhaps I should know the joke too," Dregor said in earnest.

Grimhold, still laughing, said, "Glass can't have such a luster. It doesn't polish that fine or show that fire or light within. The light in here won't tell a man's eye these things, of course. You're holding a changeling chrysoberyl and two blue elf stones that only they can fashion!"

Dregor's eyes dazzled over the gems in his hands. "How much are they worth?" Dregor asked. "I mean to say, will they cover the dueling fine and the burial?"

Grimhold stroked his braided beard and sighed. "How much is something you just can't find anymore worth?" he asked. Grimhold then went on to say, "As to your second question—yes. If Jase killed one hundred men and wanted to build a monument praising his victory, those stones would cover the cost. Just wait until the dwarf trade caravans come east to visit at harvest. You will get your money for them."

Dregor composed himself and announced in his most officious tone, "The duel between Kreg the Smith and the traveler Jase has come to a legal end!" Dregor put the stones in the pouch on his belt and, after speaking with the off-duty guards who were still present, departed suddenly.

Grimhold turned to Jase and nodded. There was something about Jase that Grimhold liked apart from his obvious generosity. *There is a bit of the old world about him*, Grimhold thought or perhaps said quietly in a hushed tone. Grimhold then said, "Now that I have a lovely new jewel of my own, I will go make something pretty for the wife!"

Jared waved as Grimhold left the tavern. Jared turned toward Jase and apologized, saying, "It seems as though this bar you have given me is worth six times its weight in gold, so you will be eating and drinking here free of charge for quite some time," Jase nodded in acknowledgement and ordered a glass of wine.

Erik finally worked up the courage to say something to the much smaller killing machine standing to his right. "So… Mr. Jase, are you elvish?" asked Erik.

Jase turned and looked up at him as he said, "Goodness! You're a big one, much larger than even the other Mountainfolk! I thought you were standing on something!"

Erik just shrugged. By this time, he was used to being larger than everyone and thought nothing of it. Erik's clumsiness and limp kept him from being considered physically imposing. Erik answered, "Only my feet, sir."

Jase looked to the floor for a moment and then replied, "I am a Quadrian elf—that means one of my parents was a half-elf, before you ask."

Erik's brow wrinkled as he though for a moment and said, "There are too few elves around these parts, in my opinion—although I believe one works at the hospital here in town."

Jase sat quietly for a moment and then said, "That would be Irilia, half-elven of the house of Feyara', I believe."

"You know her?" asked Jared and Erik at once.

"Yes, I knew her parents. They fell in the siege of the last fortress city. I brought her and a few others up this way away from the war shortly after," answered Jase.

Erik couldn't figure the number exactly but was certain that had been at least three hundred years ago. Erik stirred uncomfortably for a moment before asking, "So how long do Quadrian elves live anyway?"

Jase, clearly amused by the question, answered, "If I should ever find out, I will send word to your descendants, my friend," Jase took a sip of his wine and said, "You are not drinking, big fellow?"

"No, I saw what a mess it made of Kreg at the end of the day, and I am clumsy enough without spirits."

Jase raised his eyebrows as he thought to himself how Kreg really did end up in a mess at the end of this day and gave out a half laugh. Erik asked for a cup of water only, and Jared quickly produced it and set it on the bar.

Jase's sharp eyes then caught what Erik and Jared's did not. As Erik reached for his cup of water, it moved ever so slightly into his grasp. Jase's eyes narrowed as he said, "Well, Erik—you did not ask me the obvious question, which is why I am here in the first place."

Erik sat down the pewter cup and said politely, "So, Mr. Jase, what brings you to Hillsborough?"

Jase answered simply, "I am on somewhat of an adventure!"

They all laughed together. Erik thought that the day had been adventurous enough and that he was just being humorous.

As soon as Jase had stopped laughing, he looked Erik dead in the eyes and said coldly, "You coming?"

Chapter 3

◈ ◈ ◈

Getting a Group

E rik and Jared both fell instantly silent. Erik said quietly, almost to himself, "I have not even asked Gayle yet."

"That's the spirit," said Jase. "The more the merrier!"

Jase hopped off his stool, spun around, and declared, "This will be the moment that changes everything. Meet me in the town square just after midday. I have to see to the rest of the group." Jase then left as suddenly as he had arrived.

Erik, still not believing his ears, paused before saying at last, "I wonder if he knew I meant to say no?"

Jared shook his head and replied, "He doesn't seem the sort of fellow that takes no for an answer."

Erik sighed. So much had happened that he had not taken the time to visit the Fletchers yet. "Well, I need some rest. Tomorrow will be a strange one. I can tell," said Erik. Jared nodded and bid Erik farewell and a good night as Erik exited the Ram. Erik began to wonder how he was going to tell Gayle about this adventure, or even if he was going himself. After a short moment of thinking over it, Erik decided that he would go and was relieved that he would no longer have to look for work.

By the time Erik had labored his way to the southeast corner guard post, he could think of no reason not to go. He fumbled for the key to the post and then inserted it into the heavy lock on the door. The door opened with a loud snap as he turned the key. The dead bolt aside, he swung the door open.

Everything was dark inside, but in the moonlight, he could make out what looked to be a bunk in the corner. He entered, shutting the door behind using his staff. He then felt for the edge of the bunk, propped his staff up against the wall, and collapsed with a great thud onto the floor, and missing the bunk collapsed with a great thud onto the floor. Too tired to move for the moment, he fell asleep until morning.

He was awakened by the light of day in the room, its pale beams coming in through the small windows high in the back wall, opposite the door. Erik pushed himself up onto his knees and surveyed the room. To his left, the bunk, which he had missed the night before, had clothing laid out on it. Beyond the head of the bed was a basin and yewer with a towel folded on its edge and a razor resting on it. To his right and against the back wall there was a desk; on it he saw a note written on some rough parchment, next to a lovely golden broach in the shape of a large plum blossom with blue enameling. Erik was intrigued. After he struggled to his feet, he pulled the small stool from underneath the desk and sat down to read the note.

> *Erik,*
>
> *There are a few things you should know now that I have time to explain them. First, it was the council's decision to run Kreg out of town for unlawful business practices. Fate had other plans. The council also decided that this would be your residence until you come into your own trade and make a family. Now, as you know, your parents died in the same accident that gave you your limp. However, before you mother passed away, there were some things she wanted you to have. I have kept them until now, knowing that Kreg would take them or ruin them out of spite. The clothes were your father's, who was even larger than you, so they should fit. The broach is your mother's. Keep it well. The money I gave you yesterday was theirs as well. I will*

give you a word of caution now that you are your own to command. I
have heard tales of Jase coming and going in the past. Yet, the people
who leave with him seldom return. Stay safe, Erik the Rod.
   Sincerely,
   Dregor

Erik was happy to learn that he had something from his parents. He missed the days he had shared with his family. The heirlooms made him feel less alone in the world.

He took off his old work clothes, which were little more than rags now, and washed at the basin. He then shaved and trimmed the edges of his beard. He was delighted to have a razor and a basin. Kreg had never allowed him to have the things to groom properly. He then dressed in the clothes left for him, some large black trousers and an off-white undershirt, as well as an enormous braided leather belt and a dark leather vest with wooden toggles. They all fit perfectly. He didn't know how he looked as he sat on the bunk to put on his boots, but he felt great. Then as he bent over to tie the boots, he noticed there was something in the pocket of the vest. He put his hand in his right front pocket and pulled out a heavy gold chain, with a large, vicious-looking silvery tooth hanging from it. Erik shrugged and put it on without thinking.

He stood up confidently without the aid of his prop and let out a great breath of air. "Ahhh, I feel like my father's son today," he said with a smile. Looking down at the bunk, he noticed that it was covered not with a standard bearskin blanket but instead with a large cloak. He snatched it up, twirled it around his neck, fastened its clasp, and threw it back over his shoulders. "Well, Dad, you were sharply dressed Mountainfolk," said Erik. He grabbed his staff and left for the town square, locking the door behind him.

Now, beaming with confidence, he began to wonder whether most Mountainfolk could afford to dress this well. Perhaps if they were successful trappers, or of great standing in their family. *I have to ask Dregor more when I see him again*, Erik thought to himself. Erik greeted all whom he passed with a smile that people took notice of, being that Erik had been a shy young man until now.

Erik knew that Gayle sometimes set up shop for her father in the square. There she would set up a target and sport as a demonstration of their goods. The Fletchers were also bowyers and archers and nearly all decent hunters as well. Gayle did not hunt, but she knew all the other crafts of her family's trade. She was known best in Hillsborough as an archer.

As Erik approached the town's square, he saw that she had indeed set up a target and a cart full of goods. A small gathering of young men and women was present, all admiring her for different reasons. The senior town guardsman, Stephan, was also there.

Anytime business was done in the town's square, guards were present to deter would-be thieves. Other carts were now arriving as well, peddling different goods, mostly skins and different fruits. It would be a busy day in the square.

Erik approached Gayle's cart just as she finished loosening the last of five arrows at her target at the other end of the square. The small crowed clapped in appreciation. Her aim was excellent, all her arrows stuck in the intersection of the cross. The girls of Hillsborough admired her because instead of wearing a skirt and working at the hospital or a kitchen or as a seamstress, she was a trouser-wearing, adventurous girl. She was good enough to give the towns guardsman archery lessons. The young men liked her because she was tough, shapely of body, and very attractive.

Erik looked at her in awe. She too was wearing a leather tunic, but with a short-sleeved undershirt that showed off her muscular arms, on which she wore bracers and gloves for archery. She was currently giving a blond-haired Vanguard teenager named Jordan an archery lesson. Jordan was Erik's chief rival for Gayle's affections, in Erik's mind. However, neither was Gayle's fancy at the time. However at that moment neither had caught Gayle's eye.

Erik's presence was immediately noticed by Stephan. "Hello, Eric the Rod. You're looking like a chief among men today," said Stephan loudly. The small crowd turned its attention toward Erik, and the younger children started stroking his bearskin cloak.

Gayle turned too, and her eyes became as round as coins. "Erik?" she said, not sure of herself.

Erik smiled. "It is I."

Jordan interrupted the greeting by saying, "Well, if you are here to ask her to the dance, I have already beaten you to it, and she said yes. So why don't you find some great troll of a mountain girl to court?"

Gayle grew red in the face, clearly unhappy with Jordan's venomous tone.

"Jordan, the only thing you'll beat me to is a swift trip to the cobblestones if you upset me further," growled Erik.

"Indeed," Jordan mocked, "with the guard standing close at hand and my father on the council, you'll be beaten and in the stocks in a flash."

Erik paused. He had forgotten he was dealing with a wealthy coward who would never put himself in harm's way. "You're not worth the effort, little one. I am here to ask you a question, Gayle," said Erik grimly.

"Go ahead," said Gayle. "However, I have agreed to the dance with Jordan," she added.

"I care not," said Erik coldly and convincingly.

Gayle looked surprised for a quick moment but then composed herself and awaited Erik's question.

"My partner Jase and I are going on an adventure," said Erik. The surrounding people laughed. Erik continued unconcerned. "I thought a person with your skill would make a fine addition to the group."

Gayle seemed skeptical yet pleased and asked, "Where? To do what?"

Erik stopped for a moment and then said quickly, "We will discuss that on the road if you agree to come with us."

"Who is 'us'?" blurted Jordan. "There is just one overdressed cripple trying to seduce Ms. Gayle."

Jase, who had been listening from a ways off, approached and said, "So there is my wizard. Did you get our archer?"

Erik nodded and pointed at Gayle. She blushed and said, "So you're a wizard, Erik?"

"He will be soon enough. He has the gift. But as for you, I wanted an expert archer, not a woman child. But I guess if Erik vouches for you, you are acceptable to me," answered Jase.

"Excuse me?" Gayle yelled at Jase. Gayle grabbed her favorite bow from the cart.

Stephan stepped forward and said, "Hold there, will be no duel here. Jase has already killed a blacksmith. Let's keep this peaceful."

Gayle answered, "He must be a great archer indeed if he can insult me while at my place of business. You better be willing to prove you are a master with a bow. I'll wage ten gold scales you are not."

Jase smiled. "I am not," he said as he withdrew ten gold scales from a coin purse on his belt and laid them on the side of her cart.

Gayle took the gold and put it in her purse and said, "I thought as much."

Jase smiled again. "But I am better than any of you!" he boasted. Jase took a small bow from the cart and shoved Jordan aside. He then looked back at Gayle.

Gayle laughed. "This will be fun for me—and expensive for you, Jase." She produced two full quivers with different colored fletching and approached Jase. Gayle motioned to her brother Darren to clear the target.

"Red," Jase said. She handed him the red-feathered quiver, which he immediately shouldered. "Rules?" Jase asked.

"From the quiver, draw, shoot—no pauses," Gayle answered.

Jase turned his head to look Gayle in the eye and said, "If I win, you come with us. Agreed?"

Gayle smiled and replied, "Agreed—but I keep the gold. Now take your shot."

Jase, still looking Gayle in the eye, drew and shot an arrow with incredible speed. Gayle whipped her head toward the target just as her brother called out, "Dead center!"

Gayle's mouth hung open. *There is no way he is that good!* she thought.

"Take your shot, my lady," Jase prodded. The crowd was now quiet in disbelief. Gayle drew and loosened an arrow with great speed, but she was no match for Jase.

"One notch below dead center!" called Darren.

"A fine shot!" said Jase as he released another two arrows with amazing speed.

There was a pause from Darren before he called back, "Both the first arrows split!"

Gayle, attempting to match Jase's blinding speed, rapidly drew and shot two arrows toward the target, the first of which struck high on the cross and the second of which flew alarmingly far to the left. There was no answer from Darren, only a loud cry of pain. Darren, so confident in his sister's aim, had not taken cover as she shot and had been struck in the lower abdomen by her second arrow.

Gayle screamed and dropped her bow as she sprang forward toward her brother, as did many from the crowd who had been watching.

Jase walked up to Erik, who looked angrily down at him. Erik poked Jase in the chest and barked, "Was that necessary?"

Jase cocked an eyebrow. "I assume you can use that hand with only three fingers?" he asked. Erik stepped back, but Jase closed the distance and said, "In a word, yes—it was necessary. She would not have gone otherwise. Now, she will. She thought she was something extraordinary. Now she doesn't. She would have seen you as beneath her. Now she won't. Do not question me, boy. Although I used the word beforehand jokingly you are not a wizard yet!"

Erik apologized. He understood that it was the romantic desire inside him that made it difficult to see Gayle upset. Erik looked toward the target and saw Gayle and a few other townsfolk beginning to carry Darren toward the hospital.

Erik said back to Jase, "It does not seem she is going anywhere now with her brother so injured."

"Don't be so sure, but it is not our concern now," answered Jase coldly.

Jase looked around at the market that was now filling with people and more merchants and advised Erik to buy a large pack and fill it with provisions. He would do the same, and they would meet back at the cart in an hour.

Soon, they were fully packed for the long journey on foot and met back at the Fletchers' cart. Nearby, a fight was breaking out between two trappers over stolen pelts.

Erik looked around and said, "Well, it's just us then, I guess. Shall we be off, Mr. Jase?"

Jase paused then answered, "No and yes. There is one more, but we will meet him on the road. Let us leave now while this brawl has everyone's attention."

Chapter 4

◈ ◈ ◈

The Road South

Erik and Jase departed amid the turmoil in the street and found their way to the south gate. As they approached the gate Erik struggling to keep up asked "Mr. Jase you said I am to be our wizard. Were you just trying to impress Gayle or do I really have the gift?"

Jase not willing to take his eyes off the guards answered softly "No and yes. However, now is not the time for your instruction."

The guards at the moment seemed more concerned with reinforcing the guards at the town square than with manning the gates. The two passed through the south gate unnoticed. There just beyond its threshold, they saw Gayle wearing a gray woolen cloak and leading a giant ram by a harness. The animal already had many goods packed on his back already. Erik and Jase threw their packs on as well. The animal took the extra burden with no complaint. This breed of ram was truly monstrous, and the animal could look Jase straight in the eyes. However, the animal also seemed very even tempered and strong. "Some folk even learn to ride these," said Jase as he scratched the ram behind the ears and added, "An excellent ram!"

Gayle smiled and replied, "His name is Rammy."

Erik laughed and said, "Well, that's a well-named ram!"

Gayle snapped back at him, "Don't make fun. I was three when I named him, and it's what he answers to."

"So you have decided to join us then, Gayle?" asked Erik.

"What choice do I have now? Face my parents after having shot my brother in a contest for some extra coin? I have also damaged my reputation as a marksman as well as the quality of my family's goods," answered Gayle as she went red in the face.

It seemed to Erik that Gayle was caught somewhere in the sea of shame and anger over the contest.

"No, I think I'll spend some time on the road and let this day fade from memory," she added in a somewhat more cheerful tone.

Jase turned to Gayle and Erik both and said, "Well the road south from here is pleasant for many miles. It is good for forgetting things as well," Jase looked to have a pleasant expression, but to Gayle and Erik both his words seemed full of sorrow. Jase then turned and began to walk south at a quick pace.

It was late summer, and the best fruits were starting to ripen. All the wine and jam fruits were being collected. Now came the very best produce that the Hillsborough people traded, consumed, and sold for harvest. The municipal farmers would stop any thieves easily enough, but they took no notice of the occasional hungry traveler. The great wild rams would come south and feast on fallen fruit and become fattened and ready for culling. The sweet smell of the trees perfumed the summer air as the breeze licked the hillsides. It was truly a pleasant walk south. For many hours into the late afternoon, no one spoke a word. The walk was a moving meditation on a world at peace with itself.

At last, Erik remembered something. "You said we would meet someone on the road, didn't you?" said Erik, looking in Jase's direction.

Jase nodded as he replied, "Yes, indeed. A mighty and reckless hunter. A fine addition to the party, even if we are likely to hear him before we see him."

Gayle laughed and said, "If he doesn't make quiet of himself in the wild, he isn't much good as a hunter."

Jase also laughed, as one amused and Indignant. "Young girl, his prey does not hide, move in silence, or run when set upon."

Just as Jase finished his ominous statement, a great howl tore through the summer's quiet serenity. Gayle grabbed her bow from her ram's back and plunged two arrows lightly in the path in front of her. Jase shook his head and pointed at Rammy. "Do wolves frighten your beast?" he asked.

Just then, another howl from what sounded like the father of all wolves erupted thunderously in the air about them. Gayle looked at her ram and saw that he was perfectly still even though her own heart was pounding in her chest. Yet a third howl came rampaging from some unknown corner of the orchards and seemed to come at them from every angle.

Erik, who was almost paralyzed in fear, finally croaked out, "It's in the trees!"

Suddenly in front of them, from the great tree hanging over the path, a figure dropped down like a lightning bolt to the ground below. The earth was thrown back for several feet in every direction from the impact. The figure rose from a kneeling position. Gayle in alarm shot the arrow she had drawn back. It flew several feet, too high, and landed somewhere on the path ahead. Jase stretched out his arm and lowered her bow. Then the figure approached. It was a Hillman.

His shoulders were covered by the flayed heads of two wolves, part of the fine gray wolf-skin cape that flowed out behind him. Underneath, he was clad collar to mid-thigh in the icy blue, shimmering hide of a cold mountain drake, under which his black trousers were tucked into boots of land drake hide, of the same make as Jase's.

Erik's panic passed. Jase and the Hillman could have been cousins. The stranger possessed the same pleasant, youthful features and skin, undamaged by time or the elements. Yet there was no elvish star fire in this man's eyes, nor did he have pointed ears. There was, however, something wild about him instead.

His brown and gray hair was braided at his temples and decorated with large tribal beads of carved bone. The rest of his hair was wavy and hung freely about his shoulders. On one side of his massive silver-buckled belt hung a whip, on the other the scabbard of what could only be a long Kris blade sword. The long Kris blade sword was the traditional weapon of the Hillman dragon hunter.

Jase smiled and greeted the man loudly. "Fenrix!"

Erik couldn't believe his ears. Fenrix was a name he had heard as a child. Erik recalled what he had heard about a dragon-hunting Hillman with the head of a wolf. "You're real!" Erik gasped.

Fenrix nodded, a blank look on his face as he asked, "Why wouldn't I be?"

Erik measured the words in his mind carefully before he spoke. He did not want to offend a man whom he had thought to be a legend until ten seconds ago. Erik said, "Well, sir, I have heard that Hillmen hunted drakes in large hunting parties. However, the legend I heard of Fenrix was of a hunter who slays drakes in single combat. Also, you were supposed to have been born with the head of a wolf!"

Jase and Fenrix both laughed to the point of tears. Still red in the face, Fenrix said, "That was only a hood I used to wear made from a two-tailed dire wolf that had terrorized the eastern hills during the winter of no storms. My tribe moved closer to Hillsborough just after that. As for hunting and killing drakes in single combat, I am one of the last who do. One day I will slay a full-grown, thinking dragon. Then I will be more legend than man."

"But I have never seen you in town like the other Hillmen, and even they talk about you like they don't know you," said Erik.

Fenrix frowned for a moment. "I do not live among them. I must always be on the hunt," he said sternly. Fenrix looked over at Gayle, who was now staring dreamily at him, and said, "So you're the fool archer who damn near killed my partner."

Gayle put her hands over her mouth, dropping her bow. "I'm so sorry," she said, her voice muffled by her hands.

Fenrix let out a loud, shrill whistle through his teeth. Up from the path behind him came stomping what must have been the high lord of rams on earth, or so Erik thought. If Rammy was a giant ram, this was the greater and elder father of Rammy's breed. The animal's stride was even strangely dignified. His massive hooves made heavy and deep footfalls. He was all black and wore an armored bridle and a saddle from which hung the same icy blue scales Fenrix was wearing. A large arrow was lodged in one of the animal's truly great spiraled horns. The ram walked right past Fenrix and Jase and stopped in front of Gayle and cocked his head to one side, seeming to want the arrow's owner to remove it. Gayle dislodged the arrow with ease, for despite being shot from a great bow of yew, it had hardly penetrated the ram lord's horn at all.

"Blackhorn is his name," Fenrix finally said. "He is a lord of his kind, not seen much of at all except on the most dangerous peaks of the Northridge Mountains. These beasts have been known to drive off small drakes on their own," Blackhorn turned toward Rammy and lightly touched horns. The gesture ran a great shiver through Rammy, and he dipped his head low.

"It seems Rammy knows royalty," said Erik.

Jase shook his head and said, "Look at the difference in size. Blackhorn can nearly look you in the eye. They are different breeds. Blackhorn was just saying hello. Rammy is just a little frightened by his size is all. I swear you Mountainfolk have lost all your lore in animal husbandry."

Fenrix yawned and asked, "This is all wonderfully educational, but why the hell are we on the green path? There is no real prey for miles."

Jase raised his arms in the air. "What we are hunting is the Tree of Two Worlds!" he exclaimed.

Erik and Gayle looked at each other and shrugged while Fenrix let out a short howl and started laughing. "This is a day for legends, it seems," he said mockingly.

Jase's eyes flashed with an inner fire, and his voice was like a harmonic chorus of rushing water as he spoke: "I have seen it—in the dreams of my heart—its boughs dipped in starlight and it's great roots sipping the blood of the earth."

Fenrix visibly shivered. "The speech of Eldare' moves me, but what does it mean?" he said.

Jase spoke again in his normal voice. "Those were the words of my mentor when I was young. He visited the tree and said it was a place of the wonders of the house of Gnomare'."

Gayle clapped, and Erik smiled. This seemed like an excellent destination indeed. Fenrix only crossed his arms and said, "Well, there is no game in that adventure, but is this another hunt for your mentor, or do we mean to actually find the tree? I hear that elven women would be worth the effort should we succeed."

Gayle scoffed at Fenrix. "And what's wrong with Vanguard women, may I ask?" she said.

Fenrix replied, "I stopped hunting wolves when there was no more challenge or excitement in it."

Jase laughed at the comment and added, "Well, now we hunt a tree, but from what I remember of my mentor's story, it lies a couple days south and east of here."

Fenrix and Jase began to walk south side by side, talking about a great many things. Erik and Gayle, leading Rammy, followed a few yards behind. Blackhorn followed behind them on his own.

"That makes sense," Erik said to Gayle, who was still angry and red in the face. "That puts the tree somewhere in the elven woods beyond the orchards. Strange people, those elves. They would only ever bring a few very small carts of fruits to sell or trade. They never traded for anything but scrap metal and never once told us their names or complained about Kreg's ridiculous bartering."

Gayle, who was paying no attention to Erik, said out of nowhere, "No longer exciting! I'm exciting and challenging!"

Erik looked at her and for the first time felt the courage to tell her his feelings. "I have always thought you were. To me you are the stuff of dreams spun in starlight," he said.

Gayle stopped and looked up at Erik and said, "Erik, you barely know me," Gayle then fell silent and blushed. She felt the onset of shame for the neglect she had shown Erik in the past, never saying more than hello and goodbye despite Erik's best attempts to get to know her. "But that's not your fault at all, Erik Ironrod. You are a very sweet man, and you will make someone very happy one day," Gayle said.

Erik, who had stopped to listen, felt his heart leap and sink all in the same moment. Blackhorn stomped one of his hooves and snorted. They looked back at the giant ram to see an almost annoyed expression on his face. Erik and Gayle looked forward again. They saw that Jase and Fenrix had turned around and were staring at them too, just as annoyed.

"You will make someone happy today, and you can start by keeping up, boy!" said Fenrix.

Jase added, "And besides, Gayle can either be happy with the great wizard you will someday become or take her chances with the son of an apple merchant."

Gayle shouted back at Jase as he and Fenrix continued on ahead, "Jordan is just one man! There are others who seek my hand. I am more than just a farmer's wife-to-be!"

Jase answered over his shoulder. "I'm sure there are many trappers and leather workers who need wives too. None of them will bring magic into your life. Your eyes seek something more than what they tell you now. I know that much, girl."

Erik finally spoke up: "Let's not ruin this journey with anymore quarreling, or the first spell I shall learn is one for silence."

Fenrix let out a roar so powerful, the air around them seemed to shake. "That would be some trick!" he said.

With some considerable effort, Erik quickened his pace and caught up with Jase and Fenrix. He caught only a short part of the conversation in which Fenrix was complaining about another of Jase's dangerous searches for his old mentor. The two grew quiet as Erik approached. Erik broke the silence: "So Jase, will we meet your mentor at this tree as well?"

Jase turned and looked at Erik without expression for a moment, as if to say that he was not invited into this line of conversation. Erik took his meaning and slowed his pace a little, rejoining Gayle. Erik marveled at how the differences between Jase and Fenrix were as striking as their similarities. They were both the same height. They looked about the same age, even if it was clear that they were not. They had the same color of brown hair and the same amount of gray in it. There the similarities ended. Jase spoke with a calm, unchanging tone, even when amused or upset. The inflection of Fenrix's voice seemed to change with every word. Jase was slight of build and moved smoothly across the ground when he walked, barely disturbing the gravel. However, Fenrix's frame was as packed with as much muscle as it could hold, and his movement was a curious sort of jog; he bounced on the balls of his feet, never letting his heels touch the ground. Up ahead, the two started their conversation anew in a tongue Erik did not recognize, but he guessed it to be the tribal tongue of Fenrix.

The journey continued trouble-free for several more hours. They continued south up, down, and around the wooded hills of the orchards until the image of the hill capped with Hillsborough was one of many behind them fading in the last lights of dusk. It was now past sunset, and the moon was not shining. The air seemed to hang close about them, still and silent, void of the usual noises of a country night. Erik seemed uneasy and could not shake a feeling of dread in his mind. The caution from Dregor's letter had begin to put doubts in Erik's heart concerning his secretive new allies. Fenrix said, "We should make camp near the turn in the road ahead. It's a common stop for travelers."

Further up the road, just past the sharp left turn to the east, was a post signifying a breaking of the path. The fork led further south in one direction and east in the other, on a much smaller, almost overgrown path.

"Our journey south ends, and east begins," said Jase.

Fenrix added, "But we will not travel this way at night with a cripple and a woman child. It's too dangerous. We will stop in the clearing just ahead on the left."

Neither Gayle nor Erik had wandered down this way, and thus, they agreed despite the insult, no matter how accurate. They would go no further. The clearing was indeed a place often used. There was a pit ringed with large stones for a fire surrounded by logs for benches as well. The moon had not yet risen, and Erik's eyes told him little of what else could be there.

Jase said quietly, "Something is not right."

As soon as the words fell silent in the air, Gayle heard the hum of several bowstrings loosened. She immediately grabbed Erik and pulled him to the ground on top of her.

Fenrix let out a groan and then rushed forward into the darkness and past the small campsite, drawing his sword. Erik, trying to manage his weight so as not to crush Gayle, looked up only to see the flash of Jase's eyes and the ring of his blades as he disappeared completely into the night.

What happened next, the night told of only in a multitude of combative sounds—the loud cry of Rammy as he fell to the ground after being struck by unseen arrows, the crack of Fenrix's whip and the clatter of swordplay, and then an evil and threatening laugh from Fenrix followed by the most deafening roar Erik or Gayle had yet heard.

Then came footfalls moving quickly in Erik and Gayle's direction, followed by the sounds of more steps from the other side of the would-be fireplace. However, they stopped suddenly, followed by a gurgling sound. Erik thought he heard several elvish voices quickly whispering many strange words, and then there came a flash like lightning.

"It's safe now," Erik and Gayle heard Fenrix say.

Suddenly, they could see again. There was a fire going in the pit, and Jase was already sitting on the other side of it, wiping off his blades. Erik looked down, and Gayle was looking up at him smiling, but uncertain. Erik, with the help of his prop, picked himself up and helped Gayle to her feet. They approached the nearest bench and sat down.

A loud neigh came from Rammy as Fenrix removed an arrow from his hindquarters and pulled him into the firelight. Fenrix looked Rammy over and began removing the animal's baggage. "This one will be moving slow enough while he heals," said Fenrix. Then he sat down on the bench to the right of Jase.

Gayle looked relieved and asked where Blackhorn was. Fenrix gave out a loud whistle and Blackhorn came into the firelight with an unconscious Vanguard hanging from the ram, his mangled arm caught in one of Blackhorn's great spiraled horns. Jase rose and slashed the Vanguard's throat as he freed his arm from Blackhorn. Gayle gasped at the sight and turned her head.

"You could have spared him! He was no threat!" said Erik.

Fenrix pointed into the darkness beyond Jase and said, "Tell that to the woman and her child who lay raped and murdered just beyond that thicket. The father lies in pieces on the ground behind me. Highway men do not show mercy. They know only greed, hunger, and lust."

Jase sat down again and said, "The peace of Hillsborough is an island in a decaying world of greed. The fortress cities fell, leaving hundreds of professional killers without a home or a living. Seldom do their descendants travel this far north, but the Brigand Vanguard are ruthless. They number in the thousands, and only their fear of the unknown keeps them at bay."

"That's another reason we kill all we find. There shall be no glad tidings from the lands I hunt," Fenrix added.

Gayle's eyes welled up. "Should we look after the bodies?" she asked.

Jase nodded. "In the morning, we will stick the Brigands' heads on spikes next to the road, and we will burn all the rest."

Gayle began to cry thinking of the child. She buried her face in Erik's cloak, which Erik wrapped around her as she continued to weep.

Fenrix began to unravel the bedrolls and lay them near the fire. He sat back. "You two should rest soon. Tomorrow we head east. Elvish lands are safe enough for elves, but wild and dangerous for unwary travelers."

Chapter 5

◇　◇　◇

The Hunt Is On

Jase continued to stare into the fire. Erik noticed that it was a strange color of blue at its base and gave off a warmth that was strangely soothing and almost entrancing. Gayle laid herself down on a bedroll and looked at Erik with a smile, almost invitingly. Erik, who normally would have jumped out of his own skin to share a place of rest with Gayle, now held back.

He looked at Gayle and wished her pleasant dreams and returned to staring at the fire. Gayle quickly covered up and pretended to fall asleep. Fenrix had fallen asleep as soon as his head met the bedroll and now slept motionlessly, without even the sound of breath.

Jase looked across the fire at Erik and said, in a voice that had the resonance of many voices in harmony. "Consider this when your staff hits the ground. Can you not feel it come to life in your hand? Can you not hear the metal ring and speak? Everything created can tell you of its nature. Knowing its language is your first step."

Erik struck his staff down in front of him and heard a dull thud follow by a faint ring. He felt the staff vibrate in his hand for a moment and then touched its cold metal to his forehead. He tried to keep the sound and feeling of his staff in his head but soon fell asleep as he spread himself out over the bench.

Gayle and Erik woke to the sounds of a loud argument between Jase and Fenrix, the latter of whom was cradling the body of the dead child in his arms. The language they were using was the same strange one Erik had heard them use on the path before. The argument finally ended with Jase reaching for the young girl and Fenrix shoving him back. Jase sighed and began to pick through the other dead bodies.

Erik sat up and tried to rub the sleepiness from his eyes. To his amazement, the fire was still going but was now completely blue and very hot. The day was overcast and gray. The blue fire gave the camp a strange and magical look.

Gayle awoke suddenly and jumped out of her bedroll. "I had a terrible dream!" she said.

"Well, a new day is here, and we are with you, my lady," Erik said in the most comforting tone he could muster.

Gayle smiled but then turned her gaze toward Jase. He was decapitating one of the highway men. "The day already seems evil," she said. Jase then put the head on a makeshift wooden spear and erected the gruesome totem.

Fenrix, who was burying the body of the child, said, "These days will stay evil as long as we are away from our settlements."

Jase threw the decapitated body on the fire and said, "Give a hand with the bodies unless you plan on digging a grave like Fenrix."

Gayle helped Fenrix cover the burial stones for the child with earth and began to decorate the grave marker with flowers. Fenrix hung a thin gold chain on the marker as well. "It was her mother's," he said solemnly.

Erik helped to put the remaining bodies on the fire. The blue flames consumed the bodies in an envelope of flame as soon as they touched the now heaping mound of dead. When the last bodies were placed down, Erik said, "You must teach me about enchanted fire sometime."

"Must I?" replied Jase, who seemed genuinely sad at the sight of the pyre. Jase handed Erik a small but heavy bag. "This is your share of the spoils. You are becoming a successful adventurer, it seems."

Erik felt strange about taking it. These men had been thieves and murderers. Their valuables seemed tainted to Erik. Jase saw Erik's concern and said, "It gets easier. The spoils of conquest and combat are only as good as how you use them. Sometimes the blood washes away," Jase asked everyone to gather near the funeral pyre and said, "Here we pay our respects to the slain. Whether good or evil, they were all children of the world. May their spirits find forgiveness and peace."

Fenrix added, "Should the soul of the child walk the world again, may she find the joy deprived of her in the waking world."

Gayle was surprised to see that Fenrix thought so much of children. He was a killer down to his bones but apparently would never harm a child.

Jase turned and said, "It is time we departed this camp," And so they did.

They left behind the funeral pyre and the gruesome totems as a warning to the Brigands. That morning's journey to the east was a solemn affair. No one in the party walked swiftly; whether this was a result of the somber mood or the consideration for a cripple and a wounded beast was left unsaid.

Gayle began to notice the trees getting larger and closer to the trail, which was now little more than a forgotten footpath. After a while, the ring of Erik's staff and the heavy footfalls of Blackhorn could no longer be heard. The ground beneath the company had become a dark, soft, rich-smelling earth, yet not muddy at all.

The party continued on for hours before the silence was broken by Jase. "I meant to congratulate you on your latest hunt. It has made you some fine armor."

Fenrix cocked his head back and gave a slanted grin as he replied, "Aye, it was a great hunt. Many days tracking the great cold drake, but once it was aware of me, it all happened quickly."

Jase nodded slowly and asked, "Did you return to your tribe afterward?"

Fenrix answered, "Yes, I had to. The hide of a cold drake must be worked within days to be of any use. I was praised and paid well for what I did not keep. They even made me a chief of the hunt."

Jase frowned and said, "A kill like that would make you the natural choice for a war chief."

Fenrix sighed and began to stare into the skies and said only, "One day."

The path eastward became more and more overgrown with the lush green growth of a wild forest. They continued on. "This is no orchard at all!" said Gayle, brushing her hand over a bluish green fern. The forest on either side of them was not one of fruit-bearing trees but instead one of very large, gnarly ash and elm. It seemed like a solid wall of closely growing old trees with moss-draped branches that was occasionally interrupted by a giant sycamore or oak. These great kings of the forest would not endure their lesser cousins to grow close to them. Their giant branches thrust out from all sides, proud and foreboding. In the break in the wall of trees, underneath the odd oak or sycamore, Erik could see further into the forest on both sides. The forest underneath seemed to be an unbroken canopy for miles, a world of dim light and old growth.

"Indeed, my child, this is the border of the woods that the elvish people keep. They live off this land but are not farmers," said Jase.

"Then what are they?" asked Gayle.

Jase turned and looked at Gayle and said simply, "Elves."

Fenrix remarked, "I do not hunt here, and I avoid this place as much as possible. I do not like this forest. The air is too thick for my liking, and I have no love for these half-elves. It seems as though they are scared of their own shadows, and so is all the game in these parts." Fenrix looked uneasy and was constantly turning his head in every direction, sniffing loudly and sucking the air through his teeth.

Erik laughed to himself for a moment and asked, "Why don't you ask them where the Tree of Two Worlds is?"

Jase, who was now walking backward for the sake of conversation, replied, "I have, but I am a Quadrian of Eldare', and these folk are half-elven Gnomare', long estranged from their full-blood cousins."

Gayle rolled her eyes and said, "So what is that all supposed to mean?"

"Only that I am not completely elvish or even half, and I am from a different house. I might as well be a Mountainfolk asking these closely guarded people where they have hidden their secrets and treasures," answered Jase.

Erik took a quick breath and said, "I might as well then." Erik took a deep breath and said in a booming yet nonthreatening voice, "If there are any fold of the great house of Gnomare', or any other, can you please tell us how to find the Tree of Two Worlds?"

The sound echoed into the woods and was met with silence, after which they all laughed together. However, a moment later, a whispering voice came back from seemingly high in the trees: "East another day, look to the Sudden Valley. Only starlight will show its leaves from afar," Jase's jaw dropped open in disbelief. Fenrix cackled in delight, overcome with the humor of Jase's reaction.

Fenrix then shouted, "Since this is a day for asking, might you tell me where to find the ruins of Prime Avalon?"

"To the north, but you will not find it, good hunter. Your Fire Dragon lies far to the south. Good luck in your quest. We will not speak again," answered the voice.

Fenrix now joined Jase in stunned expression while Erik and Gayle laughed at them. "It seems the house of Gnomare' is very accommodating to its would-be guests," said Erik.

"No! That was a Feyara', or I have never heard one! She only answered because of you, Erik. Something in the air changed when you cast your spell!" replied Jase.

"Aye, I felt it too. It was the same pull as when our shaman asked our ancestors' guidance, but this was quicker and stronger," added Fenrix.

Erik stood silent and wide-eyed for a moment and then said uncertainly, "I cast a spell? I thought I just asked for directions."

Gayle tugged on Erik's sleeve and said, "I felt it too. It was like a note of music I could only feel and not hear," They all grew very quiet, and all that could be heard was the sound of Rammy and Blackhorn chewing on the vegetation.

"Well, east another day to the Sudden Valley it is," Jase declared confidently.

The pace was now quicker as the party was excited, to say the least. The mood had lightened with the distraction.

"Just imagine—in a little over a day from now, we will find one of the great elf homes, hidden since the days of the Great Wars," Jase said.

"Why are they hidden?" asked Gayle. Jase grew silent.

Fenrix at last spoke. "There was a great calamity in the mountain halls during the Great Wars. It prevented the dwarfs from completing their campaign. Although at first, the dwarfs thought it was caused by men, soon the dwarfs turned their blame to elves."

Jase went on to say, "Dwarfs had many foundries and a great crafting hall for war machines. It is just as likely their industry blew up in their faces, if you ask me. I saw that happen to them often enough in the field."

"So now the elves hide in fear of the dwarfs? That doesn't seem right to me," said Erik.

Jase answered, "The elves lost so much in the first wars that they did not want a war themselves. Everyone had suffered enough by then. The great houses went into hiding. Only the Kylvara' walk openly in the world."

Fenrix scratched his head and murmured, "I have never seen a Kylvara'. Would I have known if I did?"

Jase's eyes grew narrow, and again his voice rang out like many speaking at once some very near and threatening others that seemed to echo like a distant whisper. "They are a breed apart from the other houses. They are even larger than Erik—some are much larger—and they are darker of skin and mood than their cousins. Their prowess is unmatched by any other house. In fact, if all three of the other houses united, they still could not match the Kylvara' in strength of spirit. If you should ever meet one, you will know."

"Sounds kind of scary, if you ask me," said Erik. "So are you saying they don't hide because they don't have to, or because they don't want to?"

"Both," answered Jase. "From what I have heard, the Kylvara' have taken no interest in the worlds of men and dwarfs since the Great Fortress Wars."

Erik nodded and began to think of the magnitude of everything he had heard. The world was so much larger and more dangerous than he had thought, growing up with such people as Kreg and Jordan as his only antagonists.

The party was once again silent. Their pace east through the woods had slowed considerably. There was now no path to follow. They had only

Jase's guidance up, over, and around wooded hills and underneath an endless canopy.

The hills started to become larger and harder to manage. Then suddenly, Jase and Fenrix stopped. They began to talk in whispers to each other, and Fenrix nodded. Then with the dexterity of a wild woodland animal, Fenrix sprung up into a large nearby tree. Within moments, he was at the highest bough that would support him, looking out to the east. Fenrix soon began to skip back down between branches and landed next to Jase without a sound. After flashing a quick smile at Gayle, he turned and whispered something to Jase. Gayle marveled at how Fenrix was as nimble as a cat when he wanted to be. Jase then announced that they were nearly at their destination for now and would be stopping to eat soon.

"You found the valley, Fenrix?" asked Erik.

"No, I found a hill," replied Fenrix.

They began to move very quickly through the undergrowth. Even Erik was moving at a good pace, realizing how hungry he was. They at last came to a break in the forest, a small grassy field from which they could see their destination.

"A hill? More like a mountain cut in half!" Gayle exclaimed.

Before them was a great green mount of wooded earth several times larger than anything else around it. Yet at its top, it was completely bare stone, shining white in the daylight.

After a few more hours of a very fast pace, they arrived at its base. There it loomed in front of them, large and menacing. The sides looked steep and nonnegotiable. Where they stood was nearly a sheer face of earth.

"This is as far as we go today," said Jase. Gayle and Erik were both relieved and red in the face with exhaustion.

Fenrix said, "I will make the fire. You two rest; then prepare some supper. Tomorrow we will find some way up this thing."

Jase disappeared and returned much later as the sun was beginning to set. He reappeared holding four large gourd-like fruits of a bright orange color. He handed one to everyone in the group.

Fenrix smiled and said something in his tribal tongue as he began to shake it vigorously.

"I was fortunate to find these," Jase said. "They are prized by elves very highly and will recover your strength quickly."

Fenrix pulled the stem off his fruit and, crushing it in his hand, drank it dry. He immediately laughed merrily and threw the leathery husk in the fire. It gave off a sweet and wholesome aroma. The rest did the same.

Gayle could feel her head spin as she began to swoon and giggle. Erik began to see images dance in the fire in front of him. They both swayed back and fourth almost in unison. Then the feeling passed as quickly as it had begun. They both felt calm yet focused and immediately noticed Fenrix and Jase staring at them from across the fire.

"Perhaps next time, you two should sit down before you drink something new," said Fenrix.

Erik looked down and saw two large stones set in front of Gayle and himself.

"How long were we gone?" asked Erik as they both took a seat.

Jase laughed softly and said, "Long enough to offer no help setting up camp. Now that your strength is back, we will leave you two alone," Jase clapped his hand down on Fenrix's shoulder and motioned, with a turn of his head, to an area out of the firelight behind Erik and Gayle. Fenrix laughed and sprang from the stone he was sitting on, drawing his sword.

Gayle asked as she stood, "More Bandits?"

"No child," answered Jase. "Just a little exercise."

Gayle shrugged and sat back down. Erik and Gayle shared an awkward glance and then laughed. Then the sounds of furious turmoil between two master swordsmen began to ring out in the night—the chime of ringing blades and an occasional crack from the lash of Fenrix.

Amongst the noise, Erik and Gayle began to feel a small sense of privacy and exchange the usual pleasantries. Erik was content in her company and perfectly happy to discuss the night air, the quality of the packed rations, or feelings of homesickness, but Gayle quickly grew silent. Erik, who was used to this treatment from Gayle, went quiet too and began to study the sounds of the sparring session.

"No!" Gayle suddenly said loudly. "It isn't fair, the way I have treated you all this time. I ignored you and made fun of you when you were not around. I have been terrible to you. Here I am, an amateur archer from an average family of tradesmen, having no great wealth or position, having thought all this time that you were somehow beneath me. I am a fool, and I am sorry. You are going to be a great wizard and will know more magic and wonder than I will ever know. I admire you."

Erik's expression was blank for a moment. He was taken aback by the sudden confession, and the contest between Fenrix and Jase was now becoming thunderous, which made it harder for Erik so respond. At last he spoke. "Gayle, I am just a cripple that has been unusually lucky these last two days. I am still a cripple, still an orphan, and as far as being a wizard, I am not sure what that even means. Mr. Jase just says things, and I don't know what the hell he is talking about half the time. To be perfectly honest, the very notion of changing into something I don't understand scares me." Erik leaned closer to Gayle and put his arm around her. "You enchanted every man in Hillsborough that was anywhere near your age. You're a hard worker and made of stronger stuff than the other girls in town. I have always admired you!" added Erik.

Gayle's eyes began to tear up as she quickly stood and kissed Erik on the cheek. She gave Erik a forceful hug and then sat back down and said, "Thanks" Just then, whistling and applause from Fenrix and Jase filled the air.

Jase quickly returned to his stone opposite Erik and Gayle across the fire. "Well done!" he said.

Gayle noticed a dark red mark across Jase's cheek and said, "Looks like Fenrix won."

"No," answered Fenrix. "I lost control of my lash for a moment. It was a peaceful contest" He too returned to his seat.

Jase only smiled and said, "Though Fenrix is a masterful fighter."

"Then who won?" asked Gayle.

Fenrix answered, "If it came to killing blows, Jase would have ended me within moments, and several times over. I would have only landed one of my own much later."

"But you kill drakes singlehandedly," said Gayle, truly surprised.

Jase nodded and explained that there are several differences between fighting a young dragon and fighting another swordsman.

"Exactly what is the difference between a drake and a dragon, Fenrix, and how can you tell?" asked Gayle with a shrug.

Jase rolled his eyes and said, "And so it begins."

Fenrix shot Jase a cold glace and then smiled as he turned to Gayle and answered. "Well, I suppose the short answer to your first question is age: a dragon is a full-grown drake. Now as to your second question, there is no short answer."

"A dragon will always be larger, smarter, and faster than a drake of the same breed. A land drake is a small creature no larger than a bear before migrating to the sea. However, when it returns a full-grown land dragon, it is the size of the largest of trees. Other breeds, you can scarcely tell the difference in size between adult and juvenile. However, it is not the size that makes a dragon dangerous. A dragon is no longer a beast like a drake; it is an enemy of the world. Dragons become aware and even speak a foul language of sorts. They are clever. They can set traps and organize their young to do their bidding. Nearly all dragons have breath and venom as well. They are the most terrible of creatures to hunt. A drake is a trifle in comparison."

Gayle and Erik just nodded their heads, pretending to understand. To them, dragons and drakes seemed equally terrifying in almost every way. It was now dark. The glow of dusk was no longer in the sky, and the late summer evening was upon them. The stars above them seemed unusually bright, and the summer air was perfumed with the rich sent of the campfire.

Suddenly, the wind shifted, and a cooler breeze came across them from the north, causing the fire to dance. Fenrix and Jase's eyes widened, and looking at each other, they sprang to their feet. Jase immediately disappeared into the darkness. Fenrix jumped over the fire and threw Gayle to the ground. He then quickly laid Erik beside her and pulled Erik's cloak over them both.

Fenrix began shoveling hot ash from the fire onto Erik's cloak while mumbling, "Stupid! Stupid! Stupid! Too long hunting drakes!" Fenrix leaned down toward them and said, "I didn't notice before, but your cloak still carries the scent of a young male bear of breeding age. Now it's caught the attention of a very large dominant male. Strange this far south, but do not move or speak until we say!" Fenrix then dashed away into the dark.

The next sound that could be heard was the dying cry of a large ram. "Rammy!" Gayle said, her voice half-muffled through Erik's hand. Gayle began to sob as Erik tried to comfort her in whispers.

They were then both startled by a sudden crack of thunder accompanied by a bright flash, followed by the unmistakable groan and crackle of falling trees. Fenrix's recognizable howl echoed in the night along with the crack of his whip. However, the roar of the bear that was tracking them paralyzed Gayle and Erik both in pure terror. It sounded as though the animal was only a few feet away from Erik, who curled his body tightly around Gayle. The deafening roars and earth-shattering stomps of the giant bear were indeed getting closer with each passing moment. Yet so too were the shouts and curses from Fenrix.

Just when it seemed as though the bear was going to be right on top of them, roars turned from sharp growls to almost sad groans, followed by a heavy impact on the ground. "It's all right now, you two—the hunt is over," said Jase.

Gayle rose to her feet while Erik only rolled back to his knees. Jase came into the firelight solemnly. With his head down, he said, "I am sorry. It was on your beast before I could stop it."

Gayle swallowed the lump she felt rising in her throat and said, "Is Fenrix skinning our uninvited guest then?"

Jase looked up in wonder with a half-smile and pointed over his shoulder. Gayle then hurried to aid Fenrix in his labor with tears rolling down her cheeks. Jase sat down in front of Erik and said, "She is a strong young woman. I can see why you love her."

Erik, still in a state of shock, could only say, "I was so scared."

"It will pass. Now get some rest," answered Jase.

Chapter 6

❖ ❖ ❖

Tree of Two Worlds

Erik was jaded. His legs felt heavy, like they would no longer hold him. He rolled over onto a bedroll near the fire and shut his eyes. The sounds of the crackling fire and Jase singing softly to himself were comforting. Erik soon let his mind wander and fell asleep.

Erik woke some hours later to see that Gayle had curled up beside him. He also noticed another one of Jase's strange blue funeral pyres several yards away from their camp with what looked like the remains of a large ram in its flame. Fenrix was sleeping silently, and Jase was nowhere in sight.

Erik looked back down at Gayle and smiled. Snuggling up next to her, he could not remember ever being so happy or content. The party woke to the toothsome smell of roasting meat on wooden skewers.

Fenrix sat up immediately, saying, "Hmm—roast bear."

Gayle and Erik were comfortable and unwilling to move from their bedroll to greet the crisp late summer morning. From out of nowhere, it seemed, Jase appeared in his seat and said, "It's an exciting day for us all! Now eat something, for we shall not stop until we reach the top and survey the land by starlight."

Gayle and Erik both sat up. Erik at once grabbed a large skewer with meat on it, devoured it quickly, and grabbed another. Fenrix too was eating nonstop, one skewer after another. Gayle grabbed one hesitantly before they were all gone. She took a small bite with curiosity to find it tender and seasoned. She then abandoned her manners and began to eat like a hungry wolf in winter. Fenrix stopped only to say, "That a girl. Don't be polite in the wild. We are all animals here."

"Once you all are done eating, Fenrix and I will go ahead to make sure the way is safe," said Jase.

Jase and Fenrix began to pack up camp and load Blackhorn with the supplies and fresh water skins. Fenrix told them to follow as far behind as possible and to bring Blackhorn with them, noting, "Blackhorn will charge at anything dangerous that approaches, and if you lose sight of us, Blackhorn can follow my scent for miles."

He then removed a vial of dark brown liquid from a traveling pack on Blackhorn. He broke the seal and dipped his finger inside and began to massage it into his skin. The pungent musk of the liquid was so powerful that it made Erik's eyes water. Fenrix was amused by this discomfort but thought he owed them an explanation.

"This is the musk of several different large predators, the secret to many of my best kills. If there are any other dangerous beasts in these parts, they will come straight to me," said Fenrix.

He then resealed the vial and ran out ahead with Jase, who was already pacing along the base of the hill, looking for a place they could all climb up. Fenrix joined Jase in his search. Jase, still looking up at the unusually steep wooded hill said, "So why am I still bothered by last night's encounter?"

Fenrix answered, "Because, my friend, it should not have happened. That was an elder mountain cave bear, never seen in these parts. I can only guess why it was so far south."

Jase replied, "Guess away, good hunter."

Fenrix thought for a moment and said, "Either it was driven out by something large and terrible, or it was looking for prey because its natural home in the mountains has run out."

Jase asked, "Do you think a plague or a greater predator like a mature dragon?"

"No to both, brother. If it were plague, it would have scavenged and died or become sick. This bear was healthy and very strong. Dragons, when they become too large for the mountain, migrate to the sea," answered Fenrix. He looked around and whispered, "I have hunted everything that can be hunted in these parts. I know the smell of fear on an animal and can track it for miles. Never have I seen an elder bear show fear. They fight to the death. Yet the one last night reeked of it."

Jase whispered in reply, "So what could be the cause then? What would put terror in the heart of a fearless beast?"

Fenrix looked to the north long and unflinchingly and then said in a flat, emotionless tone, "Evil" He turned to look at Jase with deadly seriousness in his eyes.

Jase replied, "It is only a matter of time before it shows its face again."

Gayle and Erik kept a slow pace, and Jase and Fenrix quickly became small figures far ahead. Erik began to walk with a lightness in his step. Although the pain of his wound caused him to limp still, the ache was less than usual. He was happy, no matter what the next days would bring. Gayle's words were etched in his heart.

Gayle, thinking aloud said, "I wonder what they are talking about."

Erik pondered the question for some time and replied, "No idea. What do famous heroes talk about? Perhaps I would rather not know."

The journey took the party around the base of the hill for quite some time. Gayle and Erik would occasionally pass dead remains of large predatory animals so badly burned and heavily damaged that they were unrecognizable. Yet the only evidence of the killing that Erik and Gayle would observe every hour or so was a sudden flash of light.

"What in the world are they doing?" said Gayle.

"I imagine they are playing 'who can kill better.' Seems like kind of a waste to me," said Erik.

"So what would the great wizard Erik Ironrod do?" asked Gayle.

"Ask them to stop, I suppose. I don't know. I'm not a wizard," answered Erik.

At last the party had come to a place at the base of the hill where the steepness gave way to a gentle slope. Jase and Fenrix waited until Gayle and Erik joined them with Blackhorn in tow. Fenrix had his arms crossed and was tapping his foot, pretending to be impatient.

As soon as they regrouped, Jase said, "Well, it's nearly midday now thanks to taking the time to sport a little. Now the plan is to eat a big meal and camp under the stars with cold rations. I don't want firelight spoiling our chances."

They stopped, rested, and ate as much as they could hold, and after they absented themselves for the forests' version of a lavatory, the march began again. All together now, they wound their way up the very large hill. There was no straight ascent to be made without vigorous and skillful climbing, so the way up was slow. The trees became smaller and younger as they made their way up. The elm and ash trees began to give way to heartier pine and cedar. The air became rich with the fragrance of evergreen trees.

At long last, after many hours walking and climbing, they came upon the first of the stones crowning the giant hill. Jase and Fenrix both examined their surroundings and then looked at each other and shrugged before proceeding with little effort onto the large white marble–capped hilltop. Erik and Gayle were close behind. The white marble was beginning to reflect a pinkish orange hue in the light of the sunset, and the breeze that gently whipped by had an early autumn chill to it.

Jase was perched on top of a large upended slab of marble abducted from the surrounding bedrock by some ancient unseen force. "This is the place to see our stars and our tree, for sure."

Fenrix leapt to the top of the stone and looked to the east. "Brother, I see no sudden valley, just an endless canopy of trees to the east and two more giant hills," Fenrix said, pointing northeast and then southeast.

"Have faith, good hunter. The Feyara' do not lie. It is not in them to deceive—from what I have heard, anyway," answered Jase.

Fenrix jumped down and let out a yawn and said, "Well, the excitement is too much for me. Wake me up when there are elf maidens to ravish," Fenrix lay down on a bare slab of stone with his cloak wrapped tightly around him and slept.

The sun continued to set, turning the hilltop almost blood-red. Gayle and Erik unpacked Blackhorn so that he could graze further down the hill. The bedrolls were laid out and suitable stones rolled into place for chairs, and the cold rations and water skins were set down. The group, minus Fenrix, was ready to watch the stars.

Erik was beginning to open a package of dried meat when he looked up and saw Jase staring down toward the forest to the east. "So Jase, how did you and Fenrix meet, anyway?"

Jase did not respond for some time and then answered out of the awkward silence, "On a hunt."

Fenrix, rousing from his nap, sat up laughing and said, "So that's what you were doing. What were you hunting—death?"

"What do you mean?" asked Erik.

Jase began to chuckle reluctantly while Fenrix stood up.

Stretching his arms out in front of him, his hands open and palms out, Fenrix said, "So there I was hunting a large land drake, or so I thought, that was killing my tribe's oxen and other beasts. I was able to track it into the Northridge Mountains. Then the trail went crazy, tracks everywhere! Scales, blood, and scorched earth—all spoiling my hunt. I managed to follow the chaos east into the old Burial Hills. This was a bad place to hunt even for me."

Fenrix crouched and began to hunch over and tiptoe around them as he continued. "Drakes are one thing, but dragons come there to breed and make nests in the old tombs hollowed out of the rocks. I was about to turn back, knowing the danger I was heading toward, when I saw the boot prints. I have to admit I was in awe of someone who could fight off what I thought was at least two drakes and still be heading toward the breeding grounds.

"I continued on, but there were no more signs of the hunt, and I could still smell the drake blood. I had been there only once before, and it was not during breeding season like it was then. I remember that there was an enormous burial mound at the southwestern edge of the Ancients Hills, so I decided to head in that direction.

"As I approached the Great Burial Mound, I heard it—the angry cry of an elder land dragon. Climbing to the top of the eastern ridge surrounding the mound, I saw him: an insane elf man, narrowly avoiding the snapping jaws of a dragon so large it would take an army from the Ancient Wars to take down. And not only was there an elder dragon, but several young drakes were guarding the nest too, leaping like large cats, clawing and biting at him."

Fenrix stood straight up and crossed his arms while looking at Jase with a familiar nod as he went on. "In those days I kept a small dwarven ballista on Blackhorn, modified for drake hunting. I wasn't sure if I wanted to help someone that stupid, but I had no choice. A hunter in distress will find strength in the pack.

"I anchored my ballista on a giant stone loaded a harpoon and hoped for some luck as I chased Blackhorn away to the east. The death-chasing idiot was nearly surrounded, but I was able to dislodge a large boulder from the ridge above. It started a small landslide to the base of the mound and even destroyed or trapped a few drakes.

"I yelled down at the stranger, Jase, and told him to come this way, and with a large bang, the ground beneath him erupted in flame, consuming yet even more young drakes and enraging the dragon. It snapped at Jase as he lept high into the air—it was almost as if he flew to the top of the ridge. I thought if I could harpoon the elder with a tethered harpoon, that would slow it down at the cost of my ballista. It did the job. Jase flew past as I loosed the harpoon, rooting the dragon's front claw to the ridge.

"We both escaped to the west, not daring to come near our villages. The elder dragon cursed at us and sent all its nearby young after us. We traveled for weeks into the west, and we did not eat or sleep for days, fighting off land drakes.

"Through the days and nights, we fought them off. At last, the more clever older ones waited for us to tire before they attacked. Three large males came at us at night near a stream at which we had camped. They came from different directions at once, two at me and one at Jase.

"That was a hard night. We were spent and unprepared. Jase took his drake toward the stream. Drakes are good swimmers, yet not good enough to kill Jase underwater. I stayed between my two, and they eventually did enough damage to each other for me to finish them. I thought Jase was dead until I saw his drake, belly up in the stream. Jase was bleeding on the shore but still in good shape. It took weeks at my village before we were well enough to leave on our own power. From there, we went our own ways for a time."

Erik and Gayle were stunned and silent. Gayle at last said, "You saw an elder dragon, and it spoke to you? What were you even doing there, Jase? Looking for the Tree of Two Worlds?"

Jase sighed and smiled slightly. "It's a long story as to why I was there. But yes, elders can speak. They were bred by Dagoth himself and become aware and very dangerous when fully mature, as Fenrix said."

Fenrix said angrily, "Well, it cost me a dwarven ballista that I'll never come by again!"

"I promise, Fenrix, if we find the house of Gnomare', a dwarven ballista will seem like a trifle compared to what you can find," answered Jase.

The glow of dusk was gone from the night sky. The stars were now very bright, and the party's attention turned toward the forest to the east. The time seemed to pass slowly, and the silence grew with the party's anticipation.

To Erik it seemed that the glint of the stars was brighter than he was used to seeing at night in Hillsborough, yet all the patterns of stars were the same.

"This really is a beautiful night!" exclaimed Gayle to break the silence.

"Indeed," answered Jase.

Fenrix stood suddenly and said, "The stars are moving!"

They all looked into the skies directly above them. Indeed, the familiar patterns of stars they all knew began to wheel above their heads. The stars began to scintillate and flash with a myriad of spectral colors.

"It's beginning!" cried Jase.

The strange sparkling mass of lights in the night sky eventually died away, and the stars returned to their normal places. The group began to scan the dark canopy to the east, searching for something out of the ordinary.

"Where are you?" Jase said softly.

Several minutes passed, and the only thing they could see was the night forest, undisturbed and unremarkable.

Just as the phrase "Damn it!" left Jase's mouth, the party's attention was drawn skyward again.

First there was one alone, and then were three followed by another several dozen—softly wavering points of light began to slowly descend like luminous flakes of snow on a windless day. They fell quietly and beautifully toward the forest to the east and rested in the boughs of a great tree many miles off in the canopy. The lights pulsated for a moment only and then went out.

Then suddenly, the entire tree began to give off silvery blue and green lights of its own. They would light up suddenly and then slowly fade and light up somewhere else in the tree's leaves. After several minutes, the lights stopped, and the tree shined no more.

"That was beautiful! Like a dance!" said Gayle.

Jase dropped down to the ground from the rock he was perched on. He fell to his knees and let out a victorious cry in his usual, almost musical voice. "At last, elven home, I have found you! An orphan four hundred years but no more!"

Jase's happiness could not be contained, and although his face was streaked with tears, he could not stop laughing. He conjured a bright green campfire that took the shape of a tree, grabbed Gayle by the hands, and began to dance around it, singing in elvish.

Fenrix laughed at the sight and whistled for Blackhorn, who came bounding out of the darkness. Fenrix opened a large satchel on Blackhorn's back and withdrew a small mandolin, which he tuned and then used to play a lively melody. Erik smiled and began to keep rhythm by tapping his staff on the ground.

The evening went on like that for hours, sometimes with Jase or Gayle dancing alone, sometimes with all of them skipping to the tunes of the Hillman folk dances. Finally, they all sat down.

Gayle, still catching her breath, said, "You two must come to harvest dance. As much as I would love Erik all to myself, you know you would miss us!" Gayle curled her slender arms around Erik's massive left arm and rested her head on his shoulder.

"I shall be glad to be rid of you both," said Fenrix with a pause, "after the dance."

Jase only nodded and began to study the stars. Fenrix looked to the east and said, "If we get down quick enough, we could reach the tree by midday."

Erik was excited for the future. *Gayle at my side, the great mysteries of the ancient realms, and all my friends with me at harvest. This could not get any better*, Erik thought to himself.

They all grew silent and were content with the quiet. Erik stared at the enchanted green flame and let his imagination run wild. He imagined he was standing in front of the elder land dragon that had chased Fenrix and Jase with his staff at the ready. He imagined himself ready to consume the ancient serpent within his wizard's fire.

Suddenly, with a loud crackle and hiss, the campfire leapt like a serpent to the middle of Erik's staff. The fire spiraled to its top, shot high into the air, and exploded with a thunderous boom. White hot sparks rained down all around the party, sizzling on the stones.

Fenrix, who rather enjoyed mischief, was laughing hysterically while Jase, shaking his head, said, "Well, I guess they know we are here now."

Gayle also began to giggle, yet this did not comfort Erik. "I'm so sorry," he said with an expression of frozen dread on his face.

"Don't be. If we are indeed near an ancient stronghold of elvish power, we would have been discovered sooner rather than later," said Fenrix.

Jase nodded. "Indeed, your fire enchantment will probably be seen as a sign of goodwill—letting them know in advance of our presence. At least that's my hope."

Gayle yawned and said, "Well, the fire is out. I believe that means it's time to sleep."

To this they all agreed. Jase resumed his perch atop the upended slab of stone. The rest of them slept.

The following morning atop the giant hill, a touch of winter's chill was in the air. Erik and Gayle, who had curled up in the same bedroll, were shivering as they emerged. Fenrix was already finishing the last of the packing, yet Jase was nowhere to be found.

"Where is Jase?" asked Gayle.

"He went ahead to scout a quicker way down that you children can handle," replied Fenrix.

Jase reappeared and announced, "I have found a quick way down, if you all prove sturdy enough!"

Gayle packed up the bedroll, and Erik stretched out his arms and yawned. "Okay, let's go then."

Jase smiled and darted off. The rest of the group, not expecting him to move that quickly, scrambled to catch up.

The trip down the hill did not involve much walking; it was more leaping, sliding, and even falling than anything else. At one point, Erik found himself jumping into the branches of a tree at a lower shelf of rock on the hillside. The tree, however, could not support his weight, and every branch he tried to catch himself on snapped and splintered all the way down to the base of the tree. The rest of the party was waiting there, having jumped straight down. The trip down the hill involved scenes such as this for some time.

At last at the base of the hill, Erik and Gayle were both intact, aside from a few scrapes and bruises. Jase started to sprint away east. Fenrix followed swiftly with a howl and with Erik and Gayle on his heels. Through the undergrowth and between the large trunks of oak and sycamore they ran. Jase at last slowed when they reached a slight downward slope and as the trees were becoming very large.

"This makes sense. The canopy looked even from atop the hill. The trees have hidden the lay of the land," said Fenrix.

Jase was now walking slowly and cautiously to the east. "That's odd. I could have sworn we would be there, or at least be very close, by now."

The downgrade evened out, and the party began to walk to the east with care. The air began to change, and they could hear the noise of running water not far off. Jase quickened his pace ahead of the group and disappeared between the trunks of two large trees growing unusually close together.

The rest of the group started to follow, and before they reached the trees, they could hear Jase's laughter. They squeezed between the two massive trunks one by one to see Jase standing on the edge of a ridge that opened up into a quite sudden valley—and at the center of that valley was a tree that could be none other than the Tree of Two Worlds.

The valley was not very wide as valleys go. It was surrounded on all sides by a wall of red oak trees. A narrow but strong stream had carved it from the north. The deep, clear stream cascaded down a waterfall over moss-covered stones and then quickly became shallow and disappeared altogether in the moss-covered roots of the tree. The valley was quite deep and would prove difficult to descend; its banks were steep.

The tree was a true marvel of the world. Its roots formed a web that covered the majority of the valley floor. Its brown, almost-bronze-looking bark was flecked with rivulets of green throughout. Its truly titanic trunk would have filled the entire town square of Hillsborough, and it started from the valley floor and grew to the impossible height of the oaks ringing the valley. It did not produce a single branch for several hundred feet up its perilously tall trunk, and its leaves, backlit by the sun, cast a deep blue-green light over the entire valley.

Gayle gasped and said, "I never imagined something so beautiful could exist. Its bark is like gold, and its leaves are jewels."

Jase, who was once again overcome with emotion, began to talk to himself in elvish. Then he turned with tears in his eyes and a grin on his face and said, "See you at the bottom. Make sure you get there in one piece," He leapt over the edge, skipping lightly down the almost sheer face and laughing aloud as he went.

Fenrix sighed. "Aye, such a leap is beyond your ability," he said to Gayle and Erik, "but I can see a way down from here," He pointed up the valley to the north.

They made their way north to where the stream began to cut into the rock and cascade down the falls. Erik worked up the courage to go first, climbing down the rocks. But in his usual fashion, he fell most of the way and went tumbling into the stream, which washed him all the way to the shallows. There he lay inexplicably unhurt, staring up into the bluish-green canopy of the tree. He was perfectly happy to be alive and also perfectly content to lie there. Soon, his view of the canopy was interrupted by Blackhorn's snout as the animal sniffed at him, to see if he was all right. Erik stood up to see Gayle running toward him, looking panicked and worried.

"Are you all right?" she screamed, running up to hug him.

"I'm fine," answered Erik.

"Good," she said as she raised her hand into the air. She then slapped him across the face. "Don't you ever do anything that stupid again! If you need help, just ask!"

Erik was overjoyed that Gayle was so concerned, and he was not hurt in the least by her assault. "Help!" he said.

Gayle crossed her arms and, rolling her eyes, asked, "What?"

"My face hurts!" Erik bent down and pointed at his left cheek. Gayle leaned forward and kissed him on the left cheek and then smacked him lightly on the other. Erik then pointed at his right cheek.

Just as Gayle was leaning to kiss it, they heard Jase's voice. "Do you two mind? We are at the home of the house of Gnomare', and you two can find nothing better to do than court?"

Fenrix laughed as he approached and said, "Perhaps you are anxious to find your own elven maiden, Jase?"

Erik bent down and plucked his staff out of the stream and said, "What are we to do then?"

Jase pointed up into the canopy. "I saw them the Gnomare' tending to crystals hanging from the tree's branches. I cannot climb the tree. I tried, but I cannot get a hold by some enchantment. So I called up to them and asked how to get in."

"What did they say, brother?" asked Fenrix.

"Knock!" answered Jase harshly.

"So knock," said Erik.

Jase raised an eyebrow and joined Gayle and Erik in the shallows.

"I have, boy! I have knocked on the tree, its roots, the rocks, the earth. The only thing I haven't knocked on is your skull!" Jase was now staring daggers through Erik.

Erik then tapped his staff on the large slab of stone underneath the few inches of water they were standing in.

Jase and Erik began to laugh together but were interrupted by a snapping sound. As they looked around, several sections of the stone on the banks withdrew, revealing large metal hinges.

"Oh no!" shouted Erik, just as the stones beneath them swung inward like a giant door.

Fenrix, who was not standing in the stream, heard the crash and then watched as his companions disappeared into the darkness below, in a stream of rushing water. Fenrix, sensing that this might be his only opportunity, quickly jumped in without a care.

Chapter 7

◆ ◆ ◆

Elven Home

After falling into the darkness below, the travelers found themselves swept away in a shallow yet very strong current. The underground aqueduct took them spiraling down at a frightening rate but soon slowed as the angle of their descent decreased. After a few more moments, they were deposited in a small room of stainless white metal, with a grate in the floor through which the water flowed on.

First into the room dropped Erik, with a clamor that could barely be heard above the rushing water. Then Jase landing lightly on his feet beside him, with Gayle and Fenrix right behind him, landing on Erik.

Fenrix quickly jumped to his feet and said, "Woo! What a ride!" Gayle and Erik took much longer to get their bearings.

The tumult of the water behind them slowed to a quiet trickle. Jase surveyed the surroundings. The metal grating ended halfway across the room, which looked to be a natural cave. At the opposite end of the room, the roots from the great tree above opened up into an archway, above which hung a lantern made of crystal, framed with a bright silvery metal. Inside the lantern was a luminous green liquid, swirling and tempestuous.

Through the arched doorway formed by the roots, Jase could see outskirts of a great subterranean city with many elvish people therein.

"Elven home," he said to himself and then fell face first to the ground, pounding the grating with his fist. He began to speak in elvish.

Fenrix drew his sword and began to slowly approach the doorway. Gayle and Erik turned their attention to Jase, who was now shivering. Light began to rise from his body like wisps of cloud, at first faintly and then larger and brighter.

Erik looked unconcerned. However, Gayle could see that Jase was in trouble. "Jase, what's wrong?" she said as she tried to comfort him and put her hands on his shoulders. She screamed as some unseen force threw her back on her heels. Fenrix turned to see Gayle wrenching her hands and Erik standing at Jase's side, afraid to come any closer.

Fenrix sheathed his sword and came forward toward Jase, being careful not to get too close. "I have seen this once before, just after our flight from the drakes. He nearly died. One of our most powerful shaman brought him back," said Fenrix.

Everyone's attention was on Jase until they heard the sound of ringing metal followed by a loud harmonic resonance. Fenrix turned and saw them: the elves of Gnomare' had come. There stood two males clad in shimmering hauberks of metal rings, with crystal beads woven in them. Each had at the ready a large curved sword that was giving off the strange resonance the travelers had heard a moment earlier.

A beautiful, yet commanding elven voice came from behind two elves. They separated, and through the door behind stepped an elven female. Her dark green curly hair was pushed back behind her ears, framing beautiful face with a very stern expression. She was dressed in elaborately woven and intricately linked metal armor. She was taller than the two males and was obviously more important. She carried a bow in her hands, but there was a sense of power about her that no weapon could wield.

Fenrix stepped forward and was greeted by the point of the elvish swords a few inches from his face. Fenrix bowed, flourishing his hands. "Fenrix the hunter at your service," he said. The elven female said something in elvish, and the guards stepped back and sheathed their swords.

"I am Kirin, Captain of the High Guard," she said in a voice smooth, youthful and almost musical. She looked at Fenrix and smiled but then looked past him and suddenly became serious. She dashed forward, knocking Fenrix aside as she dove at Jase. Kneeling in front of him, she put her hands on his head and called for the guards. They came forward, shoving Erik and Gayle out of the way. They put their hands on Jase as if trying to keep him in place. Kirin began running her fingers through Jase's hair and whispering in his ear. She then began to sing a note in a crystalline, smooth tone.

As her voice resonated in the room, Erik felt his staff shake in his hand and begin to emit the same sound. The wispy lights rising from Jase's body began to dim and withdraw back into him. Kirin's voice began to waiver and fail and finally went silent. Just as her voice fell completely quiet, the lights radiating from Jase burst out like a roaring fire, throwing the guards back against the walls of the chamber.

The blast did not move Kirin, who was now almost enveloped by the radiating energy. She was showing pain on her face as she reared her head back and yelled with an unimaginably loud voice, "ENOCK!"

Erik, who could barely stand up near Jase, suddenly remembered Jase's words: "Everything created can tell of its nature."

Erik became resolute and said over the roaring sound of Jase's escaping spirit, "Speak of your nature!"

Erik struck his staff on the ground to produce the same tone that Kirin sang. However, he would not let it die. He held his staff out toward Jase and made the tone louder. It grew to an almost deafening volume, and his staff began to heat up in his hand, to the point it began to burn. Erik would not let it go and made the tone even louder with the sheer force of his will. With his staff glowing red hot and screaming the tone amid the screech of complaining metal, suddenly there came a flash and then silence.

The roaring light withdrew back into Jase. Erik's staff became ice cold in his hand, which at first was soothing but then began to burn. Erik dropped it to the floor, where it chimed loudly and shed its frost. It rolled to Kirin's feet, who was now staring at Erik in awe.

The guards both applauded. Fenrix, not knowing what to make if it all, joined them. Erik stepped forward, and scooping his staff off the ground with his uninjured hand, he said, "Hail! I am Erik the Ironrod."

Kirin smiled and said, "Hello, Erik Ironrod, that was a fine tuning, master sage." Kirin leaned down and began to run her fingers through Jase's hair. "A beautiful child with a powerful spirit. It would have been a shame to lose him so very young."

"Kirin?" said a powerful, almost menacing voice from outside the door.

"Yes, my Lord?" she answered.

"Bring Jase, the Quadrian of Eldare', to the House of Healing and show our guests in."

Kirin picked Jase up and cradled him in her arms as she stood. Gayle had not noticed that she was just as tall as Erik until now. Jase indeed looked like a child in her arms. She then motioned to her guards and left the room. The slightly taller of the two guards motioned to the door with a sweeping gesture and said, "Right this way."

The other guard walked through the door, motioning for them to follow. Fenrix was the first to follow; then went Erik and Gayle.

There, through the door, it opened up before them—the ancient home of the house of Gnomare'. The elder elf beckoned them forward saying with the same powerful voice that they had heard in the other room. "Come, children, behold the home of the house of Gnomare' and the city of Ellhom—the Tree of Two Worlds."

Wide-eyed and with mouths gaping open in amazement, they stepped forward past the elder and up to the marble banister to see the great wonders of elvish craft and enchantment. The Tree of Two Worlds, Ellhom, did not stop at the valley's floor, nor were its roots truly roots. Rather, they were vine-like branches, encompassing the entire cave with a lattice work of wooded and green vines.

The trunk of Ellhom did not stop at the valley floor. It proceeded downward into the cave several hundred feet below. Erik leaned over the banister to look down. What he had thought was a large ringed city in a cave surrounding the world's greatest tree was actually a gigantic marble helix of a city spiraling down several hundred feet around the length of its trunk. Ellhom's true base rested in a pool of luminous blue water at the bottom.

Gayle's gaze was fixed on the top of the cavern, where thousands of the same crystal lanterns as before were hung in the umbrella of vines supporting the cave's ceiling and walls. They mimicked the night's map of the stars perfectly and glinted several cool hues. The vines that Ellhom grew were everywhere in the first few levels. These vines assumed many utilitarian shapes—large lampposts, doorways, and benches just to name a few. The vines of Ellhom did not disrupt the structure of the city surrounding it whatsoever. Instead, they served to reinforce the flawless stone work of the Gnomare'.

"I am Enock, high lord here in the tree," said the enormous elf. Erik turned, realizing how rude he was to ignore his host. Enock looked down at Erik and patted him on the shoulder. "Do not be concerned. Ellhom is a magnificent experiment," said Enock.

Erik cocked his head back to look up at Enock, which was an unusual act for him, and said, "How can you know what I was thinking?"

"And how are you taller than a giant of a Mountainfolk?" added Fenrix, calling up at him with his hands cupped around his mouth.

"The answer to both those questions is that I am very old. Even I do not know my exact count of your years. My people do not stop growing through the ages—body, mind, or spirit," said Enock.

Enock was unusual-looking, compared to the other Gnomare'. He was indeed taller than any of the others the travelers had seen, and he almost radiated with an unseen force that even a layman could tell was incredible. He was a creature of an ancient power and grace. He had a beautiful chiseled face partially masked by metallic-looking locks of royal blue and lavender.

He wore a green and gold robe of a material that scintillated as though it were made of many jewels, and around his waist was a silvery belt of what looked like interlocked leaves. Atop his robe, green enameled epaulets were folded over his shoulders in the form of two giant metal leaves of Ellhom. He carried a staff in his left hand that looked like the wood of many trees twisted together, and at its top were many different jeweled leaves. He brushed his hair behind his right ear, revealing a glowing rune of the house of Gnomare' on his forehead, wreathed in a field of floating star like lights.

"You're so beautiful," said Gayle, mesmerized at the sight of Enock.

Enock smiled, looking deeply into Gayle's eyes. Gayle instantly blushed a rose hue and hid behind Erik, overcome with shyness.

"I have so many questions," said Fenrix, turning his head in every direction, trying to take in his surroundings.

Enock smiled and replied, "I love questions—each one is a new challenge. Fenrix the wolf, ask what you will."

Fenrix bowed and said, "If I may, my Lord, what happened to Jase? Is he in some sort of trouble? Are we? And where can I take a bath and get some food?"

Enock tapped his staff on the ground and grew a blue plum on the end of it, plucked it, and handed it to Fenrix. He did the same for Gayle and Erik. "First off, Jase is a Quadrian. His spirit and mind are immortal and will grow in strength through time, but his body will not. It is the most common demise of the Quadrians. The spirit becomes unattuned to the body," said Enock. He also explained what had happened in the well chamber: Jase's spirit, overcome with the pain of centuries of abandonment, had begun to leave his body. What Erik did was called a tuning, and it saved his life. "You did a powerful tuning," Enock said. "I was on my way up when I heard Kirin's call. You have great power in you, but a word of caution"—his tone turned foreboding—"no careless fire enchantments. The air in here is rich. It feeds the life of everything, even flame. As far as bathing, we have many well chambers, both hot and cool, as well as the pool of sky."

"What's the pool of sky?" asked Fenrix.

Pointing down over the banister, Enock answered, "A mighty enchantment. It's the life-giving water from which Ellhom grows. We also enjoy it for healing, relaxation, and loving."

"Loving?" asked Fenrix with interest.

"Yes, it's one of the three laws here, and before you ask, there are indeed curious and loving maidens here," said Enock.

Erik then asked, "What are your laws?"

Enock answered, "Now we come to it. You are guests here, but while in the city of the tree, you will obey the three devotions. You must learn. You must labor. You must love."

"All at once?" asked Fenrix laughing.

Enock nodded and said, "Only if you're any good at them," Enock called for his fellow elves and commanded them to see to the comfort of their guests. They were to wash and feed them and return them to that very spot.

A group of young elf ladies, all light green- or silver-haired and not much larger than Fenrix, began to lead him away. He turned and said, "If I do not return, tell Jase I died happy."

Erik, looking around at his beautiful hosts, saw no sign of age upon any of them and asked, "Enock, one more question. How can you tell the age of your people?"

Enock thought for a moment and said, "It is difficult to tell even for us. We do not measure or celebrate our years. Think of us like trees generally. The larger, the older. The ones that led Fenrix away, for instance, were only a few hundred years each, only adolescents in our reckoning."

Another group of elvish females came to lead Erik away. Erik looked at Gayle and seemed uneasy. "Don't worry—you are in the care of many ages of experience," said Enock.

An elven lady stepped forward and looked Erik in the eyes, brushed the hair out of his eyes, and then took his hand. Erik felt relaxed and safe almost immediately and limped away with the older elven ladies.

The elven lady guiding Erik stopped in the middle of the spiral road and turned toward Erik suddenly. She knelt and put her hands on his hips and began to slowly move them down his legs. She spoke in elvish to the ladies accompanying them. They surrounded him and began to feel his body head to toe. After they all spoke to each other again, Erik's guide picked him up with little effort, put him over her shoulder, and began to sprint away down the rings.

"Erik Ironrod, sage of Hillsborough, I am Emly. I will look after you," said the lady, completely unencumbered by his size and weight.

"Where are you taking me?" asked Erik.

"To see your friend Jase," Emly answered. After a few moments of running down the spiral road of the rings, she stopped suddenly. Turning to the left, she sat Erik down. There he saw a beautiful marble structure carved out from the cave wall. It occupied all the space between its upper and lower rings. It was columned at its entrance, with balconies above it, lanterns in its high windows, and the green vines of Ellhom spiraling its columns.

"This is the House of Healing," said Emly. Taking Erik by the hand, she led him inside. The main room of the house was made of white marble with many lamps hanging from the ceiling, giving off a bright silvery light.

The floor was completely covered with root-like vines of Ellhom and patches of soft green moss. In the far right corner was a spiral staircase, and in the center was a pool of radiant blue water. At its edge sat Jase, draped in a short white robe with feet dangling in the water. Beside him sat an elder elf lady.

Unlike the others, her hair was snow white, streaked with locks of ever-changing colors. She wore a white robe that was flowing down her body to her bare ankles at it dances with runic devices in the silvery light. Upon her brow there shined the elvish rune of the house of Feyara'. A radiance poured out of her like she was standing in the desert sun as she ran her fingers through Jase's hair and kissed him on his brow. Erik turned to Emly and said, "Jase looks like he is in good hands."

"He is. That is Ellen the sky maiden. Sister to the lady of colors and a high priestess to the Feyara'. She is ancient, powerful, and beyond compassionate," said Emly.

Erik added, "She has an unusual beauty as well. It's almost like I'm looking into the sun without my eyes burning."

Ellen laid Jase down next to the pool and shut his eyes with her fingers. She stood and looked at Erik with the bright flame of starlight in her eyes and spoke a language he had not heard before.

Erik's staff rung as if it had been struck by an unseen force and left his hand. He felt his body go numb, and he fell back, only to be caught by the vines of Ellhom that grew into a table beneath him, one that conformed to his body perfectly. "Now you are in the care of the sky maiden. I will see you soon," said Emly.

Erik felt completely numb as he stared at the ceiling. The lamp above him grew dim, and Ellen's luminous face came into view. Looking down at Erik, she said in a voice that reminded Erik of Jase's enchantments, "Sleep now, child. Your body is damaged, and I will mend it."

Erik passed into a deep sleep right away. He dreamt of a midsummer day in Hillsborough with the town full of people there to celebrate this wedding to Gayle. He dreamed of Gayle in a flowing silvery white dress covered in enchanted jewels. He dreamt of taking her into his home for a night of passion and ceaseless pleasure.

He awoke in the House of Healing with Emly on top of him in the beginning of what he thought were his marital rights. "WHAT THE—" yelled Erik, sitting up and tossing Emly off of him. She was wearing only a sheer slip dress that barely covered her mid-chest to upper thigh. "I was asleep! I love Gayle! I thought it was Gayle!" Erik yelled at the frightened elvish beauty.

Ellen descended the staircase from the upper floor and said, "What have you done, Emly?"

Emly covered her mouth, but still speaking through her hands, she answered, "I forgot! elven males do not sleep. I thought he knew it was me. He even spoke vows of love to me!"

Ellen grabbed Emly's wrist and twisted it. Emly, with a shrill yelp, fell to her knee. Ellen's face was angry but still beautiful. "Those are just dreams of men. Fantasy lives while their body rests, nothing more. You have attempted to take something that is not yours—a rare crime for a maiden but a crime in the House of Healing, nonetheless," Ellen said sternly.

It seemed to Erik that a look of complete shame overcame Emly as she said softly, "I have wronged this sage; I know I will be punished."

Erik, not now caring that he was naked, arose from the table. "No! Let her go!" said Erik with a wizard's voice. The words he spoke hung in the air and echoed back and forth in the room until there were many voices demanding one thing: "Let her go!"

Ellen unhanded her and swooned from the spell. However, instead of showing anger, she smiled. "So you changed your mind then, master sage?" she asked.

Erik paused then quickly replied, "Yes, I knew it was her. I was afraid of what Gayle would think, but I recant. I will be with Emly today," Erik walked without limping over to Emly and took her hand and said in his scratchy, deep voice, "Come here, maiden of dreams."

Erik was first to arrive back at the top of the ring, where Enock was waiting with Ellen and another elven female. Erik was walking tall, head held high with a smooth limp-less stride, staff in one hand, Emly's hand in the other. Without his limp and slouch, he stood very tall, even taller than Emly at his side. After their time together in the House of Healing and on their way back up to the top, Emly had told him that there would be a younger elf maiden waiting. It was Sarah, the only member of the house of Eldare' residing within the tree and a person of great importance.

Smiling ear to ear, Erik bowed before Sarah. "Your Majesty, I am Erik Ironrod at your service."

Sarah was young but had a quiet dignity about her that the other elves her size did not seem to possess. She had jet black hair flecked with wisps of blood red. She wore a dress of shimmering black satin with many violet iridescent runic devices that seemed to hover about the fabric. She was covered at the fingers and wrists and neck with many vivid lavender jewels, brilliantly cut and hung in deep rose gold. Erik thought she looked like the embodiment of the ancient legends of elvish beauty.

"I am Sarah. There is no need to be formal. I don't hold, nor will I hold, court in the city of the tree. In the house of Gnomare' the scholars rule above royalty," said Sarah.

"I have not impressed upon the princess the importance of her post, it seems," Enock said with a smile.

Jase's approach was hidden by Erik's massive frame. "Hello elders," he said, appearing from behind the giant man.

Sarah squeaked in delight to see the face of Jase. Springing forward, she lifted him from his feet with a bear hug. Twirling around, she kissed him several times before putting him down. Jase stood there wide-eyed and unblinking, not sure why he was so warmly greeted.

"Jase, this is Princess Sarah of the Eldare'," said Enock.

Jase's eyes filled with tears as he dropped to his knees and touched his forehead to the ground. "My dear lady, I am Jase, Quadrian of your noble house. I would have come to your service sooner had I known the way. I asked the half-elven Gnomare' and was shunned. I searched the tombs of kings and was chased by dragons. I searched the haunted dwarven vaults and battled terrors in the deeps. I have been hunted by drakes, attacked by Vanguard bandits, and assaulted by drunken Mountainfolk and have wandered long in the shadows of the wild. At last I am here to love and serve you, my princess."

Sarah, now weeping in true compassion, spoke forcefully in a tongue unknown to the elders. Enock's expression was almost one of alarm as he answered her in elvish. Then, helping Jase to his feet, Enock patted him on the back. Sarah dried her eyes with the sleeves of her gown, and then, composing herself, she withdrew a wallet from within the folds of her gown. Opening it, she plucked out a square of thin transluscent paper with the elven rune of Eldare' burning brightly on it.

"Jase, by the authority of the house of Eldare', you shall no longer walk alone in the world as an orphan. You will no longer be shunned by any lawful member of the three houses. You are an honored guest in both the houses of Gnomare' and Feyara'. I pronounce you high champion of the elvish people and a lord of the house of Eldare'!"

Touching the runed paper to Jase's forehead, she whistled a beautiful tune, ending on a powerful note that she held, and with a flash, the rune left the paper to rest on Jase's forehead.

Jase stood there shaking while all the witnesses applauded. Jase finally said haltingly, "Surely, my lady, there are more worthy than I."

"There are none. Only you and I. However, even if there were, you would always be my champion," said Sarah.

Jase shook his head. "What have I done for our people compared to any of this?" said Jase, raising his arms and taking in the majesty of Ellhom.

"You saved the lives of many of our children when the last fortress fell!" said Sarah, her eyes once again welling up with tears.

"That was so long ago. I was only fourteen years of age. There was so much hate for my mentor and me that I had to flee. The men of Northguard were hesitant to attack the Kylvara', but they wasted no time on the rest of us. I saved all the children I could in the darkness. I fought when I had to, but I grew weak, and fearing for my own life, I took the last child away to the Northroad with the rest. A paltry dozen only is what I could save. There were so many more. The city was brought down by the wrath of the Kylvara', I learned later.

"I took those poor crying children as far up the north road as I could manage with no beast of burden. At last, coming to the edge of the southernmost forest, I was stopped by the half-elves of Gnomare'. They took an elf girl, citing the final edict of Starblade, and left me to the wild road north with many scared children.

"It took days to reach a small logging settlement called Hillsborough. Out of kindness, they took in the children, but not me. Because I was covered in blood and delirious, they felt I was a bad omen, and I was left to tread the roads of men and dwarfs through the years alone," said Jase.

Enock said, "Your heroics were told to us by our half-elven cousins, Jase. I told them they had acted too rashly, but it was too late. Rumors of your travels were everywhere afterward."

"I am truly surprised that anyone even remembers them or me," replied Jase.

"Not so surprising when the child they took away was me, Lord Jase," said Sarah with a shaking voice and tears falling from her eyes.

Jase embraced Sarah. "My lady, it was my honor and duty as your humble servant." He looked up into her deep purple eyes and said, "Wow, you're taller than I!"

"Silly, you're a Quadrian. Of course, I'm taller. How you survived the wilds as a child is a feat of heroism in itself. How did you do it? Where did you go?" asked Sarah.

Jase only shook his head. Sarah turned and spoke to Enock and Ellen in the same unknown language as before, with the resonance of many harmonic voices. Ellen answered, "His mentor taught him much in a very short time; that is obvious, Princess."

Enock continued, "To fight and to defend those who cannot defend themselves. To survive with no love. To put the mission before one's self. To counter the balance of prevailing power to the last. Those are the lessons that his mentor taught him. Those are lessons of the Kylvara'. But who? I cannot guess."

"The Kylvara', I thought to be cruel, but if their lore kept our champion alive, I will greet them as friends, if they would have it so," said Sarah.

"They would not!" answered Jase and Enock simultaneously.

Erik was truly in awe of his friend Jase. Erik had thought all this time that Jase was a happy-go-lucky adventurer and treasure hunter. Jase was just another outcast orphan like him. Erik laughed and said, "Aren't we a merry bunch of misfits?"

"Who is a misfit?" said Fenrix, jumping up onto the banister from the ring below. "I am all that is, more than man and beast!" He let out a ferocious roar that could be heard echoing in every corner of the city.

Everyone except Jase and Erik was genuinely alarmed that Fenrix could leap like—and moreover sound like—a wild unknown beast many times his size.

"Our scholars of the life enchantments and our beast masters will be fascinated by you, Fenrix," said Enock.

"Thank you, and thank you again for waiting on me, great elder and, um—others," said Fenrix.

"You were not gone long, a couple hours at most, great hunter!" replied Enock.

"Hours? I have been courting at least a dozen elf maidens and am ready to die of exhaustion, and I've only been gone hours?" said Fenrix, scratching his head.

Ellen replied, "Well, I'm sure you'll get better," as she winked at him.

Everyone including Fenrix laughed. Finally, a young elven male by the name of Oberon who had been looking after Gayle appeared to announce the entrance of Gayle Vanguard, maiden of Hillsborough.

Up from the second ring she came wearing a gown of shining silver thread. She wore a circlet of true silver with a large star ruby in the center of her brow. Her neck and wrists and even her fingers were adorned with rubies set in the cunning craft of brilliant metal. Her hair had been elaborately braided and styled and her skin perfumed.

She took Oberon's hand and came forward, shooting a surprised glance at Erik standing straight, tall, and hand-in-hand with a tall elf maiden. She then greeted the elders and thanked them for their generosity. The elders and princess greeted her warmly and in earnest. They explained that there are so few guests that it's a rare pleasure to have them.

Erik and Gayle exchanged an awkward glance, but at last Erik smiled and said, "It seems you make a fine princess, Gayle."

Gayle batted her eyes and said, "Thanks. Oberon has taken good care of me."

"Your presence is a great opportunity to learn, and we will not grudge even a moment of the joy that we have enjoyed through the long years in this place," said Ellen.

Enock held out four silver chains with a flat window pane–like crystal hung from each. "These are yours," said Enock, handing one to each of the group. "These are the symbols of your learning and mastery. Among each other, we are known by what we do. These crystals will allow our people to know you by your skills and paths of learning. You must learn while in the city of the tree. We are also anxious to learn from you. So please, seek out the skills and knowledge of your desire," The elders then bowed and took their leave.

Sarah said, "Erik and Gayle, you have your guides; I shall serve as Lord Jase's. Fenrix, there are so many who desire your knowledge that I'm sure you will sniff them out, beast master."

Fenrix nodded with a mischievous grin and dropped over the banister into the lower rings.

Chapter 8

◆　◆　◆

The Path of Enchantment

E mly took Erik by the hand again and said, "Come, there is someone in the studies I was bidden to bring you to."

Erik smiled and waved goodbye to his companions and began to walk with Emly down the spiral road. Erik was somewhat regretful that he would not be spending his first moments in the tree enjoying the sights with his friends, especially Gayle. However, from his estimation, Gayle looked happy in the company of her escort, and after his own conduct in the House of Healing, he was certain that he did not deserve her company.

The Gnomare' of the city were many and busy with all sorts of work in their dwellings. Erik looked as closely as he could as he passed into the structures cut out of the cavern walls as the city spiraled downward. The buildings seemed to be an even mix of small personal dwellings and large communal structures of various purposes in every ring.

The Gnomare', being unused to having guests, usually stopped as Erik walked by with Emly, only to cast an expressionless stare back at him. The structures seemed to run deeper and deeper back into the cave as they descended down the rings. The Gnomare' as well became more numerous.

Most surprising of all to Erik was seeing very young elvish children in play clothes and decorative costumes playing in the street, running from dwelling to dwelling, laughing and causing mischief among the scholars and tradesmen who seemed genuinely glad of the momentary distraction.

After nearly an hour, at Erik's guess, of vigorous walking, they had come to the middle rings. There he heard the loud noise of ringing steel and heavy impacts of blunt force and crashing shields. Erik squeezed Emly's hand and gave her a questioning look. Emly smiled as she continued to lead him onward. She explained that these rings were the armory, smithy, and training grounds for the High Guard and their hopefuls. Erik began to study the noise as they drew near and thought he could hear the crack of a whip.

After they passed a building that Emly called the Proving Grounds, there came a large uproar of elvish voices, and many young elven males and female came running out shouting.

"Has something bad happened?" asked Erik as they passed by.

"Only if you are Lord Elwayne, our Sword Master—it seems as though a stranger called the Beast has handed him his first defeat since his duel with Elterion the Scion, our Grand Master Bowyer," answered Emly.

Erik shook his head and said, "Ah, Fenrix causing trouble already?"

As they descended further into the city, it became quiet again. Whereas the upper rings were filled with many playing children, busy tradesman, and sparring warriors, these rings were quiet. Few Gnomare' wandered the spiral road here. Instead, only a few Gnomare' were here, reading and meditating on benches grown from the vines of Ellhom next to the banister.

"This is a place for scholars," commented Erik, enjoying the peace and quiet the rings commanded.

"Indeed. Our libraries and schools of enchantment are within these rings. I am to introduce you to the head of our schools of enchantment to begin your study," answered Emly.

"So I am to become a wizard then?" said Erik. He looked at the rings that seemed to emanate a strange light of their own, separate from that of the lamps high above.

"That is up to you, Erik, although *sage* is the word in your tongue that we use for one who wields enchantment. *Wizard* is considered perhaps a vulgar term," said Emly.

At last they had come to their destination. It was the largest structure of the lowest ring dedicated to the scholars. The structure itself looked very similar in design to the House of Healing, with column and balconies visible from the outside. However, instead of the vines of Ellhom growing around the columns or entering this structure, an endless river of glowing elvish runes spiraled their way up and down the columns. It seemed to Erik that this place was to the mind what the House of Healing was to the body.

"This is the outer sanctum of the studies. This place is where the Gnomare', you might find, stop being so carefree and welcoming. So be prepared," warned Emly as she lightened her grip on Erik's hand.

Emly led Erik in through the column and the entrance. Erik could feel the air change as he entered, and he believed he could see a change in the runes as he passed.

The main room of the outer sanctum was a wide open space compared to many within the tree. On each side of the room, next to the walls, were two large crystalline mechanisms. These mechanisms had no gears or levers or parts of any kind that Erik could recognize, but consisted of many geometric and crystalline shapes hovering about each other. These devices reminded Erik of a dwarven clock that he had once seen in the market square than ran on water.

Standing opposite them in the room was a very large elven male. Emly approached cautiously with Erik by her side. This elf was unlike the others whom Erik had seen. His hair was black as night, with no sign of color in it at all. It was pulled back tightly and straight. His face was ageless and beautiful in the manner of the Gnomare', yet his eyes were a pale, but vivid green that seemed to cut Erik's consciousness like razors as he looked at him.

The enchantments surrounding him made little else about him easy to see or understand. Thin, watery pools of roiling glass-like material would swirl tempestuously around him and then terminate like paper consumed by flame. Every few seconds, Erik could see what looked like lightning jump up from the ground beneath him and weave its way into the enchantment. In his hand, the elf held a long staff of smooth, clear,

colorless crystal. At its top it looked to have the same sort of device that was on either side of the room.

Emly at last spoke. "High and Grand Master Sage Artcreft, Arch Mage of the Gnomare', may I present Erik Ironrod, Sage of Hillsborough."

Artcreft's gaze turned its intensity onto Emly as he answered, "I will be the judge of who is called 'sage' here, child. I know why you have brought him here. Now you may go."

Emly bowed and turned away. As she left, Erik looked back and sensed that someone had closed a large door nearby, even though his eyes told him nothing.

Erik immediately turned his attention back to the large, rather unpleasant elf. From his sheer height, even greater than Erik's own, Erik could only guess at his true age. Yet something about him seemed still less than Enock.

Artcreft smiled as he looked at Erik, yet it did not to seem to be an expression of happiness. "I am to begin your instruction in the elven arts of enchantment. It does not seem to me that your kind has sufficient time of life to begin, let alone complete, such training if indeed such a thing were possible."

"Nonetheless, I am glad to try and grateful for your time," answered Erik, trying to be polite.

Artcreft scowled and replied, "First, you must know the runes that give thought direction, a complete precision of thought is required before any action is taken. So you must start by thinking a great deal and speaking very little. In fact, for your current lucidity, I would recommend you speak none at all."

Erik thought to himself that this was a poor attempt to belittle him, seeing as he completely agreed, and as far as cruelty, this elf would be no match for Kreg. Erik said no word and nodded instead.

Artcreft then showed Erik through the outer sanctum, explaining the study and some of its function. The first rooms he showed Erik were filled with elven children who looked to be no older than seven or eight years, in the age and life span of the folk of Hillsborough. There they all sat at desks, not making a sound and writing on parchment.

Artcreft told Erik that this level of study is required for all Gnomare'
as a basis of language and thought. In the next room Erik was shown, a
dimly lit room, young adolescents were standing shoulder to shoulder in
a single line. These elves held in their hands small shards of light-giving
crystal the size of large pens.

One by one, down the line, an elf would draw the image of a rune
in the air with light. After the rune was complete, it would be followed
be a flash of light or sudden gust of wind and many other small effects of
light and sound. Artcreft described this process as "Light Scribing" Once
a complete understanding of the runic system has been retained, the elf
would attempt to give them form and direction in thought.

"The pens help them focus their energy, and this is where we separate
the sages from the craftsmen and warriors. Not to say that we value the latter
two any less in our society, of course," said Artcreft with a short laugh.

The next room was the last along that particular hallway of dimly lit
marble. In it there were what look to be slightly larger adolescents and adult
elves with their pens of light, drawing runes onto many different substances
throughout the room. Artcreft told Erik that here was where the Craftsmen
would learn to imbue the craft with runes through extreme repetition.

"This process requires a complete stillness of mind and unbroken
concentration before success. Then after much repetition, the rune may be
imbued to the material. This is called gifting, and with this craft we can
make cloth as hard as metal and stone as soft as cool water.. Mastering
such a feat requires many times the length of the lives of men you see, or
rather you will not perhaps."

Around the corner of the first hall there was a small ring, a faintly
growing light on the floor large enough for a few people of Erik's size to
stand within. Artcreft entered the ring first, and Erik soon followed close
behind. Erik's vision went black immediately. When sight returned to his
eyes, it was like walking out of a fog into a clear day. He found himself on
his hands and knees staring at the floor.

He was pulled to his feet by some unseen force and found himself at
the beginning of a hall very similar to the last, with Artcreft looking back
at him.

"What happened?" asked Erik.

"Indeed, that is it. We traveled in a manner that your mind could not comprehend, so your eyes could not tell you in any way what your feeble consciousness could not understand," answered Artcreft with a smirk.

Erik changed his mind and began to believe that Artcreft might indeed be a match for Kreg in the art of insult.

Next Erik was shown another dimly lit room where a small number of older elves were sitting in a circle with their eyes closed. There in the center of the circle a rune would appear, and then the effect of its nature would take hold in the room. At one moment the room would be cool and then hot, light and then dark, and at some points, it would actually rain or snow within the confines of the room. Artcreft nodded as he watched, seeming pleased by what he saw and said, "After some time, the pen is no longer needed, and the runes take form by thought alone."

Artcreft proceeded down the hall, and as he stopped, he said, "This is the last room I show you before you begin your studies and is the final stage of the outer sanctum. Understand, you will never get to this point; with the time it takes to reach this level, you would be long dead and your name forgotten by a long line of your descendants."

In this room a single elf sat in a room that was illuminated only by the shining runes hovering in the air about him as he meditated. Artcreft explained that this elf was working a complex equation of thought and that he had been there a length of time, not eating or resting. He went on to say that he would either solve the equation while his strength held or perish in an exhaustion of mind and body.

"All that are considered sages of the Gnomare' find their way to the door or die in the attempt—that is the measure of the dedication needed to become a sage," declared Artcreft.

Erik's vision went black again, and when it cleared, he found himself in a small marble room, sitting on a bunk, looking toward a desk of stone a foot or so in front of him. Erik looked to the left to see Artcreft standing just in front of a large metal door with many runes imbued on its surface.

"These are your quarters for the beginning of your study. I cannot allow you to train with the others. The cloudiness of your mind would pollute the clear direction of our elflings' thoughts. This space is not normally so crowded, but as your kind need sleep, I had to add a bed," He pointed to the corner of the room to a stack of blank parchment and said that they would serve as a start. "On your desk are some gifts from Ellen to help your study of runes. Ellen is no sage by the Gnomare' reckoning but has a fine hand for runes and is a powerful elder. I will see that food is brought to you regularly, and there are many clever devices under your bed that will serve to take care of your base functions, lest this room start to smell like a stable instead of a study," explained Artcreft.

Artcreft left the room and shut the door quickly behind him. Erik saw the runes on the door shift and knew that the door was shut beyond his ability to open. Erik laughed and thought that Artcreft might intend this to be a cruel sort of punishment, but Erik could not be happier.

Erik rose and pulled back the chair to his desk and sat down. He began to examine the objects on his desk. First, there was a book bound in leather in which there were instructions and examples of simple runes to repeat on bare parchment. The book also contained instruction for the rather unique chamber pot and washing mechanisms beneath his bed. Erik then turned his attention to an ink quill with a large red translucent feather resting in a silvery spherical ink well.

Erik sighed and said, "Well, to work then."

The following days went slowly for Erik. At first, it seemed that his hands lacked the finesse to reproduce any of the runes in the book he was given. Much of the blank parchment ended up wadded up and cast about the room in frustration.

A few days passed. Every so often, Emly would open the door to his chamber, with Artcreft beside her to bring him food, and would then leave. The meals became the highlight of his days between long patches of disappointment. Erik was able to resist the urge to sleep for a long time until at last he fell forward to his desk asleep. Erik awoke in his bunk, changed into linen sleeping cloths, and washed and approached the wooden tray of food and a small jug of wine on his desk. Erik shook his head. He had dreamed of runes in his sleep and was reluctant to begin his studies again. Erik sat at the desk and ate all the food and drank all the wine before even looking at what he had written the night before.

Erik looked down to the parchment that he had written on last. After pushing his tray aside, he saw something odd. The ink that had dried on the parchment had a silver sheen to it as he moved the parchment back and forth in the dim white lamplight. Gazing down at the parchment, he moved it to where the runes caught all the light from the lamp. The runes flashed with a brilliant light, causing Erik to drop the parchment and close his eyes. Even with his eyes closed, he could see the image of the runes burned into his eyes as if he had looked directly at the sun. When Erik opened his eyes, the image of the runes was gone from his vision and the parchment. However, when Erik closed his eyes again and thought of the runes, he could recall the exact image of what he had written. Erik thrust his arms into the air above him and let out a triumphant roar. Looking back into the book Erik, grabbed his quill and restarted his effort, invigorated by his new discovery.

After many attempts, Erik was able to duplicate the action with every page of runes in the text he was given. Emly opened the door and entered many hours later. However, this time Artcreft was not with her. She had not brought food with her, and she was wearing the same sheer, short gown that she had worn in the House of Healing when she woke Erik in the marital fashion. Emly said nothing but began to stroke Erik's hair as he clenched and relaxed his right hand in an attempt to relieve its cramping. Emly grabbed his hand and with her strong grip popped his fingers and wrist, and the pain left his arm, replaced with a cool tingling sensation. Emly thrust her fingers into Erik's skin around his shoulders and back. Erik felt all the tension leave his body.

Emly sat down on Erik's bunk and giggled while saying, "You have had enough time to study; now it's time to play."

Erik turned slightly in his chair and looked at Emly and asked, "Do you actually have feelings for me, or is this just your job?"

Emly seemed saddened by the question and answered, "You seem wise enough to know that this is my duty and profession, yet when I offer my affection, it is never feigned. I could tell you had feelings for me in the House of Healing. However, I am old enough to know it was pity."

ELDARE'
THE
FIRMAMENT

GNOMARE'
THE
EMPTY CUP

FEYARA'
THE
SPIRIT

KYLVARA
THE
COUNTERBALANCE

MANA
THE
CHANGE

VESSLE
THE
CONSTANT

SHIELD
THE
OPEN HAND

SWORD
THE
CHAMPION

FIRE
THE
PASSIONATE

WATER
THE
HEALER

WAR
THE
AMALGAM

SCION
THE
HEIR

GROWTH
INTELLIGENT
DESIGN

SIGHT
THE
OPEN
GATE

ENOCK
CHILD OF
JOY

KYLRATHA'
FLAME
BARE.

Erik lowered his eyes and replied softly, "I do pity you, but not for the reason you may think. I pity such a beautiful elf who has nothing better to do than to be with me."

Emly's expression did not change as she stood and kissed Erik on the top of the head and said, "For whatever reason, there are many things that I desire for myself as well, but your pity is not one of them. Be well, Erik Ironrod."

As she opened her hand palm outward toward the door, Erik could see the runes on it shift again, and it swung open slowly. Emly then turned and left quietly.

Putting his hands on his head and grasping a handful of his own hair in each hand, Erik shouted, "Erik the Rod, you are an idiot!"

"Yes, you are!" said Artcreft, laughing as he entered the room.

Artcreft looked about the room, which was brightened by the light of his own enchantments. Looking down at the bare parchment, he cast his glance on Erik and declared, "Had Enock not told me himself that you were to learn enchantment, I never would have guessed you had any desire to do anything intelligent. Seeing nothing but bare parchment, and watching Emly leave after you insulted her, I am sure of it. You are a fool, and you will not learn anything of consequence here."

Erik, completely unaffected by his words, looked up at Artcreft and asked, "Do you have another book of runes I can read?"

Artcreft looked furiously down at Erik and yelled, "Yes, I do, and no, I will not give it to you! You will take what time you have and study what I have given you! You will have plenty of extra time, seeing there is little chance any maiden of pleasure will visit you now, and I must send one of my own students to fetch you your meals! What a happy and worthwhile task for them!"

Artcreft departed with a flash of light and a thunderous bang. The door to the room slammed shut, and the runes on it began to glow even brighter than before. Erik sighed and wondered if he would ever be able to leave his cell and see any of the wonders of this city or his companions. While still staring at the door, Erik realized that the runes on it were not in his book and began to write them down and gift them to his memory.

Erik then began to look around the room and noticed that other objects in the room had runes on them as well. The lamp in the ceiling and even his wash basin and chamber pot had runes on them. Soon, however, all Erik had were his thoughts and nothing he could do with them. Erik could find nothing better to do than sleep.

In his dreams, again the runes began to appear. With every different one, there came an image that seemed to Erik to embody its meaning, whereas before they had been only beautiful shapes. The runes then began to form concentric rings and spin in opposite directions of their inner and outer rings.

Erik awoke to the sound of arguing outside the door to his study. At first, he could not make out the words, but as he concentrated, he could see a rune and could feel his attention drawn closer to the sounds.

The voices were that of Enock and Artcreft, and neither one sounded pleasant. "He is not suited for the path of enchantment. He is wasting his time and mine. I will waste no more of my own on him!" declared Artcreft.

"Perhaps it is his teacher that is not suited for the task he was given," responded Enock.

"If you feel that way, eldest, perhaps you should show him the way, if you can. It is no more of my concern!" snapped Artcreft.

Erik could feel the air around him growing warm, and his room began to vibrate.

Enock's voice became louder and stern yet still was smooth and melodic.

"You have over spoken in my presence. If I tell you to show this child the path, that is what you are to do, Arch Mage! It seems I could not rely on you for this simple task. Perhaps your mind has been concerned with great matters so long that the easiest of tasks eludes your brilliance."

"Have you considered what it is that you asked? To open this child's mind to the devices of enchantment that lie beyond the door, and to have the power to use them with absolutely no clarity of thought necessary to control them?" question Artcreft.

"I have considered all the uses of enchantment by all its sages since ere your sires were born to Avalon, child. Now leave my presence and set your mind to tasks it can handle!" commanded Enock.

Artcreft's voice shrank in its venomous tone as he responded, "Yes, my lord."

Erik sat up and looked at the door to his chamber. The runes on the door seemed to dissolve into wisps of light and vanish. The door opened slowly. Enock came through, and the room began to fill with the light that poured from him in gently rolling waves. Enock sat down beside Erik on the bed and placed his hands on his head. Erik could feel his body go warm, and in his mind every rune that he had committed to memory flashed out suddenly.

"Excellent!" said Enock cheerfully. "I can see the ink Ellen gave you helped memorize the basics."

Erik shook his head in agreement and answered, "I would have made no progress without it."

Enock paused then said, "I am now your teacher. The runes you have learned are devices elves use to give thought direction and magnitude, their vector, so to speak, in the old tongue. We used these vectors as conduits to siphon energy from Avalon, our last home, as well as mold this energy to our purposes. This is only one way of doing such a thing, but it is the only way that most sages are aware of. The other paths of enchantment confound them. However, they seem to come naturally to you and your companions. I will say no more on this for now."

Erik only nodded and tried to understand, but the meaning of most of Enock's words was lost on him. Enock opened up his left hand, palm out, in front of him, and before him appeared concentric rings filled with runes spinning in opposite directions.

"You have seen this, haven't you?" asked Enock.

Erik gasped and leaned forward as he replied, "Yes, I saw this in my dreams but did not understand what it was."

Enock explained that it was the Grand Runic Cipher and was the supreme achievement of runic study. With this device it was possible to accomplish nearly anything if one had the clarity of mind to use it. "There is one thing, however, that it does that is very special, and since there is little hope you will discover this in your natural lifetime, I will now show you!" declared Enock.

Enock stood and pulled Erik to his feet with his right arm. Erik could now see that the cipher had many more rings and runes than in his dreams. As the rings began to spin, the room began to resonate, and the image of the room beyond the cipher became wavering and translucent as if it were a mirage. The rings stopped spinning suddenly and locked in place, and the resonance in the room became deep; the room itself seemed to shake and waver.

Erik could see the image of a door of light appear behind the cipher, which began to spin again. The resonance in the room became loud and sharp and began to hurt Erik's ears. The cipher stopped and vanished, and the image of the door swung open and began to fill the room with blinding light. Erik could feel Enock pull him through the door a few steps and stop.

"Open your eyes, child!" commanded Enock.

Erik was almost afraid of the brilliance of the light, but it did not burn his eyes as he opened them. Erik look out ahead and could see that he was on a paved path that shimmered like gold in the sun, cutting its way through a vivid green country under a brilliant star-filled sky. The world he saw drew its light from the path rather than any celestial body, and every blade of grass, tree, and stone radiated with its light.

Erik could see small mechanisms inside everything he set his eyes on, whether rock, plant, or even the breeze that gently blew across the path. He could see everything's structure and inner working, and at that moment, it seemed so simple that he wondered why he had not noticed these things before.

"This is the shining path in the reckoning of my people," said Enock.

Erik's vision went white, and he could feel himself fall backward. When his sight returned again, he found himself sitting on the bed, swooning and tired.

Enock, now standing in front of Erik, said, "Walking the path costs a great deal of strength in body, mind, and spirit. Be careful of it. Even elders have fallen back from it withered and lessened after proceeding hastily."

Erik looked up at Enock and bowed his head. "Yes, my lord."

"Do not call me that, child. Now let us leave this place," replied Enock.

As Erik stood, he was astounded that he could see the same inner working mechanisms in the marble and other materials of the room around him.

"I can see—" said Erik with wide eyes and shaking voice.

"Then lead the way, child," responded Enock with a nod.

Erik took his staff from the corned and waved it in front of them, and as if the walls of his room were made of smoke, he and Enock passed through them and down a winding stair, into the main room of the outer sanctum. There, Artcreft stood with an expression of both awe and terror on his face as he saw them enter out of a wisp of smoke.

"What have you done?" asked Artcreft, looking at Erik.

"What you could not," answered Enock.

Erik looked toward the columns at the entrance of the outer sanctum and could perceive that the way was still shut by enchantment. Erik raised his staff toward the entrance, and many large brightly burning runes began to appear and vanish like the leaves of a book being quickly flipped through. The warding enchantments at the entrance faded completely, as did the runic devices surrounding the columns just beyond.

Erik turned back toward Artcreft, who was now scowling, clearly displeased that his gates had been disenchanted and ungifted.

"Thank you for your hospitality, Arch Mage," said Erik with a slanted grin.

Erik turned and left with Enock at his side. As they reached the spiral road, Enock halted and said, "You may go where you please in the city with one exception. Stay clear of the laboratories. Artcreft was right on one count—that your thoughts lack a certain precision, so many of your enchantments may be unpredictable. I would recommend you spend your time in our libraries and widen your knowledge."

Enock passed his hand over the crystal pane that was hanging from the chain around Erik neck and caused a series of luminous runes to appear within it.

"Go now, Master Sage, to your studies," said Enock, who then turned and hopped onto the banister. A large branch of Ellhom descended to the banister and carried Enock far upward and out of sight.

Chapter 9

◆　◆　◆

The Girl Who Would Be?

After Erik had departed with Emly toward the studies, Gayle had watched Sarah and Jase leave hand in hand, speaking in a language that sounded different from the one the Gnomare' were using.

Oberon took Gayle's hand and kissed it. "Come with me, dear lady. I will show you some of the wonders of our home."

They strolled slowly down the spiral road as Oberon explained many of the unique features of the city. He told her that the lamps in the canopy could mimic the virtues of any sort of light in the heavens. Also, he showed her how different branches of the tree were like different trees entirely and had different leaves, flowers, and fruit. In fact, there was no plant within the city of the tree that did not some how come from Ellhom.

Oberon turned and said, "Nowhere is this more evident than the arboretum. You would find it quite beautiful. Come."

Gayle walked with Oberon only a short way further down the spiral road before they stopped and turned left to a small unassuming doorway in the bedrock of the cave, almost completely covered by the flowered vines of Ellhom.

Oberon pushed the vines to the side with his right hand and with his left hand motioned Gayle forward. The small tunnel beyond the doorway was dark, cool, and moist. Gayle could hear the sound of gently running water somewhere close by. The tunnel eventually opened up into a brightly lit cave that went back into the rock a great deal further than she expected.

Oberon stepped in front of her and said, "Gayle of Hillsborough, may I present the arboretum."

Gayle flashed a smile at Oberon and stepped forward onto a cobblestone path that cut its way through an otherwise unbroken carpet of long grass-like moss. The path wound around the cave and in between many bush- and tree-like plants growing from the vines of Ellhom. Every plant seemed to be constantly in flower and bearing fruit. Gayle's eyes were drawn to several bright points of light flying about the arboretum.

"What enchantment is this?" asked Gayle, pointing at a few of the lights.

Oberon stuck his finger out, and several of the lights began to rest on the tip of his finger and give off soft chiming sounds like small bells of silver. "Pixy flies. They help keep the flowering plants healthy, I'm told. I am not sure where they come from, whether from the depths of an adjoining cave or perhaps from some experiment of Enock's. They are creatures of merry mischief, if you ask me, but the elflings love them. They chase them down with nets, and in the case of a rare success, they will keep them in jars in their dwellings."

They proceeded down the path together. Gayle was amazed at the variety of life within the arboretum. Gayle was memorized by strange transparent creatures with flower-like bodies floating through the air, giving off the light and the color of anything they floated near.

They drew near to the source of the sound of the running water after passing through a maze of hedge-like bushes. The path began to run alongside a slow-running, but deep stream of clear water. Gayle looked into the stream and could see several large silvery scaled fish swimming lazily in the current, occasionally coming to the surface to eat a seed or flower shed from the nearby tree-like plants.

"Fish!" exclaimed Gayle, genuinely surprised to see them.

Oberon smiled and asked, "Do you like fish my lady?"

Gayle shook her head affirmatively and answered, "We do not often get them at market. Sometime the dwarfs will bring them from their underground hatcheries and cook them for us. They are really tasty. Are these any good to eat?"

Oberon's eyes widened and an expression of surprise came across his face as he bowed slightly. He looked back down into the stream and then replied, "I do not know. We do not eat them, nor do many of us eat animals of any kind. However, I will inquire if these may be eaten and have some prepared for you if you wish."

Gayle now felt somewhat embarrassed and answered, "No, that is not necessary, but what do you elves eat here then?"

Oberon smiled and said, "Come, it would be easier to show you than explain. Oberon led Gayle through a small maze of hedges to a large ring in the hedge. Within the ring there were several bushes with dark single-bladed leaves, the edges of which pulsed with equal parts teal and lavender.

"Here is one example, my lady. Perhaps a closer investigation beneath the bushes will explain more," said Oberon with a soft laugh.

Gayle approached the edge of the bushes and lifted the hem of her gown in order to crouch. There, underneath the bush, to Gayle's surprise and amusement she saw a small elven girl who could not be more than two years of age dressed in a small white robe picking and eating dark maroon berries. The child's cheeks and chin as well as the front of her robe were stained red from the juice of the berries, which was still running out of her mouth as she chewed at a large mouthful. Gayle began to laugh hard at the sight and rolled back to sit down. Oberon sat next to her and held out a small handful of berries for her to sample.

As Gayle tasted them one by one, she could not compare the flavor to any of the fruits of the orchard. These berries were sweet, but they did not overpower her palate. The taste reminded her of the scent of many fragrant flowers.

The elf toddler gave out a squeal as a few pixy flies flew by. The child dropped her remaining berries and began to give chase out of the ring. Gayle watched in alarm as the elfling ran with amazing speed compared to a human child of Hillsborough of that age.

"Oberon? Your children play here unattended? What is to stop them from falling into the stream?" asked Gayle, caught somewhere between alarm and curiosity.

Oberon raised his eyebrows as he ate one of the berries and began to stare at the bright lamps in the overhead. He seemed surprised by the question but at last responded, "Nothing, and no one in the tree is unattended. As to falling into the stream, nothing stops them. They simply swim to the edge, and the fish push them back up onto the path. It's an amusing sight, and the children love playing with the fish, so they jump into the stream of their own accord regularly."

Gayle felt bad for entertaining the thought of eating such amazing fish and began to blush.

Oberon put his hand on Gayle's shoulder and asked, "So what is it that you like to study?"

Gayle hummed to herself while she thought and answered, "Well, I suppose I like to study archery. I am considered an expert where I come from, but after challenging Jase, I feel like a beginner in truth."

Oberon stood and helped Gayle to her feet and replied, "That comes as little surprise to me, even if I am no expert on the matter. The tales of Jase, however, are those of a child born into the Great Wars and left to the wild. His prowess with arms is the sole reason he lives today. Come, I will get you fitted for the ranges. Master Erlon is a good teacher, and you may learn a lot to perfect your craft."

Together they left the arboretum and ascended back up the spiral road. Oberon took Gayle to a simple marble dwelling. It was marked at the entrance with a rune of Gnomare' above the door. The stone door opened inward, on unseen hinges, into a large room with a round stone table in its center, surrounded with half a dozen marble stools.

"This is my home I have prepared quarters for you inside," said Oberon.

Oberon took her past the main room and to a smaller room in the back. In this room was a comfortable-looking bed covered in decorative satin sheets. There was also a crystal wash basin and a mirror, as well as a large wooden wardrobe grown from the vines of Ellhom. Oberon told

Gayle that these were her quarters during her stay and that he would fetch armorers to outfit her in gear suitable for the range.

Soon Gayle was joined by two silver-haired, young elf males who introduced themselves as Ketha and Jzon. At first, Gayle blushed as they began to undress her down to her under garments, but she soon noticed that they showed no interest in anything but outfitting her in the range gear. Soon Gayle was clad in soft, pliable leather with hard metal cleverly layered into it. She was also given sturdy boots and bracers with gloves for archery. Oberon appeared in the doorway once she was changed and led her out of his dwelling.

They once again strolled slowly down the spiral road. After what seemed like an hour of walking in silence, Oberon announced that they had arrived at the ranges. Gayle looked to her left and saw a large opening in the cave wall completely surrounded by the vines of Ellhom. The entrance, in fact, looked more like an opening in a wall of closely growing trees.

Oberon and Gayle proceeded up the short staircase leading up to the door that was also overgrown with the vines. Upon entering the ranges, Gayle noticed the strong scent of cedar. The lamps that lit the range were a dark green and lit the long hall of the indoor with a soft, almost twilight glow. The floor of the range, at first, was of evenly cut slate squares, almost like tiles. It gave way to a mixture of wooden chips several feet beyond the end of a long wooden bench that ran along the wall to their left.

In the range there were several targets at many distances throughout. There were both targets set on the ground and many more hung from the ceiling. From a door in the wall on the right entered a tall male elf, clad in the same gear that Gayle was wearing. He was holding a bow in his left hand and had a large quiver on his back. As soon as the elf laid eyes on Gayle, he smiled and turned to a large wooden standing closet to his left. He opened it and produced a small plain wooden bow and a cloth quiver with some white-feathered arrows protruding from it.

Oberon stepped forward and said with a bow and a sweeping gesture with his left hand toward Gayle, "Master Erlon, may I present Gayle, expert archer of Hillsborough."

Master Erlon smiled as he came forward and handed Gayle the bow and quiver.

"Thank you, Oberon. We will send for you when you are needed. As for you, Gayle of Hillsborough, you are just in time to meet the rest of your class," said Erlon.

Erlon was tall, but not as tall or nearly as large as Enock and some of the other elves she had seen. He had deep emerald green eyes and hair of the same color. What did catch Gayle's attention was that Erlon had large, sharp, almost fang-like teeth that were very apparent when he spoke. Oberon bowed and exited quietly.

Gayle turned to watch him leave and saw that several small elf children were entering the range and sitting down quietly on the bench next to the left-hand wall. They were all carrying bows and small quivers exactly like the one Gayle was holding. These children were not wearing range gear, however; rather, they were dressed in bright play clothes with bells and bright buttons of gold or silver. Others were wearing costumes of animals, such as stags or birds. Perhaps most comical was the one sitting to the far right who was dressed as a fish—with a large ridiculous fish head of cloth with large jeweled eyes for a hat. The last child to sit down on the bench was the small toddler whom Gayle had seen in the arboretum, still covered in stained clothes and dragging her bow and quiver behind her. The toddler hopped up and sat down on the bench with a plop and began to smile.

Erlon laughed and approached the bench, lifting the chin of the toddler as he spoke to her softly in elvish. The toddler nodded quietly in response. Erlon turned to Gayle and said, "I apologize for the state of my daughter. We do actually take the skill of archery quite seriously in the tree."

Gayle laughed and replied, "They're all so adorable, I just want to squeeze them."

Erlon nodded in agreement and replied, "You can do all the squeezing you like after the lesson, provided you can catch them. Now Gayle, if you would, approach the firing line to the far left so we may begin. I will be giving my commands in our tongue for the sake of the elflings. Just do as they do when commanded. Pay close attention, and you will learn much."

Gayle's heart sank—she could not believe they thought so little of her ability that they put her in a class with very small children. Gayle shouldered her quiver and thought to herself that this would be a short lesson, and soon she would be with her peers. She approached the firing line and looked to her right. Erlon began to take the elflings off the bench one at a time from the left, starting with his daughter, and lined them up to Gayle's right. After being placed on the line, the small elf girl shouldered her quiver and held her bow at the ready. The other elflings all did the same as Erlon walked them to their position.

Erlon came back to Gayle and said, "If you need assistance, just raise your hand, and I will help."

Erlon then raised his right hand and said a word in elvish. The elflings on the line all drew an arrow and shot it at the nearest target. Gayle watched as every arrow met its mark at the exact center of its shooter's target. The only exception was Erlon's daughter, who was too small to draw an arrow from her quiver. Erlon knelt down behind his daughter. Drawing an arrow from her quiver, he placed it in her hand and then pulled her platinum blond locks out of her eyes. The elfling girl then notched the arrow on the bow string, drew it back awkwardly, and released it. The arrow flew sloppily high into the air in an arch and then fell out of the air, striking her target in exact center at a peculiar downward angle.

Gayle stood stunned in complete disbelief. She was snapped out of her trance by Erlon asking if she was well. Gayle shook her head and then drew and loosed an arrow that struck her nearest target very near its dead center. Some of the elflings began to laugh, but they were quickly hushed by Erlon. Erlon raised his hand again and spoke a different word in elvish. The elflings all let an arrow fly at the next target further down range with the same result. The lesson continued like that back and forth down all the targets on the range until every one's quiver was exhausted.

Erlon then gave the signal for them all to recover their arrows. To Gayle's further horror, Erlon would go from target to target, commenting on each shot gone astray. Every elfling had a few shots on his or her furthest target that was every so slightly astray to Gayle eyes. At last Erlon came to Gayle's targets and gave the elflings a curious smile; he began to speak to them after pointing at each arrow not on target. This portion of the lesson took some time as the elflings would interrupt Erlon with laughter or to make their own comments in elvish.

Erlon then turned his attention to Gayle and said, "Perhaps more practice is needed here, and if you like, we can get you a bow you are more comfortable with."

The elflings were all dismissed. However, Erlon kept Gayle back, helping her with her posture and technique for a great deal longer, until more elf children began to enter the range. Gayle saw that these children were slightly older and were wearing the same gear that she and Erlon were wearing. Erlon looked at them and spoke to them shortly, and they began to sit down on the bench.

Erlon turned his attention to Gayle once more and placed a hand on her shoulder. "This class may be too advanced for you. I will send Oberon to fetch you when it is time for the next class."

Erlon then took her quiver and bow and walked her slowly to the door, suggesting that she relax and meditate on what she had seen and done today. Gayle wandered down the spiral road until she saw a bench next to the banister grown from the vines of Ellhom. Gayle sat and immediately began to sob.

Gayle then felt a sense of peace come over her. She noticed her body become warm and relaxed. Lifting her head, she saw a radiant image out of the corner of her eye. It was Ellen, the High Priestess, sitting beside her on the bench.

Gayle looked up at her and started to cry again, putting her head on Ellen's shoulder.

Ellen kissed Gayle on top of her head and asked, "Why the tears, child?"

"They put me with the elfling children at the range," answered Gayle. Gayle sniffed and wiped her eyes. "And they're all better then me!"

Ellen shook her head. "You poor child. Sometimes the Gnomare' are cruel without knowing. Come with me. I know what you need," said Ellen.

Ellen led Gayle to a small workshop at the very bottom ring of the city, just above the pool of sky. There in the shop and testing range, there were all sorts of bows hung on the wall, made in all different sizes and out of several different materials. Ellen disappeared into a room in the back. Gayle could hear Ellen speaking to another elf for a few moments; she returned from the back carrying a bow that she immediately handed to Gayle.

Gayle held up the bow. It was so beautiful she imagined it must be the master work of several craftsmen. The wood was hard and heavy. It was a very dark brown, almost black, with light brown streaks throughout. The gold inlay and decoration resembled the root-like vines of Ellhom. At each end of the bow was a wheel of a strange bronzey metal with a vitreous sheen. The bow string ran over these wheels in a pulley system that Gayle never would have imagined using in a bow.

"This bow carries powerful enchantments and is designed with many clever mechanisms. Its shot is true, much more so than any crude bow of the vulgar craft," said Ellen.

Gayle drew back the string with ease, yet could tell she was holding back an incredible force. She loosed the empty string, and the bow nearly sprang from her hand.

"The Lord Elterion is the tree's—and perhaps the elves'—most gifted bowyer, and he offers this to you with his best wishes," said Ellen.

Gayle's eyes became wide as she said, "Really? Where is he? I should like to thank him," She looked around the range.

"He is a grand master of one of the most prized elvish crafts. He is busy in his workshop, not wishing to be disturbed," answered Ellen.

Ellen walked over to a large wooden locker next to the entrance. Opening it, she took out a quiver made from a strange dark scaly hide and threw it over her shoulder. She then took Gayle back to the range.

Ellen returned Gayle to the firing line and stood beside her. Drawing an arrow from the quiver, she showed it to Gayle. The fletching was of exotic silvery feathers, the shaft was ironwood, and the diamond-shaped head was a bright white metal. Ellen turned the shaft between her fingers. As the arrow head turned, different runes appeared with a flash and were gone.

"This is the subtle art behind our best archers. The runes obey the mind of the rune master, making a runic archer one of the deadliest of our warriors. Now hand me your bow, child," said Ellen.

Gayle handed the bow to Ellen, who notched and fired an arrow. The arrow hit the nearest target a few dozen meters down the lamp lit tunnel of a range. The target was reduced to splinters with a loud bang. The arrow recoiled and then skipped and slid back to Ellen's feet.

"Amazing!" exclaimed Gayle, jumping up and down in excitement. "I thought you were a priest!"

"Priestess, not priest—different job entirely, my child. I am not a runic archer. However, I know much of runes. But I know little about the discipline of the bow," replied Ellen.

She handed back Gayle's bow and then put the quiver on Gayle's back and tightened the belt across her chest.

Gayle groaned. "This thing is heavy," she said with a whimper.

"Well, get used to it. The quiver is yours; you will wear it at all times. Now let's get to the House of Healing. I will begin your instruction on runes," said Ellen.

"When will I train archery with Master Erlon?" asked Gayle.

"You won't. From now on, you will take lessons from Kirin—she is a runic archer. Erlon is not. Males lack the subtlety of hand and mind for this craft," said Ellen with a laugh. Then he stopped suddenly, and her eyes grew wide as she turned to Gayle. "Don't tell Enock I said that," said Ellen in a hushed tone.

"You don't like him, do you?" asked Gayle.

Ellen shook her head. "In truth he is my hearts one desire. Yet there was a time long ago when we Elders of Prime Avalon spoke and acted as we though we no longer needed the Scions or the Saints. You see even we Elders have our superiors. The lord Elterion is one the Scions the generation that sired the elders. Enock is a Saint they are the very first in elvendom and the grand sires of the Scions. The generation between was known as the seed but they were lost to us. Why I tell you this is because you should know that when the usurper king ruled Prime Avalon we elders supported him. When Enock returned and deposed Starblade we elders were shamed . I had long held Enock in my heart and desire but after his return I had not the courage to tell him of my love. Enock is the greatest in all elvendom save the dark prince of the counter balance himself. I am only a child in the eyes of the saint of Gnomare' I am no more worthy to touch the hem of his robe that I am to hold his hand."

Gayle noticed that the light radiating from Ellen dimmed for a moment. "You don't believe he would love you in return?" Gayle asked.

"He is so great in knowledge and power that I am only a child in his eyes. Once, he was only a mighty warrior and the sword saint of the Gnomare'. Now, he is so much more. No title can define him," said Ellen.

A single luminous tear rolled off Ellen's cheek. It hit the ground and erupted into a shower of sparkling lights and fiery dispersion. Ellen smiled again and said, "Come, we have much to do."

Gayle spent what seemed like days with Ellen, sleeping and eating in the House of Healing while studying runes. Kirin would, on occasion, arrive and take Gayle to the range. Gayle showed some improvement but no ability to control the flight and very nature of her arrows as could Ellen and Kirin. Gayle would return day after day, shrugging as she looked at Ellen. This had Kirin scratching her head in frustration as she talked to Ellen after each lesson.

After several days of instruction and frustration, Gayle sat down at the table in the second floor of the house where she had been studying runes and began to cry with frustration again. The light emanating from Ellen filled the room as the priestess approached, and Gayle became calm again.

Ellen sat beside her and turned the chair that Gayle was sitting in toward her. Looking Gayle directly in the eyes, she said, "Unfortunately, learning runes and their meaning can take a very long time, and I have given out my good ink for scribing. So we must do this another way, although you might find it unpleasant. Are you willing to learn even if it hurts you?"

Gayle, not looking away from Ellen's intense gaze, answered, "Teach me."

Ellen placed her hands on each side of Gayle's head, and Gayle began to swoon. At first, Ellen's hands were warm, but soon Gayle found that her touch was beginning to burn. Images of runes began to appear in Gayle's mind one after another in an endless cycle. Gayle could fill her head begin to throb and ache with fire, and she felt stabbing pains in her eyes as each rune flashed in her mind.

This continued until Gayle was screaming at the top of her lungs, the shrieks of pain reaching out into the spiral road from the upstairs balcony of the House of Healing. Kirin soon appeared unnoticed at the door of the room to investigate but stopped. Understanding what was happening, she only stood and watched.

Gayle begged Ellen to stop, but she would not. At last, when Gayle lost the strength to scream, she fell from her seat, bleeding from her eyes, nose, mouth, and ears. Ellen rocked back in her seat and began to hold her own head. Ellen, however, quickly regained her senses and with Kirin's help brought Gayle downstairs and laid her on a bed to begin treating her wounds.

When Gayle became conscious again, she could not see, but she was in no pain. Ellen had wrapped her head in gauze, and she could hear faint voices in the room.

"Hello? Who's there?" asked Gayle.

"Rest, child," Ellen said. "You have endured something very taxing on your body. Now lie still, and you will be cared for."

Gayle quickly fell asleep and began to dream. In her dream, she could see Oberon and another elf maiden standing over her as she slept.

The elf maiden asked Oberon, "So this woman child is your responsibility to serve and love?"

Oberon grunted and replied, "Yes, Layla, that is my unhappy task."

The maiden called Layla laughed and said, "I spent some time loving the beast called Fenrix in the well house as they arrived. His body was scarred and bruised like a wounded animal, but he was a welcome amusement for me, I must say."

Oberon shook his head and said, "You may be fascinated by these lesser creatures, but their mortal fingers disgrace you. I, for one, have no desire to love or know this beastly woman child. To me, she is like a fruit rotting on the vine, already dead, yet still drawing life from the world."

Gayle woke up with a yelp and sat up. The gauze had been removed from her head. She could see that the room was empty. Kirin, having heard her yelp, came down from upstairs and asked, "Are you all right?"

Gayle, still in a state of shock, asked Kirin, "Was Oberon here?"

Kirin smiled in seeming surprise as she answered, "Yes, he was here just after you fell asleep yesterday to see if you were all right."

Gayle nodded and asked, "Was Layla with him?"

Kirin bowed her head and said, "It seems that Ellen's action have made you very perceptive. If you know her name, you know the nature of their conversation."

Gayle scowled and replied, "Yes, even for fruit dying on the vine, I can hear."

Kirin's voice became stern as she said, "So you can speak and understand our language. I will instruct that fool Oberon and his whelp to watch their tongues in the future."

Gayle shook her head and said, "I hate to disagree with you, but they were talking quite plainly, and I do not understand or speak your language."

Kirin looked alarmed as she steadied herself against the wall to her right. "My child, I hate to disagree with *you*, but you have been speaking my language since you woke. Since you do indeed understand my words, listen well. Forget the elves that work the arts of pleasure. They do so because they have talent for little else. Now that your mind is indeed awake, it is time to begin your training," Kirin helped Gayle off her bed and dressed her in her range gear.

The next days passed quickly for Gayle. Every moment at the range, Gayle became more powerful in runic archery. Even Kirin said that she had never seen anyone progress that swiftly. But Gayle's training was not without its difficulties. On one occasion, Kirin told Gayle to fire, and as she loosed her arrow all the targets on the range burst into flame. Several incidents like that happened in the following days however with each accident Gayle seem to learn a little more each time.

Perhaps the most alarming thing over the following days was Fenrix running onto the range, chasing an elvish female in some sort of game, while Gayle and Kirin were shooting. Fenrix and the female, to Gayle's and even Kirin's amazement, dodged their arrows with ease. Kirin turned and watched Fenrix chase the female out of the room.

Kirin laughed and said, "She is trouble, that one. I hope your friend knows what he is doing. However, as for you, I can see that you can progress well from this point on your own."

Gayle nodded in agreement and, giving Kirin a hug, said, "Give Ellen my love."

Kirin agreed to this and left to her duties.

Gayle then sighed and said to herself, "I am glad I am not the only one causing trouble."

Chapter 10

❖ ❖ ❖

Predators, Prey, and Provision

As Jase saw Fenrix dive over the banister and down into the city, he smiled, and Sarah shrugged. Sarah began to lead him by the hand down the spiral road.

She stopped for a moment, pulled Jase into her embrace again, and asked, "So where does our champion desire to go in this wondrous city?"

Jase answered immediately as if he had already decided his destination: "Show me where your warriors train."

Sarah, not surprised, responded, "Have a care, champion. We are house of Eldare'. Everything we do is watched closely, and because we rule, many of the older Gnomare' treat us with some resentment."

Jase laughed and replied, "At least resentment is something. I much prefer it to neglect."

Sarah giggled and let Jase go. She began to twirl Jase's hair in her fingers and said, "Well let's get you outfitted in suitable attire for a champion then."

Sarah hopped up on the banister and extended a hand toward Jase, saying that they would travel in a manner similar to his reckless friend.

Jase took her hand and hopped up beside her. Looking out over the ledge, even with his incredible dexterity and nerve, he found it to be a dizzying height. Sarah extended her hand toward the tree. A branch of the tree reached up from far below and came to rest beside the banister. The branch began to change shape into a sort of bench and foot step.

Sarah stepped onto the bench and pulled Jase on beside her as she sat. Jase marveled at her ability to control a living plant as ancient and powerful as Ellhom.

Sarah could see his surprise and told him that she was a pupil of Enock himself and had spent much of her life in his presence. She also told him that she suspected this was a further cause of resentment among the Gnomare', who covet the secrets of their ancient guardian.

The branch descended to the level of the proving grounds. Sarah and Jase hopped off the bench and onto the spiral road again. Jase looked toward the structure Sarah called the proving grounds as she explained its purpose. Jase examined the rather ordinary-looking marble structure that seemed to him nothing more than a broad stairway leading up to a stone doorway cut out of the marble. Jase could hear the sounds of combat from inside the structure and the familiar crack of a whip.

Jase sighed and said, "It seems as though Fenrix has beat me here. I hope he hasn't exhausted the best fighters already."

Sarah replied, "You think much of your friend's strength, do you?"

Jase laughed and replied, "Fenrix's strength is only one of the reasons that he is exhausting."

As they entered the halls, Jase saw that they were crowded with not only elves clad in mail but many onlookers as well. The spectators had come to watch the contests that Sarah explained would happen often.

The room itself was brightly lit with lanterns of white light. The floor was made of well-polished and unforgiving granite. The walls were of roughly hewn stone, as though hastily chipped away with no thought of aesthetics. Along the left-hand wall hung several weapons such as swords and spears of different sizes, crafted with the undeniable skill of the Gnomare'. The right-hand wall was lined with several lockers made from stainless dull gray metal. Jase could see some young elves changing out of their robes and into mail from the lockers. Jase joined them after greeting them in the best Gnomare' he could speak.

The elf adolescents greeted him warmly, and after telling him that they enjoyed his accent, they helped him change into an ensemble of mail worn by the practitioners. Making the last few adjustments to his gear, Jase approached Sarah and asked, "How do I look?"

"Like a champion, my lord," replied Sarah, becoming misty-eyed with past memories of his heroism.

Jase and Sarah proceeded farther back into the hall. On the floor the color of the granite was cut of a darker sort in large circles in the center of the hall. In every circle there would be a contest between two elves. Sarah said that the first circle would be for the beginners to attempt to progress to a higher level of competition. The farther they traveled back into the hall, the more skilled the opponent would be.

Sarah stopped and said, "The point is not victory, you understand; it is rather to know what finest of skill you wish you test your hand to."

Jase, who had been looking over the arms on the wall as they were walking, saw a pair of swords that looked like they would suit him and took them from the wall. He looked back down the hall. A long ways down the hall, he could see Fenrix sparring with a very large elf and made his way to that ring.

Sarah and Jase watched astounded as Fenrix deftly avoided every stroke of the elf's sword with ease, occasionally cracking his whip in the air near the elf's head or touching the elf lightly with the flat of his sword, unwilling to make a meaningful impact. The elf, however, was swinging with the fullness of his strength and was clearly angry about being toyed with. At last, despite the elf's best effort, he could not land a single strike and threw down his blade and bowed.

The onlookers as well as Jase and Sarah applauded. Jase called at Fenrix as he walked past, "Now I must proceed to the last rings, seeing as you have beaten all the others, friend."

Fenrix called back, "Have a care—they won't take it easy on you like I do."

Jase proceeded on with a laugh, not concerned with Fenrix's jest. He continued to the very last circle of darker granite down the hallway. It stood empty with all the spectators looking the other way.

"This is the master's circle, Jase. It is not uncommon for challengers here to receive grievous injury for their boldness," said Sarah quietly in Jase's ear.

Jase walked to the center of the circle and struck his short swords together to make them ring. At once, all other action in the hall ceased. The elves turned and looked at Jase; however, there followed nothing but silence. Jase looked back at Sarah, who now looked very alarmed. Then came the sound of ringing steel from further back in the hall, echoing out from a small open door in the wall to Jase's right.

From out of the door walked a large elf in bright mail of chain and rings carrying an enormous sword on his shoulder. His hair was as blue as the twilight air, and his eyes burned red with enchantment, as did the rune of Gnomare' on his brow. He approached slowly, apparently not sure of what to make of the much smaller Quadrian elf standing in the master's ring.

"Does this child know what he is doing, my lady?" asked the elf.

Sarah nodded and said, "Yes, Master Elwayne, this is Lord Jase of the Eldare'; he has been advised, and he wishes to test his skills here."

Elwayne laughed and replied, "I will test him then."

Elwayne entered the ring opposite Jase and looked down at him, smiling. Jase returned nothing but an expressionless gaze. The air was dead silent between the two for a few moments and then erupted with the noise of combat as the duel began.

Jase's speed and form were undeniably great even among elves, and at first, Elwayne seemed surprised be Jase's assault. Elwayne, however, was even greater in speed and much larger than Jase, standing almost twice his height. Elwayne was able to parry every single stroke from Jase as he advanced.

Soon it became evident to all who watched the contest that Elwayne was playing with Jase, and soon he began to punish him for his mistakes as he advanced. Jase would receive a cut on his arms or face and then lunge forward with even greater haste and would be knocked over, only to tumble across the floor and spring up with another furious flourish of his swords.

Elwayne eventually lost interest in the contest and began to heave Jase to the ground with every impact of his great sword, no matter how Jase tried to defend himself. Jase would rise more slowly every time he was struck down until finally he arose with a blast of what looked like lightning and blue fire from his swords. Elwayne was not caught unaware by this assault and by his own powerful enchantments sent Jase's blast back at him. The force of the impact sent Jase hurling against the weapon racks in a trail of smoke and fire with the crackling sound of dissipating electricity. Jase fell forward with a groan, dropping his weapons. Barely able to lift his head, Jase conceded a sound defeat.

Elwayne laughed mockingly and said, "A poor showing from the High Champion of Elvendom, if indeed he should retain such a hastily given title."

Sarah scolded Elwayne, saying, "Such titles are given for what they may yet accomplish, Gnomare'. You would know this if you could see anything beyond the point of your own sword."

Elwayne bowed low and replied, "My apologies, Princess. I am nothing but a master of combat and do not give judgment on such things. However, as such, I can still judge skill within the rings."

Elwayne approached Jase and, pulling him up by a handful of his hair, passed his hand over the crystal necklace given to Jase by Enock. Elwayne caused a series of runes meaning "novice" to appear in the crystal and then dropped Jase back onto his face. All the onlookers but Sarah laughed as Jase tried to pick himself up with a faint grunt. Sarah helped him to sit up.

Elwayne put his sword over his shoulder and said, "If there is nothing more I can do for your guests, Princess, I will see to my serious students."

Sarah looked up at Elwayne furiously and looked as though she was about to speak when Fenrix's voice rang out.

"Hold! There is something else, Master Elwayne. I have been seeing to your students for a while now and found nothing educational about the experience. In fact, I was wondering whether they had been taught anything at all. It's a pretty dance they do, after all, but is it fighting? No, I think not. Perhaps you can show me what you are not teaching them?"

Elwayne turned and looked the Hillman up and down, examining his garments of animal skins and crude steel weapon, and began to smile. Elwayne gestured with his left hand, palm up, toward the master's ring. Fenrix smiled, pushed past the elves in the way, and stood in the middle of the ring, facing away from Elwayne.

Fenrix shouted, "I will just wait here until someone who can handle a blade moves me."

Elwayne's face became terrible to behold; many runes began to appear and spiral around him. Elwayne dashed forward with a stroke that would have cleaved Fenrix in two but instead, all he did was scar the granite over which Fenrix was standing. A familiar howl burst out inside the hall as the contest erupted into the fullness of violence. Elwayne continued swinging furiously with deadly precision and incredible speed, which only showcased Fenrix's inability to be struck. Each time, Fenrix would leap into in to the air effortlessly, and planting his feet on the ceiling, he would rocket back down on the other side of the ring before Elwayne could recover from his previous stroke. Fenrix then began to gallop on all fours with weapons in hand, making Elwayne chase him around, thrashing his blade violently. Fenrix would stop only long enough to rake his sword across Elwayne. Fenrix's attacks were being thwarted, however, by the runes spiraling around Elwayne, throwing sparks of light across the ring.

Elwayne continued his assault, still unable to find his mark. Fenrix coiled up his body and then sprang between Elwayne's legs, cracking his whip at Elwayne on the way past him. Enraged by this, Elwayne held his left hand out toward Fenrix and caused a large brilliant rune to flash out and hang in the air in front of Fenrix.

Fenrix stood in place as if paralyzed and began to shake. Elwayne gave out a triumphant yell as he jumped forward into the air above Fenrix, with his sword above his head, ready to strike. However, the sound of his voice was stolen away by the terrifying sound that burst forth from Fenrix: Fenrix clenched his fists, whipped his head back, and let out a roar.

The roar that emanated from him sent a blast of pressure that seemed to bend the very air in waves around him. The rune holding him shattered, and the blast of force sent Elwayne shooting up into the ceiling. The blast then reverberated into the rest of the hall, knocking spectators and weapons down, shattering lamps, and denting the lockers. Elwayne dropped face-down to the floor, unconscious, and his sword fell in a shower of metal shards around him.

All those in the hall arose holding their heads, dizzy and stunned. Jase, despite blurred vision, could still make out the image of Fenrix approaching Elwayne as the latter lay helpless on the floor of the master's circle. Fenrix pulled Elwayne's head up by a handful of his hair. The silver chain holding the crystal showing Elwayne's skill and rank fell from the collar of his mail. Fenrix grabbed it and broke it free from Elwayne's neck and then dropped him.

Tying the chain to his belt, Fenrix shouted so that everyone in the hall could hear, "Master or novice, wizard or warrior, man or elf, it matters nothing. You are either predator or prey. When the time comes, what will you be?"

Fenrix turned and after patting Jase of the shoulder left the proving grounds without another word. Many of the students and High Guard rushed to Elwayne's side and began to carry him out of the hall. Others simply left the hall all together and ran out into the spiral road to tell others what they had seen.

Sarah, after shaking her head and blinking, said, "I had no idea men of Grea'nock had such power."

Jase smiled as he arose, still holding his head. "I don't think Fenrix is a man so much as a pack of angry beasts in one body. He is as great in power as any man has ever been, I believe."

Sarah took Jase by the hand and led him out of the hall, saying that she had something special to show him. The two Eldare' walked slowly through the chaos in the street outside the proving grounds and down into the city. The city once again became quite as they approached the rings dedicated to the scholars. Sarah stopped and pointed to her left. There Jase could see a large metal gate standing between two columns of marble that seemed to have a phosphorescence all their own. Jase approached the gate, and in the wavy grain patterns of the metal, he thought he could see the rune of the house of Eldare' rise to the surface as if floating to the top of a body of water.

Sarah said, "This is a warded gate to my dwelling and the palace of the Eldare' within the tree."

Sarah took Jase's hand and touched it to the door with hers. Jase could feel the sensation of being pulled through the door but could see that his body was not moving. To Jase's astonishment, one moment he was looking at the door, and the next he was standing in a room the likes of which he had never seen. Jase saw a short red marble stair leading down into a sort of courtyard. There in the air hung three windows of clear crystal on his left and right. The windows were filled with glowing white runes that slowly scrolled down them in an endless flow of information. In the floor in the middle of the room there looked to be a well of clear water giving off light in patterns that matched its rippling surface. Beyond that and up a similar set of stairs was a throne with yet another runic window of crystal floating close by on either side of it.

"These runic tablets were brought here from Prime Avalon by Enock before the Edict of Starblade commanded that we no longer travel openly in the world. They help us with our runic calculations to track the flow of energies in the world. It is the way we as Eldare' help to provide order," explained Sarah.

"I don't understand," replied Jase.

Sarah continued in, and Jase followed. As Sarah passed the tablets, she ran her fingers over them in several places, changing the order of several runes.

Sarah replied, "Nor should you understand. Enock has spent all the time I have been in the tree explaining their use as well as explaining my duties as an Eldare'. These will take time for you to understand."

Jase smiled and turned his attention to the pool of light in the middle of the room. As he approached its side, he looked down into the radiant waters. The exact depth was impossible for Jase to guess as he could see no bottom. To his surprise, however, he could see what looked like several di-ocular lenses floating in the water at various depths, turning in multiple directions at different speeds.

"What is this bewildering mechanism?" asked Jase, still gazing with a broad smile into the water.

"This is a well of sight. It is not unique to our house as the tablets are; it is a way for the houses and our cities to communicate. It can perceive as well as project images and sounds, allowing us to speak over great distances," answered Sarah.

"So you can see everywhere in Grea'nock?" asked Jase.

Sarah laughed and answered, "Not quite that far. These devices have their limits, not the least of which is the ability of the user. I have been practicing the use of the well for many long years and can scarcely see or hear any clear images outside the city, unfortunately."

Still looking into the well, Jase asked, "Can you use it now and tell me what you can see in the city?"

Sarah smiled and approached the well and stared into it intently. Jase could see all the di-ocular lenses begin to point in the same direction and give off an intense dispersion of colors.

"Oh my!" Sarah said. "It seems as though Fenrix has found his match in mischief among the citizens of the tree. Her name is Ellay, the daughter of the Lady Eltrinia who was one of the last Scions of the original seed," said Sarah, enthralled by her vision.

"I hope Lady Eltrinia doesn't mind Fenrix harassing her daughter," replied Jase.

Sarah shook her head and responded, "The lady Eltrinia died at her daughter's birth, and Ellay's father's identity is a mystery. However, Ellay has an infamously bad temper and is much larger and stronger than any other Gnomare' her age. She is in truth one of our most talented engineers and weaponsmiths, but the elders find her temper difficult to restrain. But lo! She has found Fenrix, and they now chase each other through the city in some lovers' game. What a strange happenstance." Sarah broke free from her trance and said, "I cannot hold the image long."

Sarah approached the throne and sat down. She touched the tables hovering on each side of her throne and then closed her eyes. A large runic cipher appeared above her and began to spin. Sarah told Jase that he should study the tablets and that they would contain very useful information.

During the following days, Jase and Sarah did not leave the place of Eldare'. When they were not studying, they would talk for hours on end concerning the state of Elvendom on Grea'nock and the future of their people. Jase learned many disturbing things about the abandonment of Prime Avalon and the dwindling to extinction of the house of Eldare' in the shore side lodges of Nem near its runes. He also read much from the table concerning the roles of each house in the ancient wars.

Yet Jase could find little of his former mentor mentioned in the tablets and was hesitant to tell Sarah too much of his past. After he and Sarah had spent a few more days together in the palace of the Eldare', Jase finally brought himself to raise a related subject with Sarah. "I have not heard any mention of the Kylvara'. Why not?"

Sarah grew solemn and replied, "The children of the counterbalance? I cannot see them, nor can any who desire to do so. They have always estranged themselves and have never been at one with our purposes until the most dire of circumstances. I, however, have begun to feel them moving again; it seems to me that the counterbalance is soon to put its weight on the scale again."

Jase grew quiet in thought. He began to understand why he had never been able to find his old master again though he had been searching his entire life.

Sarah, once again sitting on her throne with her eyes closed, working the grand cipher, suddenly stood and cried out, "They have come!"

Chapter 11

◇　◇　◇

From the Depths

J ase leapt to Sarah's side and took her hand. "Who has come?"
He could feel Sarah's hand quivering as she said, "The children of Dagoth."

Jase and Sarah exited the palace the same way they had come and immediately saw terror and disorder in the streets of the city. Black shapes darted through the air, up from the lower rings, and Jase and Sarah could see elves dropping lifelessly over the banister from the higher rings of the city.

The creatures seemed both bat-like and apish and gave out terrible screeches as they flew through the city, biting and clawing at all those they came near. The tree of Ellhom itself began to swat them out of the air like insects, smashing them against the walls of the cave and crushing them on the road if they dared to land. Jase drew his swords from his sheath and backed Sarah into a corner behind a column. Suddenly, a blast of radiant enchantment expanded up through the city in great spheres of light, one after the other. It was met in the higher rings by an even brighter, more intense enchantment of iridescent, vitreous sheets of radiant material pushing their way downward, accompanied by the sound of breaking glass. All the creatures flying through the air began to fall to the ground, dead and burning.

"Elders, Lords and High Guard, to the pool of sky!" echoed the voice of Enock throughout the city.

Sarah came out of the corner and said, "Come to the pool of sky."

Jase quickly asked, "Is it all right for us to be there?"

Sarah replied, "It is our duty as Eldare', my lord. Now come."

Sarah hopped up on the banister, and so did Jase. They were both carried down to the pool of sky by a branch of Ellhom. There waiting at the bottom already was Enock, with Artcreft and Ellen by his side as well as many of the other elders near at hand. Enock greeted them and explained that they were waiting for a report from the High Guard on the encroachment. Not far off, Erik appeared out of a wisp of black smoke with a rather alarmed-looking Gayle on his arm.

The group looked up as they heard a howl echoing from the very highest rings of the city and saw Fenrix free-falling through the city toward the edge of the pool of sky.

Jase looked at the tree and could see that the waters around the roots were deep, but they did not go out from the base more than a few yards before giving way to the granite floor of the cave. Gayle looked up and screamed as Fenrix, dropping out of the air, collided with the floor of the cave and disappeared into a cloud of pulverized granite dust. The shock wave created a web of cracks in the cave floor and sent ripples through the pool. Yet Fenrix strode out of the cloud of dust unharmed and smiling.

Fenrix apologized for not arriving sooner and explained that he had been looking after Ellay to make sure she was not harmed. The unrecognizably burnt corpses of the animals that littered the cave floor immediately drew his attention as he picked one up and began to examine it. A group of the High Guard came sprinting down from the lowest ring with stretchers prepared to carry away the fallen citizens of Ellhom. They arrived and knelt before Enock, with their captain conspicuously absent. Yet another patrol then issued from the cavernous doorway at the bottom ring leading down into the deep forges, and they too were without Kirin.

"Report," commanded Artcreft.

The largest elf looked up with grave concern on his face and said, "Lord Artcreft, we lost several of our adolescents. They fell defending the elflings playing in the arboretum. They elflings survived, however. Kirin got to them in time. It did not go as well for Master Erlon, who died protecting his daughter, who was also slain."

"Does Kirin know of the death of her daughter and her mate Erlon?" asked Artcreft.

Just as Artcreft spoke, a terrible and powerful scream tore through the city, clearly emanating from the ring where the range lay.

"She does now," answered Enock.

The leader of the patrol that had come up from the deep forges then spoke. "They came up from the caves beneath us, through the ventilation ducts of the deep forge. Almost all of our engineers below are slain or missing."

Artcreft looked at the creatures still smoldering on the ground about them and said, "These were only juveniles. We are lucky they did not cause more damage. There will surely be more."

Fenrix interrupted, "So you suspect there are mature darbeck near?"

"What's a darbeck?" asked Gayle.

"Bad news—they are powerful immortal beasts twisted in the first days. They are now bestial and evil. They are but some of the many children of Dagoth," said Fenrix.

A great bellowing growl echoed up from the tunnel next to the pool.

"That is no darbeck!" said Fenrix, drawing his sword.

"All the tunnels leading into the city are too small for something as large as whatever made that sound," said Artcreft.

"That may be, but something that large may possess the strength to burrow out a larger tunnel!" said Fenrix.

"Ellhom will not allow an encroachment of that size. Its vines reinforce the tunnels as well as protect them," said Enock.

"As good as a tree defending a city may sound to you all, I must be on the hunt! I'll go gather my things. Perhaps I will even find a new whip, seeing as I have broken my last taming my new pet," said Fenrix. He then left, with Gayle following close behind, telling Erik that she must change into her range gear.

Jase laughed and said, "Here we go again. If my lady will give me leave?"

Princess Sarah, with a somber look, gave a small nod of her head toward Jase and then departed up the spiral road.

Enock said, "This is brave of you, children. However, it is we elders who should strike out at this beast."

"No. Oh, Eldest, if something slips by us you are still here to defend the city it will go better than something getting by you in the caverns with only us here to defend your house." responded Jase.

Enock told them that he would gather the craftsmen for any last-minute outfitting. He then ordered the pool of sky and deep forges evacuated and High Guards officers posted there. Enock motioned at the sight of Kirin, who was now approaching with her head down and her elfling girl clutched in her arms. Kirin knelt at Enock's feet, still crying, and laid down her bow. Enock knelt down as well and held Kirin and her slain daughter to his chest and whispered something in Kirin's ear after which she stood and departed up into the city.

Artcreft growled in anger, "We shall not find a better captain to replace her."

Enock stood with and expression of rage and shook his head then pointed up the spiral road to the image of an enormous elf approaching. This elf was gigantic, standing nearly as tall as Enock himself, covered in thick plate armor glowing with runes and fashioned to make him look like some great armored insect. His deep lavender hair was pulled back and braided, covered by runic metal bands, and revealed a face that said he could have been Enock's twin. On his shoulder he carried a massive great sword of radiant blue crystal with runes scrolling down its blade; it was pulsing with light. He approached and bowed low before Enock.

Artcreft and Ellen both bowed low before him in true reverence as Artcreft said, "Greetings, Lord and Grand Master Elterion, Last Scion of the original seed. You have removed from your labors as a bowyer?"

Elterion said in a voice that made Erik's deep and booming voice seem small in comparison, "We have bows, Arch Mage. Now it seems we are in need of a captain while Kirin mourns. I offer my sword if my Lord and guardian will allow."

Enock nodded with a smile. Elterion bowed again and then departed up the spiral road to his duties. Erik looked around at the elves leaving the pool of sky and the High Guard taking their posts near the tunnel entrance. He shook his head and sat down cross-legged next to the impact crater Fenrix had made. He laid his staff down and took out a small book to study.

Enock walked over and, bending down, took up Erik's staff. Erik marveled at Enock's strength. Holding the heavy iron staff lightly between his thumb and forefinger. He whipped it through the air and twirled it between his fingers. "Wonderful!"

Erik shrugged and said, "What? It's just a bar of ordinary iron."

"That's just it. It would be just as useful as a club. It has no value for enchantment whatsoever, yet you can still focus through it. Quite remarkable," replied Enock.

"It's all I have," said Erik.

Enock laid it down next to Erik, saying, "I will see to the making of a more suitable one personally."

Erik thanked Enock and studied for a while longer until his attention was drawn to an elf maiden dressed in rough leather work clothes and a smithy apron. She was carrying a large beautifully decorated wooden chest on her right shoulder. She approached Erik and asked, "You are the one called Erik, are you not?"

"I am," replied Erik with a smile. "Fenrix should be back shortly," he added.

She sat the chest down and sat on top of it, giving an impatient grunt as she rested her cheek on her fist. After about an hour, Fenrix arrived, looking angry and with Gayle at his side, complaining, "No, I couldn't find a whip. They have no need for the lash here apparently." He was immediately tackled to the ground by Ellay. She kissed him forcefully for quite some time before she let him back up.

Helping him to his feet, she said, "I made something for you." Excitedly, she walked him over to the wooden chest. Opening it, she lifted out a large, vicious-looking mace. The head of it was made of blue-gray metal and covered with a swirl of sharp lands and grooves, and it was crowned with a long spike. At the other end was a wheel with a thin shiny chain wrapped around it that disappeared into the shaft.

"What is it?" asked Fenrix, scratching his head.

"Just watch," she said. A short way down the handle of the mace was a ring of metal inlaid with elven runes. She pointed the mace at the nearby tunnel wall and touched one of the runes on the handle. With a bang, the head shot off like an arrow and stuck into the tunnel wall.

The mace made a loud clicking sound as it paid out chain from the wheel in the back through the handle and to the head. She touched another rune, and the wheel began to turn in the other direction, taking back its chain, pulling Ellay toward the tunnel where the head was lodged. She touched the last rune, and the head dislodged from the wall and came flying back to the mace and reattached itself with a loud metal clink.

"I call it a chain mace. It's not a good name, but perhaps a good weapon, I think," said Ellay, while handing it to Fenrix.

Princess Sarah returned to the pool unnoticed while the company was admiring the new weapon. Sarah cleared her throat and spoke. "Honored guests—you take on a task that is not your own willingly and without fear," The party and the rest all turned and bowed. Sarah continued. "Evil moves across the land from the north. I can feel it growing. We are bound by edict to not walk openly in the world, leaving many evils from the ancient days unchecked.

"As you go forth, remember that if these creatures can find and disturb our hidden homes, it will not be long before your own homes will suffer. You go to the depths to seek a fight when your own houses are in danger. If you insist on aiding us now, we will do all we can when we send you forth to your own lands," declared Sarah.

The party bowed low and turned their attention to the tunnel. Jase, now holding a crystal lantern of Gnomare' and with some rope and grappling hooks slung over his shoulder, was the first to enter the tunnel. Fenrix followed behind, shouldering his new weapon. Next, Erik stood, taking Gayle by the hand, and he led her toward the darkness. They followed Jase's lamplight into the tunnel. The way was narrow and straight at first but began to widen and slope downward. The party was moving silently toward a reddish-orange light up ahead when a sudden outburst from Erik halted them.

"What the hell are we doing?" exclaimed Erik.

"Shh!" hissed Fenrix.

"Listen to me. How is it that we think we can handle some unnamed evil that Fenrix thinks he hears, rather than leaving well enough alone and getting back to Hillsborough?" said Erik.

"If that's the way you feel, then turn around," said Jase. "If it isn't enough that you are now so gifted that Lord Artcreft is afraid to teach you, I don't know what to say. As for me, these are my people, and I will defend them."

"All I live for is the hunt. That's all I will say," added Fenrix.

Gayle, drawing a glittering arrow from her quiver, said coldly, "I just want to shoot something."

Fenrix laughed under his breath as he crept forward, mace in one hand, sword in the other.

Erik sighed and said softly, "Forgive my weakness," and followed. The source of the light turned out to be the molten metal of the deep forge. They entered the large automated forge, slow and wary.

"This is some amazing engineering," said Erik.

Jase whispered, "Indeed, the Gnomare' get steel and any other molten metal they need from this forge."

"Shut the hell up, you two! We are being watched!" hissed Fenrix, pointing his sword underneath a nearby furnace.

There, two glistening points of yellow light peered at them. Gayle drew back her bow, and the light vanished; the scrambling sound of claws could be heard moving away under the automation.

"Follow," commanded Gayle as she loosed an arrow. It skipped on the ground under the furnace, throwing a shower of sparks, and disappeared under the machinery. The arrow could be heard rebounding off many surfaces before the group heard the sound of a soft impact followed by a short snarl.

A shadowy blur then fell from above the furnace. The small bat-like humanoid lay in the middle of the room with Gayle's arrow sticking out of its neck. Fenrix approached and plunged his sword into it for good measure and then withdrew Gayle's arrow. He looked at Jase questioningly and pointed to his ear.

Jase shook his head no in response.

"Okay," said Fenrix, "there are no more in the immediate area at any rate."

Gayle approached, and taking back her arrow, she examined the creature. "This is a darbeck, then?" said Gayle.

"Yes, only days old and already lethal," said Fenrix. "We were fortunate it didn't escape and warn others. The adults are much larger and very difficult to kill. A fine shot indeed, Gayle."

"Only days old? How fast do they breed?" asked Erik.

"I don't know, but they never come one or just a few at a time without hundreds following afterward. One of the southern hill tribes was wiped from the face of Grea'nock by them in my grandfather's time," answered Fenrix.

"Yes, dark days indeed, from what I recall," said Jase.

"This forge must draw its quenching water somewhere," said Erik.

"Yes, straight to the water just like a hunter, Erik," replied Fenrix while sniffing the air.

Jase looked around for a moment before pointing to some pipes in the overhead and said, "Follow those," The pipes led down through what seemed like a maze of tunnels before dropping through a hole in the cavern floor. Setting down the hooks and rope, Jase latched them over the pipe securely. Jase looked down the hole. "I can see the bottom and the edge of the water, but something is wrong with it," said Jase.

Fenrix approached the hole, sniffing repeatedly. "That air is very bad down there. You two may not like it."

"Fenrix and I will go down quickly and quietly. Erik, you next, then Gayle," said Jase in a whisper.

"If you hear fighting break out when we descend, stay here and cover any escape," added Fenrix. Then he leapt down the hole with Jase close behind.

Erik and Gayle paused for a moment, hearing nothing. Erik then worked his way down the rope the best he could while still carrying his staff. The hole opened up in to a massive cavernous room.

At one end was a subterranean pool of sickly glowing amber water. The other end of the room faded into darkness, not telling its full size. Erik finally dropped from the end of the rope with a thud.

Jase and Fenrix were positioned behind a large boulder beyond the end of the pool, shielding themselves from the dark end of the cavern. They both looked frightened and motioned wildly for Erik to get behind the boulder. As Erik joined them, Gayle skillfully slid down the rope and did the same.

"We are in serious trouble," whispered Fenrix.

"Great! Thanks. Now you understand what you got us into," said Erik.

"What is it?" asked Gayle.

Fenrix said, "Look," pointing to the glowing pool of filth. They could see dozens of egg-like cocoons just breaking its surface. "No breeding pair can produce that many young," said Fenrix.

"What can then?" asked Gayle.

"I don't know, but we must destroy them quickly before they emerge or the sire returns," said Fenrix.

"Leave that to me," said Gayle.

"There must be a hundred pods at least. I hope you brought enough arrows," replied Jase.

Gayle smiled and said, "Watch this," Notching three arrows on her bow string, she drew back her bow. "Shatter" commanded Gayle as she loosed her arrows.

As they collided with the ceiling of the cavern, they erupted into a hail of metal barbs, shredding every cocoon in the pool as they fell. The shrieks from the dying young filled the cavern, followed by a deafening roar from the other side of the cave. The heavy thump of giant footfalls began to rush toward them.

"No point in hiding now," said Fenrix as he dashed out from behind the boulder, firing his chain mace. The mace head missed the charging behemoth and lodged itself in the cavern wall behind it. Drawing the chain in, Fenrix leapt toward the red light where he thought the beast's head should be. As the mace pulled him through the air, Fenrix slashed at the beast as he flew past, but with no effect.

The beast continued its charge, sliding into the shallow waters of the pool, whipping its gigantic bat-like head from side to side. It scanned the water with a great red beam of light emanating from the giant red crystalline globe where its eyes and snout should have been. Its gaze came across the party standing in front of the boulder, and its giant jaw began to drip slime. It reached out and pointed at them with its enormous winged arm and let out a shriek.

"Pulverize!" commanded Gayle as she loosed an arrow into its hulking body. It recoiled with a groan but lunged forward instantly, slashing at them with its giant hooked claws.

Erik and Gayle dove in opposite directions, and Erik landed safely on his belly, but as he looked up, he saw Gayle catch the end of the beast's attack on the side of her head. The blow knocked her against the boulder with great force. She fell to the ground bloodied and motionless.

Jase tumbled forward and underneath the beast, slashing away at its belly and hind legs. The beast spun around and slashed at Jase time after time, getting closer with each stroke, but paying for it in flesh. Jase's blades were exacting terrible wounds with every flourish.

Erik looked down at Gayle's broken body and felt his soul catch fire. He let out a terrible scream, and striking his staff on the ground, he turned it to a white hot iron with an all-too-familiar screech. The beast slung its head around just in time to collide with Erik's staff as he had hurled it in anger.

The great globe at the center of the beast's face shattered, showering the room with luminous red crystals. The beast fell back into the pool thrashing and snarling in a hideous death rattle. The sound of several oxen and a pack of wolves being boiled alive might have been near the mark. At the same time, Erik began to swoon from his own spell.

Jase cheered for an instant before he saw Gayle. He dashed to her side and began his enchantments but was cut short. "You fools, you have interfered with my work, with my attempt to hold the counterbalance," said an icy and emotionless voice that echoed through the cavern.

Jase darted out from behind the boulder to see who was there. The crystal fragments gave the cave an uneasy red glow. The figure stood cloaked in blackness, his steely eyes shining bright in the bloody phosphorescence. His left arm was extended, holding Fenrix by the throat. Fenrix, barely conscious, was still chopping at the shadowy figure's arm with his sword.

In the newcomer's right hand was a great sword pointed at Jase. In an seemingly effortless motion, the figure tossed Fenrix toward Jase. Fenrix landed with a thump and a groan. It was all Erik could do to stay conscious and watch the contest.

Jase bounded over Fenrix and let loose with his blades, whirling them in an endless combination of flourishes, each one deflected or altogether stopped by the sword of the elven shadow. The figure did not fence, nor did he need to. He floated effortlessly in and out of the range of Jase's blades, barely moving his sword.

With a flash of light and the crackling sound of thunder, the two separated for a moment. The figure paused only to laugh maliciously and then say, "Clever boy!"

Jase yelled a curse in elvish and rushed forward, locking blades across the shadow's sword. Jase struggled against the figure with all his strength but could not move his sword. Then with a thrust of his left arm, the shadow sent the flats of Jase's blades smashing against his own chest. The impact sent Jase flying end over end into the boulder next to Erik.

The ashen-cloaked elf moved toward Jase but was stopped by the tremendous roar of the ancient beast living inside the soul of Fenrix. Fenrix attacked like an uncoiling serpent. This contest was different, every feint and half step was a lie, hoping to mask the deadly truth of Fenrix's next stroke.

The shadow was swinging furiously at Fenrix, missing only by inches each time. Bending himself backward and dropping to his knees, Fenrix just avoided being cut in half by the monstrous blade of the dark elf. Springing back up like a great cat lunging for its prey, Fenrix slammed his sword into the chest of his opponent with a loud crack.

The figure stopped. Erik thought he could see the dark elf smile as he said, "Very good, son of Shames," The elf raised his arms, and several wisps of light from throughout the cave came rushing to his hands. The air filled with a progressively intense tumult of noise.

Then came dead silence, eventually interrupted by a pronouncement: "I am Kylratha. You will now see and know the might of the counterbalance!"

The following blast of pressure threw Fenrix into the air; he landed face down in the pool's filth. Erik watched his own vision grow dark as the blast slid him across the cavern floor. For that moment, the world had become quieter, colder, and darker than ever.

Chapter 12

◇ ◇ ◇

From Darkness to Light

First, Erik felt warmth returning to his body. Then came the strange voices one often hears in dreams, like an audible whisper from a thousand yards away, faint but clear. His eyes could perceive light now, but he still had no vision. There was a sunrise-like glow, soft as if masked by clouds. Then the voices came once more, too many to count, too hard to recognize until one stood out.

It was the commanding and noble voice of Enock. "Wake up, Erik. You have survived the journey."

Erik, blinking, rubbed his eyes and sat up. There he beheld the House of Healing's lower floor. Around him were Jase, Fenrix, and Gayle, all lying on beds grown from the vines of Ellhom. The edges of their beds were raised several inches, and they were all bathed in waters from the pool of sky.

Ellen, who was standing between Jase and Gayle, was as radiant as a new dawn. She held her hands on Jase and Gayle's heads. There were signs of a great struggle on her face. She clenched her jaw and grimaced as though she could feel their pain.

Enock passed his staff over their bodies and caused the vines of Ellhom above them in the ceiling to flower and shed luminous petals onto Jase and

Gayle both. Next, Enock looked to Fenrix. Erik could see no sign of life in him; even his color was that of the dead. Enock then began to speak in a tongue Erik did not recognize. The air in the room began to tremble and change. New vines of Ellhom began to grow over the edges of Fenrix's bed. They were small, needle-like tendrils that began to pierce his skin and emit fire-like flashes of various colors.

"Will Fenrix be all right?" asked Erik in a shaky voice. Erik could feel a hand on his shoulder force him back down to his bed. Erik looked up and saw the High Sage Artcreft looking down at him gravely.

"Fenrix is an amazing creature. How he survived the magnitude of damage he received is incredible!" said Artcreft, almost sounding excited.

"Yet he has taken much effort to repair," added Enock sternly.

Ellen broke from her trance and added, "And many days of rest."

Erik sat back a moment and asked, "How long were we gone?"

Enock responded that many hours had passed before they had started to worry. Then it was decided that he would lead the elders to find the travelers. They were found in the cave all but dead near the remains of the large creature of ancient evil.

"That one-eyed gargoyle we fought was so fierce. It seemed like it knew us," said Erik.

"It was an eye of Dagoth. Both powerful and ageless, they were the messengers and scouts of the first evil. It was a great deed to have slain it. You were lucky to have survived," explained Artcreft.

Erik gave his account of everything that had happened with the eye of Dagoth, and when he was done, Artcreft and Enock both laughed. Erik looked at them both and shrugged. "What is so funny?"

Artcreft held his hands out and announced, "Behold the slayer of the eye of Dagoth, a feat of legendary prowess. So children of Dagoth, beware Erik the Ironrod, wielder of the runic enchantments and …thrower of sticks!"

Enock gave out a short cough to mask his laughter and said, "Speaking of which, I have crafted a new staff for you, Erik."

Erik had not noticed that Enock was holding not his own staff, but a long staff of smooth, almost black wood. As Enock held it out before Erik,

Erik could see a large gold band in its exact center; in the band was a large emerald with a glowing rune carved into it in intaglio fashion.

"This staff is from the heart wood of Ellhom, very difficult to extract. The emerald is called the heart of earth and is imbued with great energy. It will help you use enchantment without completely exhausting yourself. However, if you prefer, you can use it to bludgeon things," said Enock while still trying not to laugh. Erik scratched his head and took the staff sheepishly.

Erik looked up and remembered the dark elf and said, "It was that dark elf Kylratha that nearly finished us."

Enock turned with a look of concern on his face. "Kylratha, you say? How can you be sure?" said Enock skeptically.

"It was indeed my old mentor from Northguard, Lord General Kylratha," replied Jase, sitting up suddenly.

Enock shook his head and frowned. "Those are the titles that men gave him. To us he is the Warrior King, the eldest of all Elvendom within the cosmos, the sword saint and High Lord of the Kylvara'. He is the counterbalance, and if you fought him and lived, it was no accident. He spared you all," stated Enock confidently.

Jase arose from his table saying, "I know. I wronged my old master by interfering with his mission. He has only begun to punish me. We have to leave. He will not remain patient for long, and I must not be here when he comes for me." He spoke forbiddingly.

"You are not well enough to travel, child," said Ellen.

Jase began to stretch and replied, "I will be soon enough."

Erik got off his bed and added, "I will be leaving as well."

Ellen smiled, saying that it was admirable for them to concern themselves with the safety of the city. She also warned them that making any rash decisions would surely play into the hands of their enemies.

Jase thought quietly for a moment and then said, "I must speak with Sarah," He walked slowly out of the room, trying to mask his pain.

Erik slowly walked toward Gayle's table. Looking down on her, Erik could see that her wounds were healing quickly. Where there had been great a gaping claw mark slashing down from the middle of her forehead down across her right eye, only a bright red scar remained. Erik was grieved to see that her right eye was gone from its socket. Erik thought that she was more beautiful than ever but feared Gayle's reaction to her wounds.

Artcreft approached Gayle's table, and putting his hand to his chin, he murmured, "Hmm, I believe I have something that can help." Artcreft vanished in a swirl of his tempestuous enchantments like a stormy night's sky.

"He really is quite brilliant," said Enock. "He was declared the Arch Mage of our house when he was young and has never disappointed the post," Several wavering and translucent images of Artcreft entered the room moving through solid objects to join together in front of Gayle.

"Impressive—were you really in all those places at once?" exclaimed Erik as he began to scratch his head. Artcreft was holding a bright corn-flower blue jewel between his forefinger and thumb. It was a radiant sphere-shaped jewel and was imbued with a strange elven rune in its center. Whether by enchantment or some trick of light, no matter how Artcreft turned it, the elven rune was always visible to the onlooker.

Opening Gayle's eyelid with his finger, he put the gem into place. Gayle yelped but did not wake. Artcreft then began to weave enchantments with his fingers pointing toward her new jeweled eye. The air surrounding his hands began to distort the images beyond them.

Voices speaking unknown words filled the room. A sudden silence ensued, followed with a loud crash like splintering stones. Then a brilliant beacon of light flashed out from Artcreft's outstretched hands. Gayle sat up and screamed, causing Artcreft to step back and Erik to come forward. Gayle thrust her arms forward with the palms of her hands out. Erik stopped, not sure of her gesture.

Gayle began to look around in awe. "First thing I remember is the beast in the cave then darkness. Now everything is so clear. I can see... I can see everything!" Gayle said wildly.

"Calm, child," whispered Ellen softly.

Artcreft clapped and with a short laugh said, "Excellent! You have taken to your new eye perfectly."

Gayle, remembering what had happened to her, reached up and felt her scarred face. "You gave me a new eye, High Sage? Thank you so much," whispered Gayle.

"Yes my dear. You are welcome. Soon you will be as good as new," replied Artcreft with a awkward grin.

"Better," said Gayle while looking around. "I can see things, my eyes tell me, what I could never have guessed before!" she stammered.

Gayle's gaze turned to Enock, and her eyes narrowed as if looking into a bright light. Gayle gasped. "Enock, you're so beautiful. The other are not as old as you, nor are they nearly as powerful," Gale then looked to the floor and reported that Jase was with the princess in the smithy many rings down, apparently discussing the repair of his shattered blades.

"What craft have you worked here, Artcreft? She has sorceress sight now? Is this possible?" asked Ellen, who seemed truly impressed.

Artcreft gave a grim laugh and answered, "Some foolish elf maiden taught this child rune mastery to aid her archery. It seems that her skills have extended beyond that. The jewel would have only restored her sight otherwise."

Gayle looked at Ellen, and getting off her table, she leaned in and kissed her runed brow. Gayle could see Ellen's thoughts and memories. When her lips touched the rune of Feyara' on Ellen's forehead, Gayle stumbled backward to the floor.

Erik went to help her up, but she yelled, "No! This is all wrong!"

Gayle stood again and recounted aloud the images she had seen in her mind, looking at Enock. "Through countless ages Ellen walked with you! She could only watch as the deadliest warrior became the mightiest scholar. Like a child looking up at that star, she could only guess at your true nature. The mistakes of the long past have lead her through an eternity of regret," said Gayle.

From her jeweled eye there came a beam of cold blue light that shone directly to the rune of Gnomare' on Enock's forehead. Erik could now see a crown of fire hovering like a circlet around Enock's head. Gayle's eyes widened, and she became resolute.

Stepping toward Enock, she shouted, "Enock! Ellen has always loved you and always will. From the fire and light of Avalon to the roots of

Ellhom, from the shores of Nem and the towers of High Feyar, she loves you. She regrets ever doubting you. She desires nothing more in eternity than to be your mate and only lover!"

The room went silent for some time until, finally, Artcreft could hold back his amusement no longer and walked out laughing. Erik and Ellen both were still stunned and silent. Enock turned slowly toward Ellen, who was still holding Fenrix's hand, trying to revive him. Enock could see the enchanted tears of long ages welling up in the corners of her eyes, which were constantly changing color.

"Fenrix!" called Enock.

"Yes?" said Fenrix, suddenly sitting up with a violent jerk.

"Ellay waits for her hunter nervously near the pool of sky."

Fenrix sprang from his table and hurried out of the room as though he remembered nothing of what had happened.

Enock bowed his head and approached Ellen very slowly. Ellen, turning her head, let her tears fall. Her tears hit the ground with a crystal clear chime one after another. The tune that Erik thought he could make out was the saddest sound he could remember ever hearing. Enock touched his forehead to Ellen's and spoke to Ellen in the elders' tongue. Ellen could only turn her head back and forth, answering only one word at a time.

At last, Enock put his hands on the sides of her face and held her head still. Ellen only shut her eyes. Enock's words became forceful, and at last, Ellen looked Enock in the eyes. She began to cry, and her words became a song of lamentation; her tears actually did sound musical as they fell.

Gayle was overcome with sadness and began to weep quietly as she watched. Erik could feel the spell pull at him but thought quickly to counter it. Enock's words became comforting; however, Ellen continued to cry, pounding her fist on his chest. Enock shook his head and sighed and then out of nowhere began to kiss Ellen like they were long-lost lovers meeting for the first time in ages.

Ellen gave a sudden squeal and then a humming moan as she tugged at a fistful of his blue hair. The pair began to radiate with brilliant energy as they walked hand in hand past Gayle and Erik, leaving the House of Healing. There at the banister in a voice that seemed to echo off every surface in the city, Enock declared himself and Ellen mated. Raising his staff, he caused every branch and vine of Ellhom to blossom with flowers that emitted light from their petals and filled the air with a sweet perfume.

At the same time, the High Sage Artcreft changed the colors of the lanterns and sprayed the city with a prismatic luminescence. Artcreft then summoned star-like globes to hover and float about the rings, giving off a soft tune of music. It sounded like many hundreds of stringed instruments playing in perfect harmony. The Gnomare' began to leave their houses and shops and crowd the spiral road of the city.

Watching the celebration from inside, Erik turned to Gayle. He looked at her as she smiled, clearly pleased. Gayle looked back at Erik and was surprised by what she saw. Gayle gazed at Erik in wonder. Her eyes confirmed that he was a wizard.

"You are different from everything else. I can't see into you, not at all!" claimed Gayle.

With a sly smirk, Erik said, "I have a lot a padding even for your amazing gifts."

Gayle shook her head in protest. "I'm just a girl with generous friends," replied Gayle.

Erik thought for a moment and came to a conclusion. "Well, thanks to you, speaking Ellen's mind, we now have a wedding celebration to practice our dancing, it seems," said Erik. He then took Gayle's hand and led her out the spiral road.

Enock and Ellen were already dancing, as were many other of the Gnomare'. The grace of the ancient pair was unmatched, as though in all eternity they had wished for and thought of little else beyond that very moment. Fenrix and Ellay were near at hand, but they were only standing in each others arms. Ellay was much too tall for Fenrix to lead in the elven style of dance. Erik began to dance with Gayle, and it was truly awful. Erik was much too large to partner with Gayle as well, and he tripped over her feet and smashed headlong into Enock. Enock stopped, looked at him, and then embraced him with a laugh. Just as they turned to see the wonder of celebrations continue throughout the rings, the rest of the citizens of the tree issued from their homes with all manner of food and drink ready to celebrate.

In the time that followed, there was no pause in the merrymaking. At one point, almost everyone in the city would be dancing, and then at another, everyone would be feasting, and so on. Erik and Gayle began to notice that with every dance, there were fewer couples dancing and more watching.

Erik walked hand in hand with Gayle to where Fenrix was standing with Ellay's arms wrapped around him. With his eyes half-closed, Fenrix was swaying gently back and forth in Ellay's arms with a broad smile on his face and a jug of wine in his hands. Ellay, still in her rough leathery work clothes, smiled and greeted Erik and Gayle both.

Erik bowed and then, looking around, said, "I don't mean to be rude, but I am exhausted, and it seems as though many of your fellow Gnomare' have stopped dancing as well. Perhaps after loosing many of there own kin the merry making will be short lived."

Ellay laughed and answered, "You might be surprised to learn that it has been several hours in the reckoning of the surface world since the celebration began! Yet we, Gnomare', are not growing tired. This is the tradition of the wedding festival.

"First, we all dance; then we all feast. Then the elflings retire from the celebrations and watch. Then it all starts again without them. Next, it is the younglings who retire. After another longer round of dance, song, and feasting, it is the adolescents who take their leave.

"We have just finished the next cycle. Now the adults rest, and only the elders and the lords dance and feast with whomever they choose to partner with. So my partner and I are done here. After the elders and lords finish, it will be the mated couple alone. This is the wedding feast in the elven tradition."

Gayle, wiping the sweat off her brow, said, "Thank goodness it's over then! I can't dance another step or take in another meal!"

Ellay pointed behind Erik and Gayle to the road leading up to the highest ring and said, "I must remind you that if an elder or lord so chooses, you will advance to the next round of celebrations, and it is a high honor indeed!"

Erik turned to see Princess Sarah and Lord Jase approaching and said, "Oh no! They are not serious!"

Gayle spun around to see Jase whisper something in the ear of Princess Sarah as he pointed at her and Erik both. Gayle hung her head and began to lean on Erik as she said half-laughing, "I don't ever want to get married like this."

Jase came forward and with an outstretched hand said, "Gayle of Hillsborough, would you do me the honor of being my partner for the grand celebration?"

Gayle closed her eyes, took a deep breath, and then opened her eyes with a smile and took Jase's hand. "I would be honored, my lord."

Jase led Gayle by the hand up into the city. Princess Sarah then stepped forward and extended her hand toward Erik, not saying a word. Erik, realizing that Sarah was a figure of the highest importance in this culture, bowed low and took her hand without hesitation. Erik thanked Sarah many times for everything he had come to love about his time in the city.

Fenrix yelled after him as he and the princess walked away. "Well, I am taking my maiden to bed for my own celebrating, but you save your strength if you can. We will all do this again soon enough."

Erik and the princess arrived at the highest ring where they had originally entered the city. There the branches of Ellhom had grown and woven themselves into a large platform just beyond the banister. There were other vines about it, holding lanterns above it, and the globes of music were already hovering in a ring around the platform, playing another tune even more lovely and intricate than the ones before.

Stepping up lightly onto the banister, Enock and Ellen were the first to hop over onto the platform. Sarah pulled Erik up onto the banister next. They leapt more or less gracefully over to the platform, followed by Artcreft and his mistress and then Lord Jase and Gayle.

Soon all the elders followed and were assembled on the platform as it pulled away from the banister. They all began to dance without being told or cued. Princess Sarah, being taller and stronger than Gayle, made a more suitable partner for Erik, and Jase, being much smaller than Erik, also proved to be an excellent partner for Gayle in the dance.

So for at least a while, Erik and Gayle were able to look graceful in the midst of the more practiced dancers. Time seemed to stand still as the platform was raised and lowered throughout the city so that the spectators at the banister or the rings could watch.

Suddenly, three screeching points of white light darted across the ceiling of the city of Ellhom. They stopped in their flight and hung in the air with a loud gonging sound. The celebrations ceased immediately, and all the Gnomare' looked up silently.

"That's an alarm, no doubt. Now it's time for more bad news," said Jase grimly. The yelling of an elf could be heard from the top ring, along with the stomp of metal shod boots quickly running down the spiral road.

Jase looked over the edge of the balcony just as Fenrix's roar erupted below them. Enock approached the edge to see three members of the High Guard being slung over a balcony at the same time as another roar from Fenrix ripped through the city. The onlookers at the banister began to run every which way in the city trying to get a better look.

The platform lowered to the site from which the High Guards had fallen. It was the engineers' ring, and there were unconscious or wounded and bleeding High Guards lying outside the entrance to one of the larger workshops.

"What mischief is this?" said Enock in a voice loud enough for everyone in the ring to hear.

Elterion flew with the aid of his remarkable insect like armor from the ring above the platform, and landing behind Enock, he knelt. "Crime and violence," Elterion said, repeating it in elvish and then plain speech.

"Calm, child," commanded Enock.

Elterion arose, and said, "The half-elven, my Lord," with a loud gasp.

"Go on," urged Enock.

"They have been visited by some misfortune, perhaps another Darbeck attack. I could hear their screams in the night and could smell their blood on the wind," said Elterion. "I was aloft, aligning the crystals; then north from the groves of oaks came the screams. I went to find Fenrix so that he could possibly sniff out what happened and help our cousins. When I came to Ellay's shop, she and Fenrix were mating. Ellay became violent when we interrupted, and she assaulted the High Guard. She was restrained for her violence, but as we went to lead her away, Fenrix attacked. Now most of the High Guard is badly injured, and Fenrix is nowhere to be found!"

Enock sighed and said, "Ellay. Will there be no end to her foul temper? And now she has involved an outsider in violence against my house!"

"Are you surprised, eldest? This is what I foretold, dark has fallen in this house I can feel it." replied Elterion.

Enock stretched his staff out toward Ellhom, and the city began to shake. The bark of Ellhom, which at first was bronze and flecked with rivulets of emerald green, was now turned to a silvery steel, with blue veins running between the strips of its bark.

"Listen, my children, this is Ellhom's true form," shouted Enock, as he turned the lamps of the canopy to a white silvery light by the power that was in him. The city of the tree, up until that time, had been in a state of twilight, but now the light of day shone everywhere from the lamps of the mighty tree. "The darkness has passed for the moment. Fear no more violence. Instead we will look to our cousins and children as our guests determine what has transpired," commanded Enock.

Jase came to Enock's side and whispered, "I don't know what evil we started or mischief we are involved in, but we shall lead it away from here as soon as can be managed."

The city was brighter, but the mood was dark, and the Gnomare' began to murmur about their guests. Enock demanded that the Gnomare' return to their labors and studies. The crowded city streets soon became silent. Jase disappeared over the banister into one of the lower rings while Erik took leave of Sarah and apologized as he led Gayle back toward the House of Healing with Ellen close behind.

Ellen eventually joined them inside and said, "You two may no longer be safe among the Gnomare'. Enock's servants will gather your things and bring them here. It is a high crime to do anyone harm in this house."

"This is all wrong. What 's happening? This is just a misunderstanding, right?" asked Gayle.

At that moment, Fenrix was pulled through the door by Jase. "It does sound as though we have done more harm than good," said Fenrix.

"What do you mean, Fenrix?" asked Erik.

"We stopped one ancient evil and fought another," said Erik.

Fenrix rolled his eyes and replied, "That means nothing now. Even though I was only defending my lady, she had committed a crime by attacking the High Guard and is now imprisoned in the deep forge. For my actions, I am a criminal now too. Indeed it seems to me that our coming here has started something in motion and I believe the people of Ellhom may blame us for the ill fortunes."

"Very true, Fenrix. The Gnomare' however do not act without reason. Still the reasoning of the Gnomare' is still strange to me," claimed Jase. Sarah entered the house and stood behind Jase. She was carrying a large scaled scabbard, at the end of which was a hilt much like Fenrix's old sword. She beckoned Fenrix forward, which he did with a bow.

"Fenrix, high master of the sword, your sword was lost in the struggle against the overlord of the Kylvara'. Please accept this in its place," said Sarah as she held the scabbard forward.

Fenrix took and unsheathed the sword. The blade of dark gray metal had a surprising adamantine luster to it. Its shape was keris in the manner of the Hillmen, yet above the crossbar was a sphere that began to spin rapidly. The blade began to vibrate and give off a harmonic resonance.

"It is a shaping blade of the Gnomare'. May it serve a man of your skill well," said Sarah.

Fenrix happily tied the scabbard to his side and sheathed this sword, saying, "May this gift bless the hunt."

The servants of Enock began to come in one at a time, bringing backpacks full of provisions as well as a steel-bound wooden chest. Erik, after undoing the hasp and flipping the lid open, saw Gayle's gown folded at the bottom. On top of it were laid many items of jewelry. " Gayle, you will be leaving a rich woman!" teased Erik.

"I prize only my bow and quiver now," said Gayle, looking at Ellen.

Ellen's face lit up with a smile. "They are upstairs; they were saved from the blast by the stone you fell in front of," explained Ellen.

"Well, at least my armor held," said Fenrix, knuckling the drake scales of his chest piece.

Oberon arrived in the doorway and asked, "Are the mortals still hiding in here?"

Gayle spun around. "Oberon?"

Oberon immediately averted his eyes.

"I can see that you are repulsed by me, and more than that, you look to be ashamed to have loved me at all," said Gayle as a tear ran down her left cheek.

Oberon replied coldly, "I can't bear to see mortal flesh wither so swiftly. You are like a dead thing. It is something elf maidens do not do. Nor can I bear the thought of ordinary men touching our maidens. You disgrace them with your mortal fingers. I felt soiled just by touching you. I am ashamed for the maidens who loved any of you."

Gayle's face turned bright red so that her scars nearly disappeared. Gayle began to cry as she yelled, "You're a monster with fair skin and venom in your perfumed breath! You had better leave before I get my bow and decorate your flesh with shafts of my arrows and we shall see who is truly a dead thing!"

Oberon laughed mockingly and turned to leave. Ellen put her hands on Gayle and comforted her. Ellen claimed that she could not punish him for his evil words because he had not passed the doorway.

"I can!" said Erik as he walked out into the street.

Fenrix sighed and predicted that Oberon's days were over. Sarah urged Ellen to stop Erik, but she replied, "I don't believe I have the means. He has a different strength, not easily turned aside."

The scream of an elf maiden came from out in the street. Jase dashed outside, calling, "Peace, Erik! They were just words—" but then stopped and began to laugh hysterically.

Gayle left the house and beheld Erik standing in front of an elf maiden wearing Oberon's clothes. "Oberon?" questioned Gayle, pointing at the maiden.

The maiden was crying while looking at her own hands. She looked up at Erik and Gayle. They were both able to see that half of her face was sagging and withered like the skin of an elderly man.

"What have you done to me, Enock?" yelled the maiden.

"I have given you perspective, Oberon," thundered the voice of Enock from far below in the city.

"Let's see how venomous you are now, Brianna!" added Enock, standing on a branch of Ellhom that was lifting him to the edge of the banister.

Oberon yelled in protest and began to curse Erik.

Enock, interrupting, said, "You will learn the subtleties of your post from the other side of the coin. This is my house; these are my guests. You insulted my hospitality when you insulted them. I will allow you to mend your ways in a few hundred years, Brianna."

Oberon, now Brianna, hung her head, and holding her clothes up, she left down the spiral road in shame. They all reentered the House of Healing. There, Fenrix and Gayle packed for the journey and then waited while Ellen laid hands on them both, praying for a safe journey. Enock took Erik to the table where his traveling clothes were laid out. Erik took his things and went upstairs to change. Enock spoke to Jase for a while in elvish until Erik's return.

As Erik came down the stairs, Enock spoke. "Dear guests, in the months you have spent among us—"

"Months?" interrupted Gayle and Erik at the same time.

Enock only smiled and continued. "You have become lords, friends, lovers, and family. I first saw four strangers. Now I see Lord Jase, Quadrian of the Eldare'. I see Fenrix, the hunter and fighter, a High Sage of totemic channeling. I see a master of all disciplines of enchantment and, by all rights an, Arch Mage.

"I behold the lady who can see into hearts and an expert runic archer as well, a rare and deadly art. I also name you, Gayle Fletcher, a lieutenant under Elterion's command in the High Guard of the Gnomare'.

"I do not wish any of you to leave; however, the mood of my people has become dark. They may do you much harm in the trouble of their hearts. So I must send you away for now in the understanding that I may wish to see you again soon."

Gayle skipped forward and with a leap kissed Enock on the cheek.

Fenrix asked out of nowhere, "What of my elven beauty, Ellay?"

Enock's face became grave as he answered, "She must labor toward her pardon. That is our custom. She asked me to give you this," As Enock snapped his fingers, one of the Gnomare' came through the door holding a new chain mace.

As Enock's servant gave it to Fenrix, Enock said, "Ellay wishes you to know that this weapon is more powerful than the last and easier to control; she wishes that it may bless your hunt. She also says that when you wish to take a mate, she will be waiting for you and no other until your return."

"I must wait how long, oh Lord of Gnomare'?" asked Fenrix sadly.

Ellen answered this time. "You will feel your heart pull you back in a time of sorrow. The hunt will give you no joy, and the kill will have no excitement—only then will you return," Fenrix with a nod became silent. Artcreft suddenly entered the room with a flash of blinding light carrying neatly folded cloth of black material and held it out before Erik.

Erik took it and unfurled it; it was a robe black as midnight and reflected no light except for dark red metallic runes at the edges of its collar and sleeves.

Artcreft said, "You are not wholly without talent. This robe was made in the old capital, and it will ease your focus," Artcreft stepped back and then, looking somewhat uneasily around the room, vanished in plain sight.

Enock smiled. "It seems as though our angry crow has warmed up to you, Erik. Now to you, Lord Jase. The princess has commanded that you may come and go as you please. However, I suggest that you all remain together until you arrive where your journey began."

Jase saluted Enock and Ellen and then took a knee in front of Sarah, saying, "My lady, may I have leave to escort my friends on the road home?"

Sarah bent down and kissed Jase on the forehead. After whispering something in his ear, she stood and announced, "Now I bid you farewell. You have seen for your selves that the servants of Dagoth the first evil have awoke. You have also witnessed the return of the counterbalance in the world. Many great and terrible things are just over the horizon. May you all find a light within yourselves to stand against the coming darkness. I must now put a sleep on you all. You must understand that the ways in and out of the city are our most closely guarded secrets," There in the House of Healing, they would sleep their final night as the guests of city of Ellhom.

Part II

❖ ❖ ❖

Shadows of Elvendom

Prologue

❖ ❖ ❖

My sons and brothers, the following is a tale of how the war reshaped the north. I realize that such tales are commonly told through the eyes of a single hero or perhaps just a few. Being that as it may, this story is told through the eyes of many, for this is the truth of things that I have come to know. No one person sacrificed more than another in the fight for freedom in the north. To all those who fought and died as well as those who survived—we owe you our thanks, and may the deeds of the faithful and true bring honor to those who follow in your mighty memory.

Sincerely,
Erik Ironrod

Chapter 1

◇ ◇ ◇

Hunted in Dreams

They all fell into a sudden deep sleep. At first it was dark and dreamless, but then a vision came into Erik's mind. Erik was standing on a battlefield. It was littered with twisted and broken machines of war. The dead bodies of dwarfs and men covered the field, dyeing the ground red with blood. In front of Erik, in the field, stood a massive pile of dead and twisted bodies. Around the base of the grizzly mount were the shadowy figures of the Kylvara', silvery swords drawn. Atop the mount was the high lord Kylratha, his massive Gothic blade in hand, pointed down toward his brethren. He spoke in the harsh tongue of the Kylvara', yet Erik could hear him clearly in his mind.

"Brothers and sons of the counter balance, we have toiled long among men. We gave them council, and we taught them to fight with their frail hands. Yet these poor children were weak in mind and would not listen. They were weak in body and would not stand firm. Now they betray us and join with their foes against us?

"We have turned aside from our mission and the balance has been shifted by other hands. To the counterbalance we return. It's to the first evil and his servants we set our steel. Concern yourselves no longer with the business of men and dwarfs. Into the darkness we must reach with all our strength, never resting until our mission is complete. Now go!"

The Kylvara' melted into the shadows. Yet Kylratha remained, and the silvery globes of his eyes set their steely gaze upon Erik. Erik tried to turn and run, but his body would not move. He watched helplessly as Kylratha descended the mound and approached. While he stood in front of Erik, the sun set behind Kylratha, sending a cascade of wispy clouds, painted red by the sunset, flying through the skies above them.

The shadowed figure of Kylratha stood like a colossus before Erik. Dark runes adorned the heavy plates of his armor. Looking down at Erik, he put one finger of his clawed metal gauntlet on Erik's chest. "The winds have changed. You have meddled in my work. Now turn away, boy!" said the overlord in a voice like wild thunder and howling wind.

Erik felt both a stabbing pain in his chest and the sensation of his entire body burning and tearing. Erik screamed horribly as Kylratha's gauntlet plunged into Erik's chest. Withdrawing his hand, Kylratha held Erik's beating heart in front of his face. Squeezing his fist, he reduced it to pulp. Erik's vision went black, and he dreamt no more.

Erik opened his eyes and thought he was still dreaming. The autumn disguise that Ellhom wore above ground looked nothing like the Tree of the city. Its bark was dark gray, and its leaves, now a pure vermilion, were casting a red-orange glow into Erik's eyes.

As Erik stared up at the canopy of Ellhom, Jase came into view. Looking down at Erik, Jase extended an outstretched hand to help him up. Erik stood and saw Gayle and Fenrix still asleep on top of the roots of Ellhom.

Gayle woke with a scream. "The overlord is upon me!" she shouted.

Jase hurried to her side and asked what she saw.

"A giant dark elf destroying a city around me, cursing the Vanguard. He toppled towers and split the city streets with a single swing of his sword. Everywhere I ran, the city gave way beneath me. Then I fell into the dark," answered Gayle in a panic.

Fenrix sat up with an amused sort of howl. "What a fighter!" Fenrix exclaimed.

"You fought the Dark Lord in your dream, Fenrix?" asked Erik.

"No and yes, as the elves say, however only his blade was dark, but he had skin like polished steel. We laughed as we fought sword to sword before the carcass of a dead elder dragon. It was a dance of sword play like no other. I could only meet my defeat with a smile, yet he would not finish me." Fenrix stood and stretched. "I can't beat him," he declared with a long exhale.

"If he is heading north, then perhaps he is the cause of the half-elves trouble and not the darbeck if this is the case I should return home and warn Dregor," said Erik.

With heavy footfalls and a loud snort, Blackhorn let his presence be known. With his great horned head cocked to one side, he stomped his front hooves. Fenrix observed that Blackhorn was growing impatient and bored in the valley of Ellhom. Fenrix said, "Well, in any case, we should head north as quick as possible. If Kylratha is tormenting us, we should get away from the tree."

- - -

THE PARTY DECIDED TO FOLLOW the stream north, up the falls and out of the valley.

"We should go only a little ways north before we turn west again," said Fenrix while tasting the air.

The party skirted the western bank of the stream until it bent westward around a large white stone-capped hill, almost identical to the one they had climbed to the south. There the group came upon the outskirts of half-elven homes in the oak groves. The air became thick with smoke and the smell of cooking flesh. Fenrix turned and sent blackhorn north with much protest from his spiral horned companion.

At first they approached with great caution, but soon it became apparent that this village was now a gruesome reminder of evil. Every half-elven of the oak grove was dead and left hanging by the ankles, their bodies torn open and innards left to hang.

Terrified, the group walked beneath the hanging corpses into what seemed to be the center of the massacre.

"No darbeck could do this. Why, Kylratha, would you do this to the elflings? Now I have to kill you!" growled Fenrix. There were no sounds of life one would normally hear in autumn, only silence.

Gayle stepped to the front and said, "I do not like this place; we should leave."

Fenrix sniffed the air and replied, "Not until I have a look from above."

With a loud bang from his chain mace, Fenrix lodged the mace head into one of the platforms of the tree-top village and ascended.

Jase sighed and said, "And he's off. But this is strange. These bodies are mostly maidens and elflings. Where are their hunters and guards?"

Fenrix called down to Jase from one of the high platforms. "Jase, have a look!" said Fenrix as he dropped a small object.

Jase dashed forward and caught it. It was a black coin pouch. Jase stuck his hand into it and took out a handful of strange silver and gold coins. "This is Vanguard imperial coinage. I haven't seen these struck in ages," said Jase.

Erik looked at the coins curiously, moving them around in Jase's hand with his finger. Erik stroked his beard and grunted before he asked, "What would the half-elven be doing with them?"

Fenrix interrupted the conversation by leaping from the highest platform and landing with an earth-shaking thud, alarmingly close to Erik. "Many small fires still burn in the houses. However, the most interesting thing I saw was a collection of dwarven ballista. They were smashed and burning, but I would recognize those things anywhere!" said Fenrix excitedly.

Gayle clutched her hair and groaned. Erik began to stroke he hair and asked her if she was all right. She then stood and said, "My new eye was starting to burn, but I am fine now."

As the smoke cleared, Erik could see that several dozen yards up each tree, a great ringed balcony was constructed. They were all interconnected with swinging rope bridges. "This place would be charming if it were not burning down," commented Erik.

"They are here," said Gayle as she drew an arrow from her quiver.

A flight of dozens of arrows came at the party from all directions. Jase managed to easily dodge them, and the arrows aimed at Erik and

Gayle recoiled and splintered from an unseen barrier that Erik rapidly conjured. Fenrix was struck in the back and chest with little to no effect as he ascended to a high platform via his chain mace.

Several figures emerged from the smoke in the distance and began to toss grappling hooks to the lower platforms and climb up at an alarming speed. Yet more figures appeared from behind nearby trees, letting loose another volley with the same effect.

"Seek and hobble!" screamed Gayle as she let her arrow fly. The shimmering dart curved through the air, piercing the legs of three half-elves before it staked the foot of a fourth to the ground.

The half-elves were covered in strange camouflaged cloaks, and seeing their brothers fall, the others drew their weapons and advanced. Jase was the first to meet them blade to blade. The half-elves' steel weapons proved no match for the shaping blades of the Gnomare' and began to chip and shatter. Yet Jase found himself quickly surrounded, and if not for the strength of his mail, he would have received several grievous wounds. These were very skilled fighters, and Jase was no match for a dozen of them with just his blades.

A sudden flash of lightning sent several jumping back with a yelp, but then a flame cast from a taller half-elf standing away from the fight began to engulf Jase.

"Silence" Gayle whispered as she notched an arrow. She shot at the half-elf enchanter, but the arrow was repelled and fell to the ground lifelessly.

The flame died down on Jase, who was now enraged, and his movements were so swift they could not be easily seen. The half-elves near him either leapt back or were cut down. Fire began to erupt on Jase again but was immediately extinguished by sleet and rain that began to fall down in sheets.

The half-elves then began to hover in the air, kicking their legs wildly, attempting to regain their footing. The enchanter, who was also levitating, drew out an ornate dagger with many elven runes glowing down the length of its blade. He began to chant but soon dropped his dagger and reached for his throat as Erik extended his arm and made a grasping motion with his hand. With his staff held aloft in his other hand, Erik gathered the half-elves in the air above him.

Erik, speaking with a wizard's voice said, "Enough! You cannot hope to win, and enough of you have perished already!"

Three more half-elves fell from the platform above and were caught in Erik's enchantment. "Now you will sit and put down your weapons, then tell us the answer to any questions we ask. Then I will release you," commanded Erik as his voice echoed at them from every angle of the forest.

The half-elves were obliged to sit as Erik brought them down. Another half-dozen came falling down with a large piece of wooden platform. Erik also caught them as the platform crashed to the earth. After a few minutes, all the assailants were corralled in front of Erik.

Still bound by Erik's power, Jase removed their elvish cloaks and weapons and with Gayle's help placed them to the side. The beauty and youthful visage of these half-elves was much like that of their cousins from the tree. In size and power, however, they were much the lesser.

Jase stood next to Erik, still smoldering from being set ablaze and his elven rune blazing brightly on his forehead. Jase spoke in an unknown tongue, but the meaning was clear to Erik.

Jase said, "You are beaten, and by the King's speech. You will tell us all we ask of you," Jase then walked away to where the enchanter dropped his runic dagger and took it.

Fenrix dropped down from the platform above, and with his landing, he covered the half-elves who were sitting with mud.

Gayle began to giggle but became serious as she asked, "Why did you attack us?"

The enchanter answered, "I am Caine, a lord and governor of the wooded realm. I ordered the attack."

"Why?" asked Gayle again.

"Stupid girl, our maidens and elflings are dead and hanging, and you strangers were here taking our money. We thought you to be bandits. Now we see you are just fortunate fools," answered Caine.

"Fortunate fools, eh?" mocked Jase as he stood before Caine.

"You were beaten easily enough by fools," added Fenrix.

Caine laughed and said, "Fortunate fools are still dangerous when blessed by the Gnomare'. You even have an Arch Mage doing your bidding!"

"I do my own bidding, elfling!" said Erik as he pointed at Caine menacingly.

"Where did you get the dwarven ballista, and why would you even want such a thing?" asked Fenrix, pointing up at the platforms.

Caine answered, "From the trade caravans. The Vanguard and dwarfs have formed a new empire and are rebuilding the cities. We have even heard that the foundries have been rebuilt and relit. They pass this way with many goods for trade and we need the ballista."

"Why?" repeated Jase and Fenrix in unison.

Caine looked to the trees and said, "There is a strange new breed of drake in the forest. They can change their color and glide through the treetops. Their venom is deadly to all within seconds. We needed the ballista to defend our villages and city."

"Villages—city? Isn't this just an oak grove beyond the borders of the Hillsborough orchards?" asked Erik.

"This is the wooded realm, hidden from the eyes and minds of men through enchantment, although it is no longer hidden from your eye, Arch Mage," answered Caine.

Fenrix asked anxiously, "Are there many of this new breed, Caine?"

Caine told him of every encounter and guessed that there must be dozens but noted that he had yet to slay one. "We were hunting deep in the realm for days. When we returned, we came upon this disaster," said Caine.

"We had nothing to do with what happened here," Erik said. "We were heading north to our village. Elterion, captain of the High Guard, told us of your plight, so we came to see if we could aid you."

Caine managed to struggle against Erik's spell well enough to ask, "Then do you know who is responsible for this?"

Jase bent over and looked Caine straight in the eyes and said with a smile, "Kylratha."

Caine laughed and said, "Ghost stories. Kylratha died when Northguard fell around him this is no act of the counterbalance."

Jase shook his head slowly, not breaking eye contact with Caine as he answered. "Kylratha was very much alive when I left him in Northguard. He was also just as alive when I crossed swords with him under the Tree of Two Worlds."

"Why would the overlord do this to us?" asked Caine.

Jase emptied the coin pouch in front of Caine, spilling the imperial coinage on the muddy ground. "Because that's what the Vanguard did to us four hundred years ago. Now you are trading with them and taking them to your homes more willingly than a half-dead Quadrian and a cart full of scarred half-elven children!" screamed Jase, his eyes now burning with an inner fire.

The drops of rain and sleet began to sizzle and vaporize before they could touch Jase. Now breathing heavily, Jase had death in his eyes.

Caine smiled, perceiving no real threat. He stood and stared down at Jase. "Yes, I remember you, and I would still do business with the Vanguard, both before and after Northguard fell. I supplied and sheltered them in our realm for years after. They needed my protection; it was something we could use to our advantage. I knew I would need their future trade more than I would need hungry mouths of the bastard children of Eldare' and Feyara'."

Those were the last words Caine spoke before Jase's blade passed through his neck. Caine's head rolled back off his shoulders and his body fell lifelessly into the mud.

Jase, turning around, eyes ablaze with star fire, shouted, "Release them, Erik! I want them to run!"

Erik said while looking at Jase intently. "No!"

"Fine, they die where they sit!" roared Jase.

Caine's body burst into an eerie blue flame that spread with a flash to the half-elves sitting in Erik's trance. They screamed as they burned in place. Jase cocked his head back and yelled out a burning enchantment with the runed dagger pulsating in his hand and his rune blazing on his brow. Erik tried to counter the spell but failed, nor could he silence or bind

Jase when using the King's speech, the ancient language of the house of Eldare'. The hanging bodies began to burn, as did the platforms high in the trees. The flame could not be quenched even when Erik caused the sky to pour down ice and hail.

Fenrix grabbed Jase and walked away, yelling, "We'll head north— follow!" With his arm over Jase's shoulder, he led Jase away into the forest, speaking in the Hillman tongue. Erik looked up at the village being consumed in blue flame. Horrified, he turned to Gayle, who was herself horrified with the destruction.

"We have to go!" Erik shouted above the noise of the rising flames and falling water. Gayle turned her head toward Erik and nodded. Erik and Gayle began to run after Fenrix and Jase, though being careful not to get too close to the pair as they began to talk.

"What happened back there? Has Jase gone completely mad?" said Erik, half-whispering.

"Jase and his kin must have suffered greatly at the hands of my people," answered Gayle.

"I really had no idea what trials Jase had gone through in his youth. I believe, however, that I am only beginning to know the depths of the suffering he has seen in his life," said Erik, looking ahead.

Up ahead, Fenrix, with his arm still around Jase, said, "Why do you keep your hate for so long? It will destroy you every day you carry it. I despise the Vanguard too, but it is a fire I light only when I must."

Jase's eyes flashed as he spoke in many voices. "Soon these people will cover this world, and then what? When they have covered every field, felled every tree, killed everyone different from themselves? If you could see what they were going to do, would you ever put your fire out?"

"What are you saying, brother?" asked Fenrix.

"When I slept under the tree, my old mentor came to me. He dragged me by the arm to the top of a black tower of twisted steel and red glowing lamps. There he showed Grea'nock as it will be if the servants of Dagoth are defeated, and the new empire is allowed to thrive.

"Great cities of stone and steel will plague the land. War machines larger and more deadly than any before will roam the streets and the open places, crushing anything they pass. The same machines roar through the air like dragons, spewing fire and foul smoke. The war machines even roam the depths and sink the war ships of enemy nations.

"The empire will crush the elven houses without the might of Kylvara' to aid them and chase the Hillmen and Mountainfolk into the deep wilds to die. The half-elves and dwarfs will lose their uniqueness in the bloodlines of the Vanguard, until only one evil and sickly race remains to consume Grea'nock.

"Then he showed me the world as it would be if he fell, and the Kylvara' dispersed. The world was a twisted nightmare realm. The servants of Dagoth swept over the land like a pestilence. The dragons burned down the elven homes; great horned beasts issued from the mountains and trampled the Mountainfolk into the dust.

"The darbeck haunted and infested the foundries of the dwarfs. The corpses of men began to rise and feed on the flesh of the living. The Kylvara' began to quarrel amongst themselves and then ally themselves with the servants of Dagoth and even lock themselves in a never-ending war between evil immortals.

"All surviving men and dwarfs became like frightened animals living in holes, afraid to live in the open among the demons of Dagoth and the vampire-like Kylvara' who went drinking the blood of mortals and living in towers of blackened bone.

"The elves shed their bodies, too weak to return to Avalon. They wandered the wastes as wisplike spirits mourning the world that was.

"After showing me both visions of the future, he put his hand on me and said 'See, child, there is no victory,'" Jase concluded solemnly.

Fenrix looked genuinely alarmed by Jase's dream and asked, "Do you trust Kylratha's visions in your dream?"

Jase thought for a moment and grasped Fenrix's hand on his shoulder. "I do not often sleep or dream, but I do trust these visions.It seems to me the the counter balance is shifted too far and if there is to be true victory I must wear the mantle of power"

Fenrix looked to the north and said, "Then what is to be done, brother?"

Jase scowled as he said grimly, "I must slay Kylratha, my old mentor, and then destroy this new empire."

Fenrix laughed and wiped the rain from his brow with the backside of his left hand and said, "Is that all? I was starting to worry."

Fenrix beckoned Erik and Gayle to come closer so that they could travel together. Erik and Gayle were flirting with one another and trying to forget that their friend and companion had just killed a dozen people in cold blood. They were somewhat reluctant to approach Jase and Fenrix.

Fenrix smiled and said, "Lord Jase is his usual charming self again—I think. Those half-elves back there were the very ones who abandoned Jase and a dozen starving children to the road and death; the children would have died were it not for Jase. Trust not in this new empire or those who have dealings with them. Mark my words, only bad things will happen if you do."

Gayle replied, "I'm sorry for your pains, Jase. Four hundred years is a long time to carry a weight like that. As far as this empire, my grandmother used to read to us from her ancestor's childhood journal. Believe me, I do not wish to return to the dark ways of fortress cities."

"I, for one, do not wish to take part in any more needless killing," declared Erik.

"You can't solve all your problems with wizardry, Erik," warned Jase. "You can turn every unfriendly arrow to flowers and every brigand to a maiden, but you will be weak on your conjuring in a day and be dead in a year. Mortals cannot live by the arts and survive long."

"As far as needless killing, if you would have released those half-elves and turned away, they would have shot you dead for the contents of your pockets," added Fenrix.

"I could see that desire in their eyes as well but wasn't sure if I should say anything," said Gayle, casting a glance south over her shoulder.

Fenrix stopped and said, "Your sight is a rare gift. If I had my way, you would tell me everything you see, and Jase everything he hears. Then I would be the perfect hunter. We should head west now. Follow me quickly."

They followed Fenrix, running through the undergrowth. The pace was exhausting, and for hours they scrambled through the dense vegetation without rest. Erik and Gayle began to fall behind, so Fenrix slowed to a stop.

Just then, Gayle ran headfirst into a tree. Rubbing her nose with an uneasy laugh, she said, "Sorry. I forgot, just because I can see through things doesn't mean they are not there."

Fenrix turned and said to Erik as he came stomping up, "I sent Blackhorn to the crossroads as soon as we came near the wooden realm, sensing the danger. Now that we are near the crossroads, we must be quiet. Blackhorn was carrying some food and water as well as the chest with your valuables. I fear he might have been captured."

"Would any bandit just kill him for the meat?" asked Erik.

"Perhaps, but not if they had any sense. A Ramlord is a rare creature, tough and intelligent, worth much more alive," answered Fenrix.

Jase added, "Well, it's getting dark beneath the trees; sunset is not far away."

Fenrix put his finger over his mouth and said, "Now, you all follow, quick but quiet."

They followed Fenrix west and slightly south through the trees, the forest was growing thinner. Gayle, who once had been skeptical of the stealth of Fenrix, was now amazed. He slipped through the forest barely stirring a plant and not making a sound. Even Jase was finding it difficult to match Fenrix's speed without making an incredible amount of noise. Fenrix, slowing a little, began to look over his shoulder with angry glances. After a while, the sun set, and the noise the group was making was too much for Fenrix. He stopped and spun around and put his hand out.

"In the hills we would be dead in the breeding season. Do you all sleep as soon as the sun sets, never to walk a step under the stars? From here we walk. Gayle, you in front with me—at least you can still see your feet. We creep slow and silent. We are not far from the crossroads, and I can smell our prey's cooking," lectured Fenrix.

"You don't know they are unfriendly," said Erik.

Fenrix sniffed the air sadly and replied, "Yes, I do."

From there they crept carefully southwest until they could see a bright orange glow between the trees. Fenrix approached the trunk of a large sycamore and crouched behind it. The others joined him at its base.

Fenrix looked at Jase and pointed to his ear. Jase nodded and said, "At least a dozen, and a few occasionally speak a word or two of the dwarven tongue. We are not close enough for them to hear us over the noise they are making."

Erik could barely hear anything but his own breath, but he could smell the aroma of cooking meat, and it made him hungry. "What is that smell there, Fenrix? It's delicious," said Erik.

Fenrix became very grim as he said, "It's Blackhorn they are cooking, and I'm sure he is delicious. But I will eat their leader's heart first."

Jase stopped himself from laughing out of respect. Fenrix looked back toward the glow and said, "Gayle, you will be my eyes before I strike. We are near the clearing. Stay low and in the shadow of the trees."

Fenrix stalked his way toward the edge of the clearing. Gayle followed just behind while Erik and Jase stayed further back. Fenrix finally stopped behind a very tall tree and motioned for Gayle. Gayle approached Fenrix now in a crouched position and knelt behind him, putting her hands on his shoulders.

Fenrix whispered, "Tell me what you see, archer. Can you poke your head out and have a look without being noticed?"

Gayle giggled in his ear and answered, "I can do better than that!"

Gayle, staring directly through the tree, said, "There are fourteen of them, thirteen of the Vanguard and a single dwarf. They are sitting near a fire over which a very large ram is roasting. They are mostly drunk, gambling over my jewelry, and that damn dwarf is wearing my gown. He dies first!"

Fenrix looked back at Gayle as she notched an arrow with blinding speed. "This is my revenge, so shoot for the head; leave their hearts to me," said Fenrix as he scrambled up the tree.

Gayle pulled her string back and waited. The sound of a humming blade whispered down to her from the treetop, and then a monstrous howl echoed in the night. Gayle could see the thieves stand up and start to grab their weapons and look in every direction.

Gayle yelled, "Seek and kill!" and then loosed her arrow. It flashed through the night air and collided with the dwarf's head, reducing it to a fragmented spray of flesh and bone.

The Vanguard, now cursing and facing the forest where Gale had appeared, began to approach very slowly. Out of the night air, Fenrix descended upon them, killing the lead man with his landing. Resonating keris sword and chain mace in hand, Fenrix went to work, spinning and twisting his body one way and then the other, passing his weapons over or through his quarry.

In a moment, one stood alone, only to be cut in half by a flash of white light as Gayle yelled, "Sever!"

Fenrix laughed as the blood sprayed him. Erik and Jase then appeared next to Gayle in the firelight, and together they hurried to Fenrix's side. Fenrix was smiling as he began to stack the bodies a few at a time near the fire.

"These will have to do for benches, except the dwarf, of course," said Fenrix as he took a knife from his belt and began to carve at the body of the dwarf. Withdrawing the heart from the dwarf's body, he began to eat it as he sat on a pile of bodies next to the fire.

Gayle grabbed a jug of wine from a small table at which the thieves had been gambling. Taking a large draught from the jug, Gayle sat down next to Fenrix and sighed.

Erik, unwilling to sit on stacked corpses, stood across from Fenrix. Raising his arms and then letting them fall back to his side with a slap, he realized he didn't quite know what to say.

Jase sat on a stack of bodies and started to look around. "These are not common thieves. They are all in uniform," he said, looking down at the bodies.

"Why couldn't we have talked to them? We might have persuaded them to return Gayle's jewels," said Erik.

"They killed my friend and companion, and you want me to hold my blade? Boy, I live for the hunt, and I have killed for less. I needed no other reason," growled Fenrix.

"They have horses tied up not far away, and there is a strange crest on their leather jerkins," observed Jase.

"I still don't see why you couldn't have taken your revenge on just one.

Instead you cut down a dozen people for the sake of a beast of burden!"
yelled Erik.

"There are heavy wagon tracks leading away north," announced Jase.

"He was not a beast of burden—he was a loyal friend who saved my
life many times!" screamed Fenrix as he rose and began to carve a piece of
meat off Blackhorn and eat it.

"And now you're eating him. Hell's blast, man?" bellowed Erik.

"Idiots! Shut up!" yelled Jase over Erik and Fenrix both. "I understand
you have lost a dear friend, Fenrix; however, Erik and Gayle hold people
above beasts and do not share a kinship of spirit with them as you do.

"Second, it is the custom of the Hillmen to eat the bodies of their most
loyal and prized beasts when they die, to share their strength.

"Last, and this is important, shut the hell up!" demanded Jase.

Jase stood and walked to the crossroads, yelling back to his companions
to join him on the road. They came to his side after exchanging awkward
glances amongst themselves.

Gayle looked down at the road. Pointing her finger to the large tracks
in the dirt, she said, "Whatever made these wheel tracks had to have been
very heavy."

Fenrix knelt and sniffed at a handful of dirt and said, "Yes, and drawn
by great plains oxen. Very large beasts indeed."

Jase looked back toward the fire and explained that the crest on the
men they had killed was that of the Northguard. Also, he had seen tracks
like that before.

"It's a war wagon, an armored personnel carrier. If you want to move
heavy infantry a good distance and want them to have the strength to fight,
it's the best way, for the Vanguard at any rate. This group of men here were
light cavalry left in the rear guard in case it goes ill," said Jase, pointing to
the road south, where nearly a dozen horses were tied up.

"What goes ill?" asked Erik.

Jase gave Erik a strange look, not believing he was still that naive.
Jase answered, "The half-elves told us there is now a new empire. The first
thing it will do is set its borders. These war wagons have one destination
and purpose: the subjugation of Hillsborough."

Chapter 2

◆ ◆ ◆

Returning to Darkness

Erik was hovering somewhere in his mind between fear and anger. Struggling to see the trail left by the war wagons, he asked, "How many and how long ago?"

Jase looked down and shook his head.

"At least four wagons," said Gayle.

"And about a half a day or so from the smell of the tracks," added Fenrix.

Erik, thinking aloud, said, "Fifty heavily armed men against half a dozen night guardsmen. They will have control of the whole town by now. We must make haste."

Gayle, who was beginning to panic, asked if anyone knew how to ride a horse. Jase and Fenrix shook their heads no.

"Then I must make haste!" declared Erik.

"I can travel faster than any horse, but it will still take me hours to get there," said Fenrix.

"Then go," begged Gayle. "Protect my family until I get there. The Fletchers live next to the Millers, south of town square."

Erik threw off his pack and brought out his runic robes and began to change.

Jase, laying on Erik's pack the runic dagger he had taken earlier, said, "I'm not sure what you're planning, but the dagger is a powerful device for channeling."

Erik finished dressing. The red metallic runes woven into the ornate mantle of his robe gave him an almost sinister look in the firelight. Erik grasped his staff in his right hand, and the air began to fill with tension. He then bent down and took the crystalline dagger, and immediately its runes began to pulse with light.

The night was filled with turbulent noise, almost ripping through the air like a rusty saw blade through hard wood. The horses tied up nearby began to go mad and break their restraints and run. Jase put his hands over his ears and shouted with his voice distorted by the spell, "What are you doing?"

"Making haste," answered Erik. "I give speed to the mechanism," said Erik in his wizard's voice. As he said this, eerie tendrils of dark bluish energy shot out of his hands like angry serpents, piercing the chest of himself and his companions.

Gayle screamed at first and then began to laugh and almost howl in delight. Jase could feel his blood rushing like a wild river through his veins as his heart began to pound too hard and fast to count the beats. Fenrix only smiled as though he had felt this sensation before. With a flash, the tendrils disappeared, leaving a cloud of sparkling mist around them. As they breathed it in, their lungs began to cool, and they regained their senses.

Erik stood tall, looming dark and sorcerous in the night. In his wizard's voice, he said, "Now, follow me!"

The wizard dashed up the north road like an arrow in the dark. The others, astounded by the cumbersome giant's newfound speed, ran off after him. They sprinted into the night and up the north road with incredible speed. Gayle could barely feel her feet touch the ground as she moved.

Fenrix laughed and yelled above the air whipping past his ears, "Now I have a pack to run with!"

Within moments the town of Hillsborough was visible high in the foothills. Fenrix's speed was now so great that he was literally springing from hilltop to hilltop with a great thunderous boom crashing out when he leapt. Up in the distance, Erik could see Fenrix stop at the base of the hill on which the town rested. The remainder of the group ran as fast as the enchantment would allow them, yet it took several minutes to reach Fenrix. Coming to a sliding halt, the three of them kicked up earth and gravel for yards in every direction, including that of Fenrix. Fenrix shook the dirt off, muttering something about grace.

"Slow the mechanism," commanded Erik in his wizard's voice. They all began to feel normal again, yet a sense of fatigue set in immediately.

"It is the sleep the great cats must take in after the killing charge," said Fenrix.

"We have no time for that," said Erik as he raised his staff. The jewel on his staff began to hum as it blossomed with fruit laden branches. The branches produced strange small apples that looked black in the starlight.

"Eat these quickly!" said Erik as he plucked one from his staff and bit into it.

They all took one and ate it. As soon as the nectar of the fruit hit Erik's stomach, he felt full of energy and strength.

Erik looked up toward Hillsborough. He could already hear screams of terror in the night.

"Damn, they arrived before the gates were closed! I was hoping to break a siege, not fight in the streets!" growled Jase.

"We kill any Vanguard or dwarf holding a weapon and in heavy armor! Agreed?" said Fenrix.

The rest turned to him and nodded. The night breeze blew down from the mountains at them. The city loomed dark and menacing, capping the top of the wooded hill with a black monument still echoing of screams in the night.

Fenrix drew his sword suddenly and said grimly, "Something is very wrong! I can smell death—old death," Fenrix began to run up the hill, and the party followed swiftly behind him.

The noise of combat and screams of frightened voices pleading for help began to grow as they approached. The gate was half raised and dark.

No watch lamps were lit, and the sounds of fighting and wailing in terror could be heard beyond. Fenrix stopped a dozen yards short of the gate and began to smell the air.

The party joined him within moments. "What do you see?" asked Jase.

"I can smell death everywhere! Three men died right here only moments ago, but there are no bodies," said Fenrix.

"Yes, I see the spray of blood from where they fell, yet I see no bodies lying in the streets," added Gayle.

"I can hear terror in the voice of everyone beyond that gate and other voices I don't recognize," said Jase, bending down on all fours and putting an ear to the ground.

"Well, this city must be saved, and the ones to do it might as well be us!" proclaimed Erik.

"Here they come!" said Gayle, pointing at the gate.

With an earth-shaking roar, Fenrix went in. Erik followed behind, with Jase at his side. Gayle notched three arrows at once and then stepped through the gate. In the dim evening light, they could see the silhouettes of four heavy infantry advancing toward the gate. They stopped just in front of Fenrix, pointing their pole arms at him.

"Sir, let us pass. This place is cursed. If you had any sense, you would leave before the dead devour you," said the frightened soldier of the empire.

At that very moment, a dozen figures came into sight from behind the men, howling and shrieking as they lurched forward. The group realized that they were looking at the walking dead. The soldiers spun around and prepared to take the charge from the undead. As they came closer, Erik thought he recognized one of the dead as Stephan, the town guardsman, but couldn't be sure.

"What devilry is at work here?" asked Erik not believing his eyes.

"The darkest sort of enchantment, death itself has been turned on its head," answered Jase as he readied his blades.

Gayle stepped around Erik and fired her arrows as the word "Shatter!" left her lips. Her arrows exploded behind the soldiers in a tidal wave of runic crystalline shards, paying no heed to metal armor or risen flesh. The shower of murderous metal cut everything, including the soldiers, into ribbons of flesh and metal. The street was silent and littered with flesh, blood, and bone. The bloodied walls were now scintillating with the shards of Gayle's arrows embedded in the stone.

The sounds of battle could still be heard from the town square. Fenrix crept forward, his sword and mace at the ready. Jase followed close behind him, blades drawn and wary. Gayle notched another arrow and followed them with Erik at her side.

Several more of the undead rounded the main street corner from the town square. The ones who made it past Gayle's arrows were cut to pieces by Jase and Fenrix or hurled against the city walls to be pulverized by the force of Erik's enchantments.

The party advanced slowly to the corner of the square. The building on their left was the town's only mill. It was a taller building with no windows and offered no view of the square. The sounds of combat were lessening, but still fierce. Fenrix and Jase crouched at the corner, springing into action when the dead passed and then withdrawing behind the corner again.

"What do you see?" asked Erik, getting close enough to Jase not to raise his voice.

"The dead have the square. Some of the townsfolk and the Vanguard are resisting, but there are few," answered Jase.

More undead rounded the corner, now aware of the group's presence. Erik, in anger, launched them high into the air to fall ruinously somewhere beyond the walls of the city.

"We must cut our way in toward the townsfolk and save who we can!" said Erik above the noise. Fenrix howled and leapt around the corner, and Jase dashed to his side. The two were immediately met by dozens of living dead and were pushed back.

Erik rounded the corner to see the two master swordsmen nearly overcome by a wall of putrid dead climbing over each other just for a chance to bite and claw at Fenrix and Jase. In the distance, Erik could see only the twisted silhouettes of the dead back lit against a single dim red lantern from the town hall. To Erik, it seemed the town he knew was now a grotesque mosaic of black figures in dim red lamplight.

Suddenly, a voice came down upon the town in a thunderous echo as clear as day. "Traitors, betrayers, usurpers, and kin slayers! You came upon your brethren to the north with sword and spear to put them under the yoke of your old empire. Now you will know your own darkness. Even as your dead fall, they will rise and devour you!" said Kylratha ominously.

Fenrix let loose an earth-shattering roar, so powerful it split the stones beneath his feet and caused his companions to stop their ears. The onslaught of the dead advancing on him began to quiver as if paralyzed, and with that, Jase issued a flash of lightning and blue flame. The dead were thrown back by the force of the enchantment. The flame began spreading among the dead, illuminating the square.

Gayle rounded the corner loosing two arrows and screaming, "Whirl and cleave!" Her arrows spiraled in tight circles through the square, cutting down everything they touched with a flash of white light.

Erik could now see the south end of the square. Standing outside his smithy, Grimhold, in full dwarven heraldic plate, with a massive hammer in each hand, was pummeling any undead that approached him. Near him stood a few of the surviving town guard, including Dareth, Dregor's younger stepbrother.

"Left, to the south end! Just follow the dwarf chanting curses!" shouted Erik. It was easy enough to do; Grimhold could be heard cursing above the noise quite well.

Fenrix and Jase began to fight their way through the ever-advancing dead toward Grimhold's smithy. Erik caused the dead to smash into each other, ending up in twitching heaps of flesh on the ground.

Out of the night air there came a terrible shriek from Gayle. Erik spun around, fearing the dead had gotten to her. There, in the plaza, Gayle knelt over the remains of her family, screaming. The undead began to surround her. Erik acted quickly, causing them all to collapse in on themselves as they got close enough to touch her.

Gayle's jeweled eye flashed as she stood. She began drawing and loosing arrows with blinding speed. Some splintered into hundreds of darts, piercing everything they touched; others erupted in explosions throughout the square, sending stone, undead, and Vanguard tumbling through the air. Gayle's jeweled eye flashed again, and she put her hand over it and screamed in pain. She then looked up into the crowded square with a beam of cold light emanating from her eye. She surveyed the crowd silently for a moment and then reached for another arrow. Finally, Gayle notched an arrow whose head began to burst into a dispersion of all known colors as she drew it back. She pointed her arrow to the northern sky, and her voice shrieked through the square: "Greater mythic crusher!"

Erik could feel the awesome power behind the command but did not expect what happened next. The arrow tore through the night air with a roar like an angry dragon. After the prismatic dart reached its zenith, the light became even more intense as it rocketed down onto the town hall. The explosion shook the entire town as the arrow grew into a spherical blast of arcane energy, completely destroying the town hall. The raining debris and blast of pressure obliterated everyone and everything in the northern half of the town square. Erik quickly shielded his companions from the blast with a barrier of enchantment.

"Clever girl," said Kylratha, hovering like a cloud of black storms in the air above the square. "But look—even more of the dead come from your crypt!" added Kylratha as he pointed to the westward mausoleum.

The living dead began to issue from the structure's dark doorway. Fenrix continued to the smithy and began to sniff the debris in search for survivors of the blast.

Faintly glowing wisps of dark energy began to rise from the ground and tighten around Erik. Gasping and shaking his head, he dropped his weapons and fell to the ground.

Jase, looking up at Kylratha, began to yell out in the King's speech. Then, erupting into a bright orange flame, he leapt into the air after Kylratha.

"Petulant child!" growled Kylratha as he swatted Jase out of the air with the back of his hand.

The impact of Kylratha's blow seemed unreal. It sent Jase rocketing like a fiery arrow into the mausoleum. Jase disappeared with a tremendous thud into the rubble of the collapsing stone structure. Fenrix, after helping Grimhold and Dareth out of the wreckage of dead bodies and shattered

stones, turned and launched his chain mace at Kylratha with a bang. Kylratha avoided the attack by simply descending to the ground. "Son of Shames! We meet again," said Kylratha with a smirk.

Fenrix leapt forward, and the two began their contest with blue fire still burning in the debris around them. It was almost like a dance. Each combatant's swing of his sword was perfectly matched by the other in speed and intensity.

Gayle drew back another arrow, but the movements of the two swordsmen were so fast and deadly that even she was not sure of her shot. There were no pauses and no talk between the two. The fight became an endless succession of ringing steel.

At last, Fenrix slipped in and with a leap struck Kylratha across the face with the pommel of his sword. Kylratha quickly countered, disarming Fenrix of both his weapons in the blink of an eye. Then striking Fenrix on the shoulder with the flat of his great sword, Kylratha forced Fenrix to his knees. With the edge of Kylratha's blade at his neck, Fenrix looked up and laughed.

"The night is yours, Kylratha. Strike true, but if you will spare the little ones," said Fenrix as a tear rolled down his face.

Kylratha drew back his blade but instead kicked Fenrix in the chest, sending him spiraling into the air to land on the roof of Grimhold's smithy. "Go in peace, child, son of Shames," said Kylratha mockingly.

Gayle had Kylratha's back in her sights, but after seeing him spare Fenrix, when she loosed the arrow, she said only, "Just go away."

Kylratha turned and caught the arrow in his right gauntlet. The force of the arrow drove him back several feet. He stared at it curiously before tossing it back to Gayle's feet. Gayle looked down at her arrow and saw that the rune on it had changed. When she looked up, Kylratha was gone. The bands of energy slowly disappeared from around Erik as he stood up gasping for air. He put his hands on his knees and took in a deep breath.

"He is too powerful. I can't begin to counter his strength!" exclaimed Erik.

Gayle looked around and said softly, "He is gone."

Erik launched a flare from the end of his staff into the air. Gayle looked to the sky and then, notching an arrow, said, "Light!" Her arrow erupted in a spray of light like the silvery lamplight's of Ellhom. The artificial stars hung in the sky low and bright, creating a false daylight by which to search for their companions. The stones of the rubble began to stir as the dead began to rise again. The first out of the rubble were Dregor and the other guards who had been cut down by the invading Vanguard. The undead began to look around and actually help each other out of the wreckage.

Gayle notched another arrow and yelled, "Is there no end to this nightmare?"

"Stop!" shouted Erik, raising his staff and dagger above his head. A white hot arch of energy began to pulse between the two objects like a lasting bolt of lightning. Above the crackle and hiss of his enchantment, he said, "Bring your leader forth, you who walk again!"

Dregor stepped forward, incapable of speech, and raised his hand.

Erik looked into the milky eyes of his old friend and said with his wizard's voice, "Lead the dead away from here, Dregor, or I will show all of you a second death so horrible that Hell itself will greet you kindly."

Dregor turned slowly around, and lifting his sword, he let out a hideous croaking groan. All the dead still intact rose and began to form ranks. When the formation was complete, Dregor motioned toward the hole Gayle had blown in the town wall. Column by column, they marched out of the town. When the last column had left, Dregor turned and nodded at Erik.

Dareth came running up and without a care embraced his dead brother, saying, "I promise I will avenge you!" Dregor pushed Dareth away and shook his head slowly. Then looking down, he removed his captain's crest from around his neck. Dregor hung it around Dareth's neck and poked him in the chest with his gauntlet. After taking a few steps backward, Dregor turned and followed the columns north.

Dareth turned to Erik and asked, "Will we see them again?"

Erik's eyes grew wide, not expecting that question. "I have no idea."

Chapter 3

◈ ◈ ◈

Rebuilding

Grimhold finally approached after double-checking his home and smithy. "Erik, is that you?"

"Yes, Grim, it is. What do you think about leading the reconstruction?" answered Erik.

"Well, I would say that clearing the wreckage and seeing to the dead that did not rise again would be a start," replied Grimhold.

Erik tapped his staff on the ground and said, "I can help with that."

With a drawn-out grunt, Erik filled the air with tension, and with a flash from his eyes runes appeared in the air and then vanished. The rubble all over the city began to float just a few feet above the ground as if weightless. Erik explained, "As soon as they are set back to the ground, they will stay where you lay them."

Grimhold let out a laugh at the sight. Erik instructed Dareth that as the new captain of the city, it was his job to check the homes of Hillsborough to see who had survived. He also told him to bring all the tradesmen he found to Grimhold for instruction. Grimhold went to work straight away, moving the largest blocks he could find back to the north wall to began to mend the damage.

Gayle began a search to recover her arrows. She began by picking up the one Kylratha had cast before her. Picking it up, she walked over to Erik and asked as she turned the shaft in her fingers, "What does this rune say?"

Erik saw the arrowhead flash a dark violet rune for a moment. "Kylratha," answered Erik.

Turning away to the center of the square, Erik said, "Put it away," over his shoulder. Taken aback by Erik's coldness, Gayle began to search for her arrows. It was something for her to do. She was afraid of what would happen when she had to stop and think about what had transpired.

Erik began to chant in the middle of the town square. Gayle could hear his wizard's voice echoing throughout the square. She could see black clouds begin to swirl at his feet and rise to his waist. A sudden and powerful wind came up. Gayle watched in horror at the gruesome sight that followed. All of the spilled blood, torn flesh, broken bones, and severed limbs began moving toward Erik. When all the remains and putrescence of death were gathered in front of Erik, he ignited the pile in a blue flame.

Dareth had gathered a dozen tradesmen and reentered the town square just as the funeral pyre was lit. It was the first time the townsfolk had seen Erik in months. And now there he was, standing tall behind a giant blue fire and wearing a runic robe, with a luminous dagger and staff in hand and large stones hovering in the air around him.

Dareth came forward with the craftsmen in tow. "Erik! Good news! Most of the families are safe, yet some do not want to leave their homes until real daylight. However, it does seem that most of the carnage was centralized in the square. We do have a few people unaccounted for. I will continue to search," said Dareth, trying to sound confident.

Erik explained what Grimhold was doing and asked the tradesmen for their help.

Thanks to her enchanted vision, Gayle was able to recover every arrow that had not shattered or splintered, including the prismatic arrow she called crusher.

The fire burned until nearly dawn. Thanks to Erik's enchantment, once the mortar was mixed, the wall was repaired in hours. The rest of the stones that could be used were put in various stacks where the town hall used to be; the unusable debris was piled outside the gate. Erik looked at the cleared mausoleum site and saw no sign of Jase. He turned and shouted to Gayle, who was herself looking everywhere in the city.

"Have you seen Jase?" asked Erik.

Gayle yelled back, "No! Nor Fenrix either. They are not here in town."

Erik's mind raced. Had they left unnoticed, or had they risen as undead, forever to walk in the shadows? Erik decided to stay busy for now. He too was afraid of what would happen if he had to stop and think about the events. Gayle and Erik put out the lights above the city and waited for dawn. After the ash from the fire had been swept away into the sky by a small whirlwind that Erik conjured, one could hardly tell there had been a terrible battle there at all. For the rest of the time before sunrise, Erik discussed the reconstruction with Grimhold, while Dareth and Gayle had a conversation about the town's defenses.

The new day dawned with a red sun spilling its light over the northern wall. Gayle and Erik stood next to each other, hand in hand, watching the new day begin. Grimhold asked Dareth to assemble the townsfolk in the square as soon as he could. Grimhold himself began to ring the bell outside the hospital. It was a signal for emergency, and he hoped it would get people out of their homes.

Soon people began to gather in the square. Most of them were in awe of the destruction; others seemed afraid and looked around nervously, fearing what may yet come.

Grimhold returned to Erik's side and with Dareth, who had just returned, hushed the crowds. Dareth began to speak, and immediately, the townspeople, especially those on the town council, began to interrupt him. They were asking what right a child of seventeen years had to assemble a town meeting.

Erik stood forward, and as he tapped his staff on the ground, the city shook around them. The crowds became silent, and Erik spoke with his voice bolstered by enchantment. Even the people furthest away heard him clearly. "Dareth took up arms and defended this town when most of you stayed huddled in your homes. He is now the new captain of the guard of this town, and when he speaks, you will either listen or leave. But if you choose to walk away, then do so now, and you will not be welcome within these walls!"

Many of the town council reminded Erik that they decided who was welcome in town. Erik replied, "Were the Vanguard that attacked us last night welcome? Were the dead that rose from their graves to assail the living welcome? No, they were not! You did nothing but cower in your homes while the town guard fell defending you! The Fletchers and Millers, as well as Erilian half-elven, among others, stood their ground to defend this place while you men of the council did nothing!

"That which does nothing is nothing! There is no town council! I disband it here and now! The trades guild will remain, but all public matters will be decided by the people at meetings such as this, not by a few cowardly politicians who have hidden from an honest living so long they have forgotten their trade!"

The council members in the crowd protested for a short time but were silenced by their fellow townsfolk. The crowd was primarily composed of tradesmen and their families, which agreed for the most part with what Erik said. But the people began to insist that a tradesman be appointed as a representative for the town.

To that Erik said, "For now, Grimhold will be your mayor. He is a fine tradesman and stood his ground beside Dareth in the battle. If you should elect another mayor in the future, the only thing I can tell you is that he must be a tradesman in good standing with the guild and must continue in his trade while elected."

One of the former councilmen stepped forward and said angrily, "What of the councilmen? What are we to do?"

Erik laughed and answered, "Whatever seems good to you to make a living. You will no longer have a pension, so if your trade skills are indeed gone, I'm sure the new mayor can find work for you."

Grimhold began to speak, telling the crowd everything that had happened the night before—the attack of the Vanguard, the fall of Dregor, the rise of the dead, and then finally the arrival of the group of heroes who stopped the attack and fought the ancient dark elf. Grimhold had a way with words, and the crowd was spellbound by his story, at the conclusion of which they cheered for Gayle, and for Erik as well, but in the mind of the townsfolk, they had their new champion.

Gayle had been popular in town beforehand, but now she was royalty in their eyes, and they all began to call her Lady and Princess.

Dareth called the crowd to silence once more and told them of his need for guardsmen, and to that end, Grimhold promised not only better wages but also better equipment—the finest armor and weapons he could craft.

Still, the tradesmen were reluctant, and the council would have no part in this new guard. Finally, many of the younger men, and even a few women, volunteered. All barely out of childhood, they swore to stand the watch. The councilmen laughed, saying that men had been replaced with children, but few listened. Grimhold then announced that there would be a memorial that night for the fallen.

The day had barely began, but Erik and Gayle were exhausted. Gayle took Erik by the hand and led him to her house. There she swung the door open and pulled Erik in. Slamming the door behind her, she led him to her bedroom. Slinging him down on the bed, she then curled up beside him and wept. She cried over so many things. She cried over her family that she secretly had been dreading seeing again. Now she felt only shame for not saying goodbye. She wept too for Fenrix and Jase, and she wept over her torn face and her empty house. She missed the Gnomare' and wished they hadn't had to leave the tree.

Erik stroked her hair and pulled her head to his chest. He wept softly while Gayle cried aloud. Gayle, Dregor, Jase, and Fenrix were all the family he really knew, and he was already missing the city of Ellhom as well.

The two slept for quite some time and awoke at sunset to the sound of a knock at Gayle's door. Gayle sat up suddenly with tears still in her eyes. To Erik it seemed as though she was still in the trance of a nightmare. At the door were a few of the new town guard. They had brought three traveler's packs from outside the city gate. They asked if they were Gayle's.

She nodded and opened her door. The guards laid the packs down in her den, saluted, and left, wishing their princess a good night.

Gayle chuckled but then looked down at the packs and became grave. "That's Jase's pack," she said sadly.

Erik tried to be cheerful and said, "Well, we will keep it here until his return."

Erik had begun digging through the pack when they were suddenly greeted from the open door by Grimhold and Jared from the Grey Ram. The men bowed before Gayle and smiled. "Good evening, Princess!" said Grimhold.

"So you're the cause of this princess business, Grim?" accused Gayle.

Grim shook his head while Jared answered, "It was the people who decided they wanted a princess. We wanted someone we could believe in and trust, something better than a group of greedy old men. We went through the records of the town council in the wreckage. They were no better than thieves. They had money that should have gone to the town for upkeep, to the guards for equipment and training. It was stashed away in a private vault like a treasure horde. They are all in chains now, some in the stables, others in the stocks. Dareth and Grim had it done straight after the truth was discovered. Now we have a princess we can love and bestow treasures on because we love her."

Erik withdrew his mother's pin from his pack and said, "Then allow me to be the first!" as he pinned the blue-enameled golden plum blossom to her vest.

Gayle blushed, and her jeweled eye began to glow brightly. Grimhold then asked them to join them in the town square for the wake and memorial.

The memorial started as a solemn event at first, but because most people of the town decided to drink the troubles away, the evening was soon filled with the ruckus of a wake.

Seeing that the mood had shifted to glad remembrance rather than despair, Gayle made up her mind about an announcement. "Grim, the first task I give you is to pronounce Erik and I to be engaged!" commanded Gayle.

"What? Here? Now?" questioned Grimhold.

"Yes, now in the Gnomare' fashion," said Gayle. Erik scratching the back of his head looked suddenly down at Gayle . His eyes began to tear up as the woman he loved smiled back at him. Erik took Gayle's hand and squeezed it. He could feel every word he had ever wished to say stick in his throat. As he looked back at Grimhold all he could do is nod his head happily with a short exhale.

Grimhold was, after some time, able to get the attention of the townspeople, and when he had it, he declared Gayle, the Princess of Hillsborough, and the wizard Erik Ironrod engaged. Gayle and Erik greeted their well-wishers gladly. After some time, they withdrew while the celebration continued and returned to Gayle's house to enjoy their night. Erik, as the door shut behind them, said, "This is all I've ever wanted!"

— — —

THE FOLLOWING YEARS PASSED SWIFTLY. There was much to do in the city and at first few hands to do it. However, with the help of Grimhold's kin of the Iron Cap clan from the eastern delving, there was plenty of knowledge for reconstruction, as well as ideas for improvement of the city.

The vacant mill became a water tower and still, and at Jared's bidding, he was allowed a microbrewery as well.

Grimhold's engineering became instantly famous when every home was given clean, hot and cold running water.

The people at first wanted to make the remains of the town hall into a manor for their princess, but Gayle refused and instead ordered the building of a much larger structure.

Grimhold showed the local masons how to reenforce buildings with a steel frame, allowing for much larger, stronger buildings. With Erik's ability to levitate large objects, construction was easy and quick. Within months, the city was almost completely redesigned.

The hospital was larger, and where the town hall had stood, there was now a massive building five stories high. It had a proper barracks and training hall for the guards, a school for children, a meeting hall, and a trades guild headquarters.

The new city saw its share of troubles in the first years. There were attacks by the new empire that met disaster at the hands of Erik and Gayle. Strange beasts came down from the mountains to waylay farmers in the orchards, and for the first few years, almost no trade caravans came; only the Hillmen and mountain people came to trade.

Despite the difficulties life in the newly named Hillsbrand went well.. Grimhold and his wife had a daughter named Emry. Dareth caused a scandal by marrying one of his female guards, Jilian. Erik and Gayle married and had a son they called Jetherion after a black smith of ancient legend.

The town guard grew to a full complement of fifty, and the city defenses became fortified by ballista and other contraptions of Grimhold's design. The efforts in reconstruction were greatly aided by Erik, who helped Grimhold in the construction of a steel mill, much like the deep forges of Gnomare'.

The following sixteen years passed peacefully, for the most part, and the city grew in population and industry. The guards had even taken to riding horses to patrol the orchards.

Trade from the eastern clan houses or Delves as the dwarves call them began to come in greater number than in past years, and life in Hillsbrand became blessed with good fortune.

Many new inventions were crafted by Grimhold and Erik as they mixed the dwarven and elvish crafts. Gayle and Erik told Grimhold what they knew of runes, and in return he taught them of dwarven sigils. Through their combined craft, they were also able to make powerful articles of armor and weaponry for the city guard and imbue the city gate and walls with many enchanted properties.

In the later years, the empire had stopped sending troops and had started sending spies and assassins instead, none of which were able to slip past Gayle's watchful eye or Erik's enchantments. After Erik had rested from conjuring for several months, he had the strength to lay an enchantment down over the entire township of Hillsbrand, the orchards, and the woods, so that he Gayle, Grimhold, and Dareth would be alerted to approaching danger. For the time being, the city was secured and prosperous. Yet something continued to loom in Erik's mind, a growing feeling of uneasiness with each passing year.

Gayle continued to say that darkness stood unbroken in her vision in

all directions upon the horizon. In all that time, what Erik found most
disturbing, however, was the disappearance of his companions and friends.
Fenrix and Jase were too powerful in his mind to have passed from the
world unnoticed, yet he had heard no news of them. Even his friend
Dregor, who had left as a captain of the dead, he had a desire to see again
for some reason. Time passed like the waters of a swift-running stream,
quick and unremarkable—until one day at long last, magic returned to
Hillsbrand.

Chapter 4

◇　◇　◇

A Time of Majick

At the crossroads, the paths diverged. The east road headed toward the wooded realm, the southern imperial way, and north up the green path to the enchanted city of Hillsbrand, where they said no force of arms could enter.

A lone woman stood upon the crossroads, brushing her silvery blue hair out of her gorgeous elven face and tucking it behind her right ear. She looked north and south at her choices. She blinked her large silver eyes and wiped the sweat off her brow, runed with the brightly glowing mark of the Gnomare'.

Her wolfskin cloak openly flapped in the hot summer breeze, revealing her impressive attire. She was clad in a bright red, scaled armor breastpiece and tasset; her bare thighs were muscular and smooth; and the rest of each leg, knee to toe, was covered in a silvery plated greave cleverly adorned with red-enameled filigree and gifted with runic enchantment. She wore a keris-bladed sword sheathed on her left hip and a chain mace on the other. Around her neck was a silver chain on which hung a clear crystal like a window pane, with three glowing runes on each side.

The woman was stunning, a creature of unparalleled physical beauty. At only sixteen years of age, she had been pronounced a lady of the

House of Gnomare'. Though only half-elven, she already stood as tall as her mother, Ellay, and for some reason was more than her match in strength.

She looked again north and then south and said to herself, "South to his end, or north to his beginning?"

Soon she saw a large covered wagon coming up from the south road, drawn by two large oxen. As it approached, she could see that it was being driven by two Vanguard men. They stopped suddenly at the crossroads.

"Where are you off to, young lady?" the driver on the left asked.

"I'm not sure. Maybe north or maybe south?" she said playfully.

"Well, it best not be north; no one returns from there, they say. A wizard holds their princess captive in that fortress of a city. Everyone the empire has sent to rescue her has been killed," said the merchant.

She giggled and waved them along, saying, "This I must see."

The merchant called after her as she left. "You're an elf, aren't you?" he asked.

She turned around and smiled. "You're half right," she said as the rune on her forehead flashed a bright rose hue.

"What's your name, girl, in case I never see your lovely face again?" said the merchant.

She laughed and shook the hair back over her face and said, "Majick!" She began to sprint effortlessly up the road, excited to see whether the merchant was speaking the truth.

Moving like a bolt of lightning from a clear sky, she tore up the green path as she ran. She thought she could see shadowy figures moving within the woods on either side of the path but dismissed it. She continued to run north on the greenway, still kicking up the earth as her boots tore through the ground. Majick began to sense something as she approached the orchards. No normal woman or half-elf maiden could have seen it, yet it was clear as day to Majick.

"A warning enchantment!" exclaimed Majick, as she laughed, genuinely amused. She unbuckled her cloak and turned it inside out and rebuckled it. After she put her hood up, the small pearly iridescent scales of the cloak's lining began to turn color and match her background from every angle.

She moved forward through the field, still giggling. Unless someone were paying attention to a curious shadow on the ground cast by no cloud, bird, or tree, they would not have noticed any signs of her.

Passing through the field, she could feel a spell being cast but gave it no mind for she knew they would not see or hear her approach. She could now see the beginnings of the city of Hillsbrand and quickened her stride. Her speed could not be matched by any beast on foot or in the air.

Soon she was standing in front of the gate, and to her surprise there was a great deal of traffic coming in and out of the gate, but none headed south. Instead, the dwarven caravans headed toward the east on a newly paved road that twisted as far as the eye could see to the west.

To the west was a glistening white gravel road, which the Hillmen took to their tribal homes. As she looked around, she also saw many gravel walking paths through the orchards to both sides of the green path, with armed guards on horseback leisurely trotting up and down them.

"Doesn't seem like a dark fortress," Majick said to herself. She unbuckled her cloak and turned it back around. She then proceeded through the gate. Dareth's wife, Jilian, was on watch. Locking eyes with Majick, she became entranced. Jilian took her crested helm off, letting her softly curled locks of red fall down over her shoulders and breastplate.

Jilian was a beauty herself, her pale skin neither ravaged by time nor parched by the sun, and her pale green eyes locked on the shimmering silver of Majick's. Her full red lips hung open in awe of the elven beauty.

"So beautiful," said Jilian softly as Majick approached. Majick smiled and with a wink licked the end of her pointer finger and lightly ran it across Jilian's lips as she passed. Jilian's eyebrows raised quickly, her only response as she watched Majick walk by. Jilian took no notice that Majick was armed, and that was exactly the sort of thing she was supposed to prevent.

"Hold!" called a voice from down the main road, which was now called "the shimmering way" because it was still embedded with the years-old shards from Gayle's arrows. "I cannot allow you to enter Hillsbrand armed!" said Dareth in his deep yet pleasant voice.

began to gasp. Emry then swung her hammer, still hot from the forge, up into Jetherion's chest, causing him to stumble back and collapse onto the stone fence. Emry, now standing on the fence, pointed her finger down at him and lectured, "I'm hot, sweaty, and dirty, and I smell like leather and coal!"

Jetherion smiled with a bloody grin up at her and replied, "That's the way I like you!"

The next thing Jetherion saw was the flat edge of Emry's hammer— then darkness.

Chapter 6

◆ ◆ ◆

Majick's Mischief

The first thing Majick saw upon awaking was the face of Gayle, who was looking down at her, smiling. Erik was standing behind her, propped on his staff and looking at Majick with a strange grin.

"DIE!" shouted Majick as she lurched forward and wrapped her hands around Gayle's neck with an iron grip. Erik panicked and, not sure what to do, smacked Majick on top of the head with his staff with all of his strength.

The next time Majick woke, the first thing she saw was Gayle's face scowling at her with Erik standing beside her, staff at the ready. Majick growled and flexed her muscular arms, and the leather straps holding her to the bed began to crackle and smolder.

"Silence her before she burns the hospital down!" said Gayle.

"I can't. She is not casting a spell—she is channeling. I can't counter that. It's what made her father so deadly," answered Erik.

"You knew my father?" asked Majick, suddenly wide-eyed and smiling.

"Yes, you are surely the daughter of Fenrix the great and Ellay of the Gnomare'!" said Erik happily.

"They were quite a couple!" added Gayle, managing to smile again.

"So I have heard," responded Majick as she sat up, snapping her restraints.

Gayle jumped back out of her reach while Erik stepped forward. Erik ran his fingers over the scales on her chest piece. The scales had a blood-red hue but seemed coated with an adamantine luster; underneath was a deep blue aventuresence, like sparkling pin holes of the afternoon sky. Majick looked down at Erik's fingers and purred while Gayle looked on angrily with a grunt.

Erik withdrew his hand quickly and said, "I am Erik Ironrod. This is my wife, Princess Gayle."

Majick laughingly said, "So you're the wizard who has the princess in bondage?"

"Only the bonds of love," sang Gayle as she hugged Erik at the waist.

"I can see Fenrix has slain his dragon. Please pass our congratulations on to your father next time you see him," said Erik.

Majick's face became sad as she answered, "I cannot; my father died of his wounds."

Gayle stepped back slowly and then sank into the corner and started to sob. Erik's face twisted with anger at himself for not being there for his friend. Silence filled the room. He clenched his jaw and managed to hiss out, "Tell me what happened."

Majick told them of Fenrix's return to the tree, how he had arrived to find Ellay pregnant with his child. Upon learning of the pregnancy, he was overjoyed and swore to bring his new family back treasures from the wild. He left for the hunt with Ellay's blessing.

He returned several months later with the hide of an elder fire dragon in his clutches. He was burnt and bloodied but proud to greet his child as Fenrix the dragon slayer. But something was wrong; Ellay was already in labor and was bleeding badly.

Majick paused in her story for a moment and choked back her tears before continuing. "I was born cold and lifeless. My mother was heartbroken but said to my father that there was still time to have a family. My father would not have it. I am told he grasped my tiny hand and passed all the strength of his spirit into my body. When I opened my eyes, I am told that he kissed me on the head, and said, 'Hello, my elfling.'

"Then, turning to my mother, he kissed her and said, 'Goodbye, my love!' My father collapsed lifeless on the floor, cold and still. All the might of Enock and Ellay could not revive him. The spark of his heart rested in me now."

Erik fought back his tears for many minutes before at last he said, "Fenrix was a champion for all children. To harm one in his presence was certain death. It was only natural he would give his life for his only daughter."

"First Jase, now Fenrix. Are we to lose everyone we love?" lamented Gayle.

"Jase isn't dead," replied Majick with a smile.

Gayle wiped her eyes and shouted, "What?"

"We have heard no word from him in all this time," said Erik.

Majick again seemed sad as she replied, "That does not surprise me at all. He returned to the city of the tree shortly after my father left for the hunt. His body was broken, but his spirit was raging. Much of his body, the Gnomare' encased or replaced with enchanted armor. It took him years to get used to it, but he was tireless. He worked night and day to master his new body and soon found that he was stronger than ever.

"He defeated High Master Elwayne in every match, each time easier than the last. He even fought to a draw the grandmaster, Elterion, in their only contest. But Jase was not satisfied. He became obsessed with becoming stronger and soon became as versed in the elemental enchantments as Artcreft himself.

"Against the princess's wish, he left the city of the tree, vowing that he would stop Kylratha and shift the counterbalance in order to destroy the new empire. He was so dark yet so masterful—I fell in love with him so easily. The princess has sent me to recover him and take him back to the tree to live life in peace until his heart heals. If I succeed, Jase will be my ward and mate by the order of the princess."

Erik just stood wide-eyed with his mouth hanging open, not sure what to say.

Gayle stood up in the corner and said, "That's the most insane thing I have ever heard. I can see it must be true."

Erik snapped out of his daze. "Well, you bear the rune upon your brow, so you must carry the favor of Gnomare'. I see from your learning pendant that you are the grand master of no less than six disciplines. That is no small feat even for an elder."

Majick had a broad grin on her face as she said, "They say I am the most gifted pupil since Erik Ironrod. Artcreft even calls me 'his arrogant little bastard.' In truth, my father passed more than his spirit to me. I know many things without being taught. This has always baffled the Gnomare'. I was given the title of lady, and I attend to the princess as my duty while in the city of Ellhom."

"How are Enock and Ellen?" asked Gayle.

Majick smirked and rolled her eyes as she replied, "As intolerably perfect as ever. Enock is so gorgeous, and Ellen has him all to herself. Well, at least I'll have my Jase. Oh, by the way, my mother said if I should ever find you, Erik, to tell you that Oberon has finally taken to wearing dresses and now sings to entertain the males; he is Artcreft's favorite!"

"Well, I can see you have inherited your parents, er—lust for life," teased Gayle.

Majick nodded. "The young male elves find me too rough to love," explained Majick with a frown. Just then, Majick looked around the plain stone room. There was nothing but an iron-bound oak door and a large window letting the afternoon light in.

"Where am I?" asked Majick, rubbing the knot on her head.

"You're in the trauma room," answered Erik.

There came a sudden and forceful knock from the door, and as Erik opened it, Dareth and Jilian came in, dragging the bloodied and beaten Jetherion. Gayle rushed to her son's side, asking what had happened as Majick sprang from the bed. Dareth explained that it was a result of another of Emry's meltdowns.

"Again?" said Erik and Gayle together. Erik helped Dareth lay his son on the bed. His face was swollen and cut, his nose crooked and still bleeding.

Majick moved Dareth to the side and said, "Allow me."

Majick began to sing a beautiful elvish tune that made all in the room feel like their hair was standing on end. Majick leaned in and kissed Jetherion on the nose and forehead. Jetherion's wounds melted away. It was as if he had never been touched.

"Grand master of the life enchantments, indeed!" said Erik.

"Even I am not that rough!" said Majick. Majick looked down at Jetherion and saw what she considered a man of exceptional beauty. Majick leaned in and kissed him softly and slowly on the lips and then began to purr like an actual feline and licked his neck.

"Is that a healing enchantment too?" asked Dareth, not having seen the healing arts practiced in the elven fashion.

"No, I just really like the way he tastes," answered Majick.

"My son already has one violent maiden in his life; he can ill afford another, no matter how beautiful. So there will be no more licking today," warned Gayle.

Majick giggled and said she was sorry. "I should have bitten him instead," Gayle smiled and told Dareth to return Majick's weapons, which he did reluctantly.

"Will you behave yourself within the walls?" asked Dareth.

"No, she will not. Fenrix the dragon slayer brought his mischief to the tree. His daughter has my permission to misbehave here," declared Gayle.

Dareth bowed, and with a sigh, he said, "Well, my days should be full of excitement then," Dareth then departed with a salute.

Once the door shut behind him, Jilian pulled Majick to her by the hand and kissed her forcefully on the lips then shook her head. Then casting a strange glance in Gayle's direction, she left in a hurry.

"What was that?" asked Erik.

"I may have put a charm on her as I passed through the gate, so that she would let me pass. It seems to have had a lingering effect," answered Majick playfully.

"You can cast charms on women?" questioned Erik, not knowing much of charms himself.

"It seems my father passed much of his magnetism to me as well. Many of the young maidens of the tree told me they could feel it quite strongly at times. I won't say that I don't enjoy the attention. I do however promise that I will cause no unnecessary trouble while I am here. I must find Jase, and I'm hoping you can help."

Gayle smiled and replied, "We will gladly help, and I think I might know where to begin. But first, I think I might need your help with a matter of love."

Majick's ears perked up as she gently ran her fingers across Jetherion's chest and said, "I'm listening."

Majick left the hospital after speaking with Gayle. Erik and Gayle stayed with their son, waiting for him to regain consciousness. Majick cast her gaze about the town square. Only a few people still did business outdoors in the square, now that there was a large indoor trade hall that stayed cool in the summer. She saw only a few casual strollers as well as a guard walking his patrol through the city. As she looked to her right, she took notice of a cute young dwarf maiden working outdoors at a fenced-in smithy. Majick stretched and gave out a sinister little laugh before walking slowly to the edge of the smithy with a mischievous grin. Emry noticed her and looked up in wonder, for she had not seen an elf maiden before.

"Did you just come from the hospital?" asked Emry with a curious look.

"Yes, there was a beautiful young man there I had to nurse back to health," said Majick while playing with her hair.

"Oh?" Emry replied with interest.

"Do you know him? I think his name is Jetherion. He has a body like chiseled stone smoothed by running water, sky-blue eyes, and lips that look sad but taste like honey wine," said Majick, pursing her lips to taste them.

"What?" exclaimed Emry with a growl.

Majick shifted all her weight to one side and put her hands on her hips and said, "You didn't know? We elf maidens heal our men by making love to them. He was most grateful. He even let me give him a bath."

Emry, now turning red with anger, charged at her with her hammer in hand, growling as she came. Emry jumped to the top of the stone fence and leapt at Majick, preparing to smash the elf over the head with her oversized smithing hammer.

Majick clotheslined Emry midair with a punch that would have splintered a door. Emry fell flat on her back, with Majick immediately taking a mounted position. Majick rained down a withering amount of abuse on Emry for several minutes.

Emry was strong and proud, but she had no leverage to get Majick off of her and wasn't quick or strong enough to parry any of Majick's assault. Majick hit Emry with closed fists and open hands over and over and would not relent. Emry struggled against the assault until her nose was broken, her lips split and bleeding, both eyes cut above and below, and her teeth loosened.

At last Emry cried out, "Stop!" with a spray of blood leaving her mouth.

Majick stood after stroking Emry's hair gently. "You look terrible. You should go to the hospital," mocked Majick.

Emry, still being a girl full of pride, picked herself up slowly and dizzily staggered toward the hospital. Majick sniffed the air as she spun around. There was something in the air she recognized, and she went to search for it.

Chapter 7

◇ ◇ ◇

Family, Friends, and Foes

Gayle and Erik stared down at their son together. "I'm so happy that he has your looks, Gayle, even if Emry tries to ruin them every time he upsets her," said Erik.

Gayle stroked her son's hair and said, "I wish Emry would treat him better. He is a gentle giant like his father. I think I'll need to have a talk with them both—whenever my baby decides to wake."

Erik put his hand on Gayle's shoulder. "It may take some time. The life enchantments take much of a person's strength. What were you discussing with Majick outside, anyway?"

Gayle giggled and said that she had convinced Majick to make Emry jealous by saying she was going to be his sweetheart. Maybe a little friendly competition might force Emry to be better to Jetherion.

A soft, clawing knock came from the door. When Gayle opened it, Emry stumbled in. Her face was still bleeding in several places. The blood was running down her smithing apron and dripping on the floor. Emry lifted her head and could barely see Jetherion lying on the bed.

Erik and Gayle were both startled at the sight of the battered and bloodied Emry. With a frown, Erik turned to Gayle and shook his head. Emry limped to the bed where Jetherion was lying and hopped up to sit on it. She leaned over, curled her arms around his left arm, pressed her bloody face against his shoulder, and cried.

"What's wrong with the women of this city?" whispered Erik. He walked over to the bed and passed his staff over Emry. A soft hum filled the air, and Emry fell asleep as her wounds closed. Erik touched his staff to the ceiling above Emry and Jetherion. The vines of Ellhom grew out of the end of his staff and onto the ceiling and began to blossom. After a few minutes, the petals of the blossoms of Ellhom began to fall and rest on Emry, and after a few seconds more, the petals started to disappear with a soft light.

Gayle said softly, "Ahhh, you learned that from Enock, didn't you?"

Erik smiled and said, "Yes, kind of. In truth I can't pull that off without the staff he gave me," Erik sighed as he leaned on his staff.

"You don't want to be here when she wakes up, do you?" asked Gayle.

"No. I love Grimhold like a brother, but I really don't like Emry. She reminds me of someone I would rather forget," answered Erik.

Gayle stopped herself from laughing and said, "Go ahead, I'll finish up here. Perhaps there is something in Jase's traveler's pack that can help Majick."

Erik turned to leave but then turned back and asked, "Um, where is it again?"

Gayle's jeweled eye widened as she turned in the direction of their house. Her eye flashed, and she said, "Oh! There it is! In the chest in the den," pointing straight into the wall.

Erik, with a blank expression on his face, said, "Thanks" and then left.

At last, every blossom of Ellhom shed its petals, and Emry began to stir. She sat up and rubbed her eyes. Then looking down at Jetherion covered in dried blood, she began to cry.

"What's wrong, Emry?" asked Gayle skeptically.

"I'm an idiot!" replied Emry.

"Go on," said Gayle with a wave of her hand.

"It's just that dwarf women are very rough with our men. It's in our blood," explained Emry.

"And what do dwarf men do in response?" asked Gayle.

"My dad has started wearing armor around the house. In our culture, the mother controls the home with an iron fist. The harder we are to live with, the harder our men work, and the longer they stay at work, the more successful the home is," answered Emry.

"Barbaric! Why would a dwarf work so hard to build a home he can't enjoy?" asked Gayle with a scowl.

"It's not all bad. Once a month, there is a homecoming. The wife plans everything perfectly for her mate's return—all his favorite music, food, drink, whatever he desires," replied Emry.

Gayle shook her head and said, "It's not enough. If you wish to be with my son, you will be kind. Every day is a homecoming in my city, and for my son. Treat him kindly, and he will work hard to please you. Fail to do so, and I will not allow you to see or court him. And if you attack him again, you will be put in the stocks!"

Tears began to roll down Emry's face as she said, "I didn't want to lie to him. I, like most dwarf women, have a terrible temper. In my insanity, I guess I thought that if he was with me as I truly am, and still loved me, then I knew he would be 'the one'."

Gayle rolled her eyes and replied, "He is not a dwarf. Do you really want him to be gone all the time because you're too honest to control your temper? That's insane! Look, having things done your way doesn't require violence if you can make that small step," Gayle paused and sighed. "That will be enough for now."

Emry nodded and said, "Yes, Princess. He really is a prince and so very handsome. Did that elf woman really make love to him? She also said she gave him a bath, and I see that's not true."

Gayle laughed and denied the claim, noting that she was standing in the room. "She did kiss him though."

"She did?" exclaimed Emry with a growl, as she balled up her fists. "That dirty wench!"

"I'm sorry if she hurt you, Emry," admitted Gayle.

"It's okay. I think I tried to kill her first. She is too tough for me. Did she attack anyone else?" asked Emry.

"She knocked out Dareth before I put her down," answered Gayle with a wink.

"You're as powerful as they say! So now I don't feel so bad about being beaten up. I deserved it for what I've done to my prince," said Emry, stroking Jetherion's hair.

"Gayle?" said Emry.

"What?"

"Can I give him a bath?" said Emry with a huge grin.

Gayle blushed for a moment and replied, "As long as you don't hit him anymore, especially anywhere tender. I want grandchildren!" There was an awkward pause before Gayle blurted, "But not now—eventually. Just a bath. Nothing else. I don't want to know if—" Gayle stopped herself and turned and left the room, going red in the face.

After stopping by Grimhold's smithy to explain what had transpired Erik returned home. Erik stepped through the door of his house and could tell something was wrong. The air was different somehow; it smelled like the wild forests. He heard a sniffling sound coming from the den. As Erik rounded the corner, he cloaked himself with enchantment. He looked inside the den, and there in front of his favorite chair was Jase's travel pack, with most of its contents spilled out on the floor. He could see nothing but could still hear the sniffling and was sure there was someone in the room.

Stepping out of his enchantment and thrusting his staff forward, Erik sent a blast of pressure through the room. The spell threw most of the contents of the room, along with a very surprised Majick, across the den and into the back wall. She landed with a long, deep groan. Erik rushed forward to see if she was okay.

Already smiling, she picked up a small book from Jase's pack and then looked up wide-eyed and dizzy. "I think I found something!"

Gayle, who appeared around the corner at just that moment, yelped upon seeing the room and then said, "Well, you'll be staying for dinner? That may give you a chance to help my naughty wizard clean the den."

Chapter 8

◆ ◆ ◆

Reclaiming Old Strength

Erik looked down at Majick as she stood up, her body still mostly camouflaged by her cloak. She unbuckled her cloak and turned it so that the wolf skin side faced out. Erik apologized for blasting her and began to admire her cloak.

"That is clever," said Erik, feeling the liner of the cloak.

"It's the skin of the forest drake. The half-elves of the wooded realm make cloaks with the skins they shed. I have found that fresh works much better—a secret only I have discovered, seeing as how those simpletons have yet to slay one," Majick opened the small book she had found in Jase's travel pack and showed it to Erik. "I can't read the runes in this," said Majick anxiously.

Erik tapped his staff on the ground twice, and the misplaced objects in the room returned to their original positions. Erik's curiosity was aroused, and taking the book, he sat down in his favorite chair. Majick sat cross-legged on the floor in front of him, looking up at Erik in interest.

Though he was momentarily distracted by the display of Majick's voluptuous and bare inner thighs, Erik quickly came to his senses. He studied the first few pages and looked up. "The runes are Kylvara'. I can read only a few of them, but reading them wouldn't do me much good anyway because this is a runic cipher of sorts. I can't begin to decode it without a key word or phrase."

Majick gave out a squeal of delight and replied, "This should be a fun mystery—and what is more important is that it still has a strong scent from Jase on it!"

Erik closed the book and asked, "At least it's a start. Did you find anything else of interest in Jase's pack?"

Majick held her hand out and showed a small black stone that sparkled with red pinpoints of light. Majick studied the stone with an uncertain look and said, "I'm pretty sure this is Avalonian iron. It's quite rare, but I'm not sure what it means," Majick searched through the rest of the pack, holding everything to her nose and inhaling deeply. "I love his scent!" she said as she closed her eyes.

Erik smiled, and looking at the ceiling and trying to remember, he said, "I don't remember Jase having a scent at all."

Majick frowned and replied, "Of course not. Your own scent is too strong, especially with a bearskin cloak that hasn't been treated properly."

"Hey, I take good care of this cloak!" argued Erik.

Majick rolled her eyes and put her head in her hand. She didn't feel like explaining the fine pints of skinning.

Gayle poked her head around the corner, smiling. She was pleased to see the den back together. Gayle, with a strange theatrical voice sang, "Dinner's almost ready."

Majick sprang to her feet, unbuckled her cloak, and began to take her scaled armor and tasset off. Erik tried not to look but soon saw that Gayle was also staring at Majick and so went ahead and looked. Majick, now in her undergarments, pulled a small bundle of cloth from her own pack.

"What are you doing?" asked Gayle with a horrified look on her face.

"Changing for dinner," answered Majick.

"Not in front of my husband next time," barked Gayle.

"Is he your husband?" asked Majick sarcastically.

Gayle rounded the corner and said, "Yes, that's obvious."

"Then what are you worried about?" teased Majick.

Erik quickly walked Gayle out of the room to calm her, reminding her that Majick was from the tree, and elves do not wear their shame on their skin.

Erik sat down at the head of the table while Gayle started to set out the dishes for dinner. Majick walked in wearing a beautiful silky slip dress that left little to the imagination. She was wearing many red jewels on her body that seemed to glow with an inner fire.

Majick sat down to Erik's left and said, "I am hungry. It all smells so good!"

Erik rubbed his belly, which was actually now quite flat, and said, "Gayle, for some reason, can cook everything to perfection. If she said to me 'Honey, we are having rocks for dinner,' I would say, 'Mmm, rocks!'"

Gayle gave out a short laugh and kissed Erik on the top of the head. The large oak table was now filled with food— apple-glazed ram, seasoned potatoes, roasted onions with garlic and mushrooms, and even fresh flat bread, which was a treat in Hillsbrand, seeing as grain from the south was in short supply.

"I hope I didn't prepare too much!" said Gayle.

"No, indeed, I could eat much more!" answered Majick.

"And put it where?" said Gayle, pulling away the low neckline of her dress.

Majick started to purr again while Gayle giggled at her. Gayle apologized for being short with Majick, recounting her experiences in the tree and noting that Majick's behavior was in no way offensive. Majick explained that she thought it was strange how people of Hillsbrand hide their bodies and their love.

Gayle sat down to Erik's right and said, "Well, we don't hide our love for food, so dig in!"

They suddenly heard the front door open and close, and the two sets of footsteps revealed their owners as Jetherion and Emry entered the dining room. Jetherion was grinning from ear to ear. Emry had a slight smile on her face as she held Jetherion's hand and stroked his arm with her other hand.

Gayle turned slightly and looked at Emry. As the two made eye contact, Emry blushed and looked to the floor and giggled quietly. Gayle's eyes grew wide as she turned a bright red as well. Erik noticed the awkward moment and shrugged as he looked at Jetherion. Jetherion only shrugged in return and raised his eyebrows but kept smiling.

Majick sniffed the air and asked, "Did you two enjoy mating?"

Erik leaned backward and fell out of his seat, while Gayle yelled, "Emry! I said a bath only!"

Erik stood up quickly and shouted, "A what? You let these two share a bath?"

Gayle looked up sheepishly at Erik and winced as she answered, "Not exactly."

"Then what exactly?" demanded Erik.

Majick cleared her throat and said, "By the way Emly sends her regards and says that she misses you company very much."

Erik's expression was blank as he stood in a room of questioning stares and uncomfortable silence.

"Who is Emly, Dad?" asked Jetherion, half-laughing.

Erik picked his chair up and plopped down in it with a sudden grin. "My first lover, a maiden of pleasure in the city of Ellhom. I though she was your mother at first, in my defense," accounted Erik.

Jetherion, with the same smirk, sat at the foot of the table after helping Emry to her seat and looked over at Majick. "I can understand that. Mom looks absolutely nothing like an elf, after all!"

Erik scowled at Jetherion and began to point his finger but was interrupted by Gayle's mention of Oberon.

"He was my lover while in the city of the tree, and I knew he wasn't your father—although it seems he did not actually care for me," admitted Gayle.

Jetherion and Emry both gasped. Then Jetherion said, "So! You two acted well, young once? I would not have believed it if it hadn't come from your own mouths."

Erik bobbed his head and explained the differences in Gnomare' society.

Majick also added, "So you see, if elves are not mated as a pair, we make love to whom we please, and quite often—almost every day for the first hundred years or so, if possible."

Jetherion's mouth hung open as he tried to imagine and then asked, "Wouldn't you get bored?"

"Not if you love each other," said Gayle confidently while nudging Erik.

"Nonsense. They get bored and change partners constantly, almost daily for some. A mated pair is a rare thing in the tree," declared Majick.

"But a mated pair is a wonderful thing, and Enock and Ellen are a fine couple," argued Gayle.

"Oh, indeed, they are a perfect pair!" agreed Majick.

Jetherion took a bite of bread and said, "That's an exciting thing to imagine."

Gayle decided to dissuade her son by saying, "Now imagine your father and me."

Jetherion stopped chewing and groaned while rolling his eyes. Emry only laughed and started to eat. The supper conversation continued with amusing accounts of past adventures, interrupted by the occasional parental lecture.

After every scrap of food on the table had been eaten, which was a feat achieved mostly due to Jetherion and Majick, Jetherion asked, "So why are you here, Majick?"

Majick recounted the tale as she had earlier for Gayle and Erik.

Jetherion was amazed at her story and said, "Jase and Fenrix were both just people in stories my parents would tell me at night. Now the daughter of Fenrix the great is here in Hillsbrand, seeking out Lord Jase of the Eldare'. That's amazing to say the least!"

Majick stood and replied, "We believe we have found something that might help." She walked back into the den and returned quickly with a small book.

Emry stood and said, "I must be going now. Mother will be wondering where I have been," Jetherion walked her to the door and then returned and began to clear dishes from the table.

Majick sat the book in front of Erik, and with a wave of his wand, it opened and its pages slowly began to turn. Erik explained to Gayle that it was a runic cipher in Kylvara'.

"Without the key word or phrase, and a complete understanding of the runes of Kylvara', this book can't tell me much," said Erik.

"The root word is 'Kylratha,'" answered Gayle, as she studied the book.

"How can you tell that?" asked Majick.

"It's hidden in the pages' overlapping images," answered Gayle.

Gayle picked up the book and grabbed the pages between her thumb and forefinger and flipped them quickly in front of their eyes. A vivid lavender glowing rune flashed in front of them.

"Amazing, as usual, my lady," commented Erik.

"Will this allow us to decipher it?" asked Majick.

Erik shook his head, disappointed, and replied, "I don't think so. Maybe Artcreft or Enock could do it. I don't know these runes."

"Well, I enjoy a good mystery, so what's the harm in trying?" declared Gayle.

Jetherion bid them all goodnight sleepily, hobbled to the stairs, and climbed up them gorged with food. But Erik, Gayle, and Majick stayed up studying the book for hours with no success. After a while, Majick yawned and said she was weak from getting blasted and stunned.

Erik scratched his head and blinked at the book sleepily.

"You can make the den your place of rest tonight; there is a bedroll in the chest," said Gayle.

Majick thanked Gayle and left the room silently. Erik rose, knocking his chair over again. His eyes crossing with drowsiness as he wished his wife goodnight, he stumbled noisily up the stairs.

Gayle, undeterred, pulled the book in front of her and began to study it. Controlling certain runes had become more effortless for her as she had grown older. Finally, after another few hours, she gave up. "Damn the runes of Kylvara'. The only one I've ever seen is on my arrow!" Gayle said to herself. Gayle stood up and retrieved her quiver from the hallway closet and with it returned to her seat.

Withdrawing the arrow that Kylratha had changed, she rolled the shaft between her fingers, and the rune flashed before her eyes. A strange mist-like aura began to radiate from the head of the arrow. Gayle could feel the arrow become heavy in her hand. As she let her hand fall slowly toward the book, lightning-like arcs of an unusual dark light began to leap from the arrowhead to the book, dancing over its pages as they turned. Gayle watched as the runes on the pages began to move freely within the book.

For some reason Gayle didn't understand, she felt compelled to say the name "Kylratha." Her voice resonated throughout her home and echoed out into the street. Gayle covered her mouth, alarmed at the volume of her own voice. She then watched the runes on the book arrange themselves.

The overlaid image of Kylratha's name was gone from the book, and nothing took its place. Gayle assumed that the cipher had been decoded and was pleased but now was curious as to what it might say.

As she debated in her mind whether to wake Erik, she was startled by a deep, metallic, and hollow voice. "Kylratha," the voice said ominously.

Through the wall, Gayle could see a dark figure standing in the center of the square, but she could not see past the shadowy aura surrounding him. Gayle shouldered her quiver and went to the closet to retrieve her bow. Rushing out into the square, she saw the figure wrapped in a cloak of shadow with a clawed hand stretched out to his side.

There were already three night guardsmen unconscious at his feet. Gayle ran her fingers down her bow string and drew an arrow. The figure turned in the dim lantern light. Even Gayle could see nothing through the shadowy cloak but two burning orange eyes.

Notching an arrow, she loosed it at the blackened silhouette and shouted, "Stun!" Gayle's arrow shot out with a flash, only to be swept up in a tempest of fiery smoke wreathed in lightning.

The sight of the colossal glowing pillar was terrifying, yet it vanished quickly, leaving only the faint smell of ash. Gayle quickly drew another arrow, but the figure had advanced and was now staring at Gayle from barely arm's reach away.

"Gayle? You haven't aged a day!" said the mechanical voice.

Gayle looked closely at the figure, and through his shadowy presence, she saw the rune of Eldare. "Jase?" Gayle said in a questioning tone.

The figure nodded affirmatively.

"Jase! Where have you been? We have missed you so much!" exclaimed Gayle, skipping forward and embracing him. She had to jump to kiss him on the steel mask covering his mouth and nose. A metallic, clinking chuckle came from Jase as he wrapped his arms around Gayle. "What did you do to my guards, Jase?" asked Gayle.

Jase released his embrace and answered, "Nothing really. They only sleep and will wake with no memory of this night."

"You're such a bad boy, Jase," Gayle said, laughing as she took a hold of his vicious-looking clawed gauntlet. Gayle pulled him by the arm to her house. They arrived in time to see Jetherion sneaking back into his window. "Big trouble!" shouted Gayle before she opened the front door.

They stepped inside and continued into the dining room. Erik was there sleepily scratching his head, until he noticed the sinister figure brooding behind Gayle, encompassed by a shadowy mist. Jase was staring at Erik with fiery reddish-orange, luminous eyes. Erik, not having his staff, readied his hands in front of him and tried to look as threatening as possible in a nightgown.

A clinking and metallic laugh issued from Jase.

"Honey, it's Jase!" said Gayle happily.

"Jase, you're—um, scary, and well, taller than me even," said Erik, unsure of himself.

Jase turned his head to an alarming degree to the right with a loud ratcheting sound and said, "Yes, new body and all. This one is quite a bit larger than my original. Took some serious getting used to."

"Jase! Yes, new body and all. The wounds Kylratha inflicted could not be healed such is his power.!" yelled Majick as she leapt around the corner from the den. She dove at Jase, meaning to tackle him. She collided with him and sank to the ground as if she had hit a wall, clutching her shoulder. She groaned and then, with a flash from her eyes, rotated her arm and stood.

"Meddling little girl, why the hell are you here?" said Jase, in a cold and menacing tone.

Majick shrank back at first but then stood tall and cleared her throat.

"By order of Princess Sarah, of the house of Eldare', and first lady of the city of Ellhom, you are commanded, Lord Jase, to return with me at once to the tree and explain your disobedience. There, if pardoned, you shall be my ward and live in the city of the tree until—" Majick words were lost as Jase struck her with the back of his gauntlet, knocking her to the ground.

"Jase!" yelled Erik.

"Silence, boy! This is an elven matter. This stupid little girl has just attempted to serve a summons beyond the authority of her house and rank!" said Jase coldly.

Majick stood up and growled. As she looked up at Jase, her open and bleeding wounds sealed up. Majick, not saying a word, turned and left toward the den.

"That was uncalled for!" shouted Erik, waving an open hand through the air.

"I will not explain it further. Just know that she is on a fool's errand, and she will be dealt with harshly should she continue!"declared Jase.

Jase looked at Erik with a piercing stare. Erik did not see the fire that reminded him of starlight. Just the hot coals of anger filled his gaze. Erik knew that from the time they had first met, Jase had said nothing that he did not mean. Something about Jase was different now, inside as well as obviously outside. Jase seemed darker, wiser, sadder, and more than anything, infinitely more deadly. Erik smiled and sat down at the head of the table.

"Well, now that you're here, please, our home is yours, brother. Please sit, tell us of your journeys." requested Gayle trying to ease the tension.

Jase nodded and took a step forward just as Majick slipped in from around the corner wearing her armor, and with chain mace in hand, she took a swing at Jase. Jase extended his hand, and Majick's mace rebounded harmlessly. Gripping her around the throat with his other hand, he lifted her from her feet. He held her head close to the vents on his steel mask as they opened, and blasts of a steam-like mist shot out. Upon breathing it in, Majick hung limp in his grip. Jase dropped her to the floor.

"Is this what you did to my guards, Jase?" asked Gayle.

"Yes, but more severe. She will remember nothing of her fool's errand," answered Jase, as he sat down. Gayle then joined them at the table.

"Almost like old times," said Erik as he scratched his head, seeming somewhat confused.

"Unfortunately, things can never be as they once were," replied Jase, looking down at Majick.

"We miss him too. Life was never dull with Fenrix the great—the dragon slayer," commented Gayle.

"Jase, where have you been all this time?" asked Erik. "Majick told us only that you returned to the tree to heal and learn and then left."

"It was four years ago when I left. I went south secretly to see what the 'United Empire,' as they call it, was up to. Out of the sixteen fortress cities, eight have been rebuilt, none as grand as before, save one. Their so-called capital city, Mason Prime, is a spiraling metropolis. Its governing lord, however, is not the emperor.

"Though the city's army numbers over one hundred thousand, the real power in the empire is farther south in Under Hold, a giant fortress city built into the side of a mountain and under it. The emperor resides there, a fair young dwarf innovator called Gearhart. Though the army of Under Hold is only tens of thousands strong, its real might lies in its war machines and siege engines. No standing infantry or cavalry would last a day against it. Neither would your precious city, Princess."

"So it's a return to the dark days of war, isn't it?" asked Gayle.

Jase brooded in dark thought for a moment and then answered, "Yes, the emperor Gearhart is content to delve into his mountains for treasure and expansion. However, Ayden the cruel, as he is known, is king of Mason prime, and his greed for land and wealth knows no bounds. The resistance of Hillsbrand has reached his ears.

"To tell a man that greedy and lustful that he can't have something is an invitation for hostilities. That is exactly what you have done here with your enchanted city. It's only a matter of time. The city of Northguard, just days to the south, is rebuilt and capable of holding vast armies."

"What are we to do then? Perhaps we should seek an alliance?" asked Gayle.

"That would be your death. The governing lords who resisted at first and then parlayed were killed along with their servants and kin and replaced with someone Ayden could manage," replied Jase.

Jase explained that the only force that could oppose this coming scourge was the three houses united under the banner of Eldare'. The only thing for the people to do was resist and ally with what friends they had until the houses come forward.

"Surely we can ally with the western tribes and the eastern delves and form a strong opposing kingdom," suggested Gayle.

Jase shook his head in disagreement. "Perhaps in a couple hundred years, but your resources are few, and the time to fight is near, Princess." Jase told them that their only advantage was mighty enchantments and difficult terrain, along with the fact that Gearhart would not send his war machines this far north.

He also told them of many merchants being sent into the wooded realm. "I spent the last couple of years disrupting their supply lines, but their numbers are so vast that for every caravan I destroy, there are ten to take its place."

"You have been busy, old friend. So why did you come here?" asked Erik.

Jase looked down at the book of Kylvara' cipher and said, "I thought that I had heard the voice of Kylratha, but it was only a silly girl meddling with something she didn't understand," Jase grabbed the book with his clawed gauntlet and stuffed it somewhere inside his long black cloak dancing with wisps of smoke and shadow.

Gayle, slightly embarrassed, began to apologize but was stopped when the image of many rows of light infantry marching up the green path flashed through her mind. Gayle and Erik stood and looked at each other with an expression of terror.

"The Alarming Barrier!" shouted Erik.

"Ah, yes, quite clever in fact. How many hundreds have they sent?" asked Jase.

"Not hundreds, old friend, many thousands!" replied Gayle anxiously.

Jase stood, and jets of steam hissed from his mask as said he said grimly in his threatening metal voice, "So it begins!"

Chapter 9

◇ ◇ ◇

The Hard Press of Darkness

Erik scrambled up to his room to change. Gayle's mind filled with fear and doubt, and her eyes began to brim with tears. She turned slowly to Jase and said, "You've seen this before right, Jase? And you survived. Tell me that my city will survive, Jase!"

Jase, standing tall, eyes and rune aglow like fire, wreathed in smoke and shadow, clenched his steel-shod fist and said defiantly in a metallic echo of supreme confidence, "We will overcome!"

Gayle, comforted by the declaration from her sorcerous old friend, became stern and wiped the tears from her eyes. Jetherion came down from his room and entered the dining room. Stopping suddenly at the sight of the dark lord Jase, Jetherion raised his arms and balled his fists.

"Kylratha, you have come to the wrong house!" said Jetherion defiantly.

Gayle laughed. "Babykin, this is our friend Jase, here to help us fight the enemy. Now go get Emry and protect her!" said Gayle firmly.

Jetherion stood staring at the dark elf lord. The visitor's gray hair was flowing down about his luminous eyes, and his pale gray skin glowed, with the rune of Eldare' burning like a hot coal. His eyes, like fire, cast an eerie light down over his plated armor, affixed with luminous runes of several ancient languages. His steel fists, with spiked knuckles and clawed fingers, were clenched at his side. The cloak of shadow wrapped around him, whirling with smoke as if caught in a breeze, hid most of his menacing presence at will. Jetherion found him very frightening, and without a word, he swallowed the lump rising in his throat and left for Grimhold's smithy.

Jase looked down at Majick and said, "Wake up, child."

Majick sat up and yawned as Erik came down dressed in his robe, with staff in hand and with the dagger Jase had given him sheathed on his belt.

"Hello, Jase, where are we?" asked Majick.

"We are in the city of Hillsbrand, about to help them fight a war against the United Empire," answered Jase.

Majick sprang to her feet and growled but then asked, "Hello, Erik and Gayle—how do I know you?"

"They are old friends. They asked us for our help before we return to the tree," replied Jase.

"Oh!" exclaimed Majick, and she rounded the corner toward the den.

"You overdid it, brother!" said Erik, wrinkling his brow.

Majick returned with her cloak on and her sword on her hip. Gayle went to change while Erik and the others left for the square.

They entered the square to see Grimhold ringing the new bell, while Dareth yelled in his booming voice, "To arms! To arms! To arms!"

Erik and the others joined Grimhold at the bell. Dareth had the guards send their two fastest riders to the eastern delves and to the western Hillman tribes for aid. When the citizens of Hillsbrand had assembled, Grimhold had the city nurses take the seniors and children into the basement of the training halls, underneath the trades guild, with food and medicine. The rest of the able-bodied men and women stayed.

Gayle emerged from her house wearing the range gear she had obtained in the city of Ellhom. It had been badly damage in the battle upon their return home. So Grimhold as one of many wedding presents refashioned it with many feathery leaves of metal that shimmered in the starlight as she moved.

She stomped down the stairs leading from her house in steel-plated boots. With her bow in hand and quiver on her back, she stood before the hospital bell and shouted, "Lights!" as she loosed two arrows into the air. Her missiles went screaming into the air and erupted in a thunderous crash, filling the sky above Hillsbrand with silvery stars.

The crowd fell silent, and Gayle began to speak, with her voice amplified by Erik's enchantment. It echoed throughout Hillsbrand.

"The southern empire has set its ambition on our fair city! Even now an army of thousands marches up the green path to subjugate the town! They will come to slay me and all those loyal to me! They will drive the rest under the lash to feed the greed of their empire. We have barely hundreds to meet them with, but when it comes time to put our steel to theirs, they will have crawled through rivers of their own dead to meet us! They will be filled with terror, and we will cut them down to the last man! They will know the torment of fire, shadow, lightning, and metal. We will let them know. We are Hillsbrand, and we will not yield!" thundered Gayle.

The people gave out a roar of enthusiastic bravado. Grimhold immediately went to work lining the men up at the smithy to be outfitted by Emry and his wife Ruby. Dareth organized the guard and put them at general quarters to repel attackers. Some stood with pole arms behind the shut gates, with Jilian at their lead. Others manned the ballista in the towers built atop the corners of the city walls. The remaining guards took up bows and pole arms to defend the walls and gate from above.

Gayle sent the younger women to the bowyer, armed them with bows and crossbows, and stationed them on top of the guild hall as a last defense for the skirmishers gathering in the square and for the children inside the building. The older women were sent back into the hospital to tend the wounded.

Grimhold told Dareth and Gayle that he would be firing up the steel mill and water furnace as well. "I have some nasty surprises for them!" he said with an evil sort of grin.

Gayle told him not to act until given word. She reintroduced Jase to Grimhold as her strategist general and asked them to coordinate a plan and then join her and Erik in the tower above the gate.

Erik and Gayle hurried away to the southeast tower. Where a small wooden door used to guard the entrance to the guard post was now a large iron-bound oak door instead. Swinging it open, they faced a staircase spiraling up three levels above the outer wall. At the top was a small room with a window facing south and a small doorway to the west, leading to a ladder going down to the walkway across the gate and around the top of the outer wall.

Dareth was there looking through the window with the spyglass Grimhold had made for him. "I don't see them yet, my lady!" said Dareth.

Gayle looked out the window. Even with her star lights in the air, the night was dim. Her eye flashed as she said, "They are moving slowly."

Jase appeared suddenly through the western doorway to the alarm of everyone in the room. He looked at the ladder leading to the top of the tower, where a ballista was mounted. "You all won't see anything in this room. Join me on the wall next to the gate!"

Jase then dropped out of the western-facing door.

Gayle followed in a much more careful manner, climbing down the three floors via ladder, as did Dareth. Erik descended by safely levitating down next to Jase. Gayle and Dareth crossed over the narrow walkway that the gate serves as when fully shut and joined them atop the wall. The wall was topped with an additional lip of stone to protect the guards from the flight of unfriendly arrows.

"Where is Majick?" asked Gayle.

"She insisted on speaking to the western tribes. Like her father, she embodies the spirits of their entire totem. If they will listen to anyone, it will be her. She is faster than any horse. She will have reached them by now," answered Jase. Looking over the city, he slowly added, "I have instructed your ballista crews and archers on what to do. We will match volume with precision. Grimhold is an engineering genius. His efforts in the reconstruction will prove very useful."

A guard called up from the city streets, reporting that the militia was assembled in the square. Jase asked Dareth to tell them to stand by and to bring him a bow and several hundred arrows.

Gayle turned and smiled as Dareth passed along Jase's orders. "Another contest of archery then?" asked Gayle.

"Yes, save your runic arrows until the need is dire. There is not an arrow to waste. They will try to keep our heads down with their archers while they bring their equipment forward to scale our walls and breach the gate. The one who kills the most archers wins!" said Jase.

Gayle laughed. "If I start losing, I'll cheat!" said Gayle mischievously.

"As will I," answered Jase with a nod.

The first ranks of the imperial army now could be seen atop the furthest hill in the distance. Dareth lowered his glass. "There they are!" he said excitedly.

"Calm down, boy, you will need your strength for the morning!" said Jase.

Another guard called down from the tower. "The preparations have been made, and your equipment is ready!" said the guard as he lowered a bow bundled with many arrows. Several more bundles of arrows were lowered as Jase took the bow and first bundle. Gayle and Jase spent the next few minutes setting arrows out for quick use.

As Gayle notched an arrow and Jase looked at his recurve bow, he asked, "You really intend to start before the first column is in range?"

Gayle nodded and then shot an arrow into the distance. Jase, looking down range, and Dareth, looking through his glass, watched two light infantry fall by her arrow.

"Excellent shot, Princess!" said Dareth.

Jase shook his head and growled, "Not the infantry!" as he drew back and loosed his own arrow at a nearby tree. A camouflaged half-elf dropped to the ground dead from its branches.

"Hells blast! They are in the trees!" yelled Dareth.

Gayle's eye flashed as she scanned the nearby trees. She saw hundreds of half-elf archers in the trees, readying their bows. "Tell the militia to take cover!" screamed Gayle.

"Too late!" said Erik, as a flight of arrows flew toward the city. The arrows were foiled by an unseen enchantment and clattered harmlessly about them atop the wall. "Extra arrows anyone?" asked Erik with a grin.

"Save your strength for enchantments until we have exhausted the conventional means of war!" barked Jase.

Jase commanded Dareth to tell the archers to fire into the trees, even without a clear shot, and gave word for the militia to take cover in the first floor of the trades hall. The city guard in all four towers began to shoot at anything that looked suspicious.

Jase and Gayle began to fire at their targets, one after another with great success. After they had shot hundreds of arrows at archers hidden within the surrounding orchards, they were still receiving return fire. Two guards had already been wounded by the arrows. Gayle lost patience and drew two runic arrows from her quiver, shouting, "Shatter!" as they flew.

The scintillation of metal shards rocketing through the orchard in a fanning arch was bewildering to the eye. The trees, now terribly wounded, shed most of their leaves and archers.

"You win, Princess! I believe we can get the rest," said Jase, loosing arrow after arrow. Jase then instructed Dareth to pass the word not to shoot the front lines of infantry until they had passed and to shoot behind them.

The night had the chill of autumn air, and the approaching stomp of armored feet beat back the usual silence. Shortly, the front lines of the United Empire were upon them, row after row of mail-clad Vanguard, all with steel helms shining in the faint silvery lights.

"Should we fire on them, or should they come right up and knock?" inquired Gayle desperately.

"Knock!" replied Jase abruptly.

The light infantry started to charge, revealing two large battering rams for the gate. One row of infantry, on each side of the two battering rams, began its sprint, accompanied by an extra row of infantry holding shields high to protect the runners.

"Archers! Fire at the infantry behind the battering rams!" commanded Jase.

Dareth repeated the order with a furious roar. The city's archers let loose, and the infantry that followed the battering rams slowly began to speed up, seeing that the bearers were taking no fire. The infantry still further back thought that a charge had been ordered and advanced hastily. By the time the infantry with its rams was at the gate, nearly a full company was charging up the hill behind it.

With an evil, cackling laugh, Jase yelled, "Grimhold, light the forge!" His metallic voice rang out tremendously loud through the city as blast of steam shot out from his mask.

Gayle watched two large pipes extend from the city wall on either side of the gate. Then, after only a few seconds, red-hot molten iron began to gush from the pipes, showering the infantry with burning death. The sheer volume turned the greenway into a glowing stream of hot iron. All the members of the infantry at the gate met their death by arrows or iron; none escaped.

"Clever old Grim," said Erik to himself, just now realizing why Grimhold was so fascinated by the Gnomare' deep forge designs that he had drawn for him. The counterattack had made the gate unapproachable. The hot iron began to spill over the sides of the path and skirt the walls of the city, sizzling and giving off the smell of burnt grass and earth.

"Now they will try to surround us with small groups and scale the walls while their siege engines try to hit us from a distance. Dareth, have the preparations been made?" asked Jase.

"Yes! The stables outside the northern wall have been emptied and saturated with lamp oil!" answered Dareth.

"Excellent, this should be fun! Your ballista will most likely have a greater range than their crude catapults. However, Princess, you must destroy anything they cannot, understand?" said Jase.

Gayle nodded and began to feel comforted that Jase had seen this type of warfare before.

"No mercy killing! Save your arrows—let them burn!" yelled Dareth up at the towers.

The molten iron had now begun to spill off the path further down the road, catching surrounding trees on fire.

"For once I'm glad our city is all steel and stone!" said Gayle as the cinders started to fly.

Approaching the gate was now impossible, so as Jase said, the invading force began to move more light infantry through the now-blazing orchards and wheel around the base of the hill. Upon gathering at the hill's northern side, several platoons of infantry charged the north wall. Climbing to the top of the stables, they began to throw grappling hooks and hoist ladders.

Jase, who had moved like a flash to the top of the trades hall, joined the young women. He had a perfect view of the attack from the hall and sent word to the north towers not to shoot until he gave word. When Jase saw that the imperial infantry had their ladders ready to scale and were assembled on top of the stable, he shot a burning arrow down at them. It caught fire and spread throughout the stables in seconds. Jase gave the command to shoot, and those not burning quickly fell.

On the south wall, Gayle could see a catapult being pulled by two gigantic horned beasts far too large to be oxen. She thought she would amuse herself by testing their hardihood. She drew back a runic arrow and shouted, "Pain!" as she let it fly.

The arrow flew into the night air and pierced one of the beast's ears and lodged itself in the beast's shoulder. The enormous animal immediately panicked and began to run, turning away from the road. The other beast followed, and being at the top of a distant hill, they stumbled and fell, pulling the catapult with them, which tumbled end over end down the side of the hill, crashing into the trees below.

Gayle was able to repeat this several times before the men began pushing the siege engines from behind. When the first siege engines had finally come within range of the ballista, they were obliterated before preparing a single shot. Carts full of barrels of burning oils and explosive powders soon made easy targets for Gayle and began to burn and explode around the approaching army.

"Beautifully done, Princess!" exclaimed Jase, appearing from the shadows sounding almost happy, even if robotic.

The advance of the army was in complete disarray. Up from the rear, their commander came charging on horseback with dozens of cavalry behind him. The inspiring sight caused the infantry to reform and charge behind them. The commander, along with his cavalry, stopped well short of the gate in fear of the still-cooling iron, but motioned his troops forward. Moving quickly with ladders and hooks in hand, they advanced under the cover of fire from their own crossbows.

Jase called for everyone to take cover from the bolts, but it was too late, for one guard in the tower overlooking the gate fell out the window to his death. The infantry, even as their boots began to burn on the ground, started to raise ladders and throw hooks over the walls.

"Light the forge!" commanded Jase.

This time, molten silver spewed out of the pipes in front of the gate. The infantrymen who were not scalded to death turned to watch their cavalry and commander get mowed down by two of Gayle's whirling arrows.

The flashes of light and sprays of blood from both horse and man painted the night air with the essence of death. The remaining infantry ran wildly away from the city. Most were shot dead in their retreat, and others ran into the burning orchards to be overcome with smoke and flame.

"I see no more approaching, only those in the rear leaving," said Gayle.

"That was just a taste. The scouts are now reporting to the main host. The rest should be here by dawn," replied Jase.

Erik called up a storm, and it began to rain lightly.

"What are you doing, fool?" roared Jase.

"I do not wish to see all of Hillsbrand burned!" answered Erik.

Jase shook his head and said, "It's just as well. I can work wonders with storms!" Jase surveyed the surrounding landscape. "Something feels very wrong," he said almost to himself. He gave instructions for everyone to rest but remain wary. "We have a few hours until dawn. Let's get some rest." With that, he jumped with ease high up into the tower chamber.

Erik grabbed Gayle and joined Jase in the same manner. There, in the small tower guard post, Jase stood next to the south-facing window. Three guards from the ballista crew were huddled together on the stairs, mourning the loss of their comrade. Erik and Gayle entered the room and immediately sat down on the floor next to each other.

Dareth at last joined them. "I wish I could travel as easily as you fine people," he said as he entered through the door. Dareth joined his fellow guardsmen on the stairs and threw his arms over their shoulders.

The room was silent, save the noise of rain. Throughout the city, people had heeded the instruction to rest while they could. Jase stared out the window with his glowing ember-like eyes unblinking. He clutched the window's edge with his claws, making an unsettling scraping sound on the stone. Erik and Gayle, as well as the guards, began to drift off into an uncomfortable sleep.

Erik didn't dream. He just drifted in a floating grayness of thought, the grand runic cipher spinning in his mind. Everyone in the room woke in what seemed like only moments later to Erik to the sound of heavy footfalls coming up the stairs. Dareth perked up first and hurried the guards off the steps.

It was Grimhold with his wife Ruby. Still in his smithing attire, Grimhold wiped the sweat from his forehead and smiled. Erik and Gayle stood and applauded him. The guards and Jase even joined in. Jase turned back around to see the pale beams of dawn pierce the overcast sky.

"Well done indeed, Lord Grimhold!" commended Gayle.

"Lord? I'm just a public servant, Princess," answered Grimhold.

"I am the princess of Hillsbrand. I may ennoble whomever I like. Mayor Grimhold, you are the Forge Lord of Hillsbrand, and your eldest child will carry your title here. Dareth, your guards are now the knights of Hillsbrand, and you are their captain and Arch Knight. Your titles will be yours alone, and only guards will follow you, unless they are promoted for their valor. These are my commands," declared Gayle.

Grimhold bowed while the knights saluted. "Princess, thanks to a generous donation from the citizens of Hillsbrand, we have two full vats of bronze to greet our next attackers with, along with a few more nasty surprises," boasted Lord Grimhold.

Ruby stepped forward with a tray of tea and began to offer it around. The knights were grateful for the refreshments, as were Erik and Gayle.

Ruby was a pretty redheaded dwarf lady with a fiery temper, but now she was polite and smiling as she passed the tray around. "Dark Lord, would you care for tea?" asked Ruby, staring up at Jase's back. Grimhold gasped in terror at Ruby's choice of words and put his head in his hands. Jase ratcheted his head completely around and cocked it down at her.

His eyes burning bright, he peered down at the dwarf woman as she shrank back. "No, madam. I would not," Jase then spun his head back around to the window.

Grimhold hurried Ruby out of the room with an awkward laugh. As he left, he said, "I thought you should know, Emry has crafted some mighty armor for Prince Jetherion. He is standing by the gate with Jilian and the other knights, ready to skirmish."

Gayle paused and stood in silence. In her mind, her son was still a child, even if he was larger than everyone else and unnaturally strong. She fought back tears and with a smile said, "Very well."

"The main host approaches," said Jase grimly.

Gayle immediately headed toward the door and left. Jase instructed Dareth to pass the word for all archers and ballista crews to shoot only at the flanking forces and make them pay dearly for surrounding the city. As Dareth left down the stairs, Erik and Jase left out the door to the wall.

In the new dawn, Gayle witnessed the devastation. The beautiful white gravel paths throughout the orchards were littered with bodies and stained with blood and ash. Hundreds of burnt and dead bodies were swirled in a mix of black and silver metallic death spilled from above the gate. Throughout the orchards and down the green path, hundreds lay dead among the twisted wreckage of the would-be machines of war.

"This will be a gruesome sight to march an army through," said Gayle.

"Indeed, but behold the black banners of Mason Prime," said Jase, pointing south to a hill in the distance. "These soldiers have seen and performed countless atrocities in the name of their new empire. They are not the sheltered sort from Northguard. I have seen their work in the south—they will come like a plague, and we will be surrounded within hours."

The banners of Mason Prime continued to advance until they had come to the place where the siege engines of Northguard had been stopped and destroyed.

"What are they waiting for?" asked Dareth.

"They are advancing through the trees and around the hills on both sides," said Gayle.

"Yes, they will amass a force on all sides and attack at once, figuring we do not have the strength to hold them off. And they are right." Jase laughed.

"This is funny to you, Jase?" asked Erik, looking at Jase in wonder.

The imperial troops could now be seen moving quickly between the trees on both sides of the city.

"That's why you should have let the forest burn! Now bring back your storm, wizard!" commanded Jase harshly.

Erik waved his staff through into the air, blackening the sky with angry clouds. "Fire!" shouted Jase.

The ballista and the archers began to fire at the imperial soldiers advancing through the orchards. Gayle began to fire arrows repeatedly into the orchards as well. She had become so sure, strong, and masterful that her movements were lost on all but the keenest eyes.

Erik, tired of standing by, began to hurl the advancing soldiers into the air high enough so as to make the return to the ground deadly, or crippling at best. Still, the soldiers poured into the orchards on both sides of the city.

Jase pulled his head back and began to growl, the palms of his steely clawed gauntlets facing upward. The vaporous ribbons of smoke and shadow surrounding him began to rise and grow. His eyes flashed, and their radiance grew in its intensity. Then out of the black rolling clouds above crashed bolts of lightning on all sides of the city.

Erik immediately joined in the enchantment, and the city began to dance with tremendous flashes of lightning and shake with unending thunder. Everyone else had to stop their ears and shut their eyes, the clamor was so great.

As suddenly as it started, the lightning bombardment stopped. Jase began to slouch, and Erik leaned on his staff, breathing heavily.

Opening her eyes, Gayle could see the orchards smoldering in the rain. The orchard grounds were almost completely covered with the dead. Yet to the horror of everyone, more soldiers immediately began to move through the orchards to the north. A knight from the city below called up to Dareth, reporting that already a large imperial force had gathered on the north slope.

"What?" shouted Gayle.

"It's as I said—they will surround us and then attack. They just gave us a small force to play with while they marched a large force far around," explained Jase.

Gayle looked at the troops in the distance and yelled, "Damn cowards! Even a snake attacks with its head in front!"

"We are running out of arrows, and the south ballista are out of bolts!" said Dareth.

"Bring the knights down from the towers and up from the gates, with sword and shield ready to defend from atop the walls!" commanded Jase.

Gayle turned around and saw Grimhold on top of the water tower turning wheels and pulling levers. "What is Grim up to, Jase?" asked Gayle.

"He is preparing a warm welcome for our guests," answered Jase.

In only a few moments' time, a large organized force was mustered on each side of the hill, surrounding Hillsbrand.

All was quiet while the surrounding forces seemed to wait for a signal to attack, and soon the signal came. The sound of horns began to resonate throughout the hills, and the imperial army advanced for its final blow.

"Wait for the main column before you shoot the crusher I know you're saving, and put it right in the middle of them!" said Jase.

Gayle grinned slightly as she scanned the distant troops, hoping to see their commanders. The surrounding forces charged and under the cover of their own archers were soon at the base of the walls and at the gate, with rams, ladders, and grappling hooks.

"Light the forge, Grim!" echoed Jase's voice.

The city immediately began to groan and creak with the complaining of expanding metal and shifting stone. The pipes above the gates began to douse the soldiers below with molten bronze. The flow was constant for many minutes, until the southern wall was rimmed with the glow of molten bronze. Only the bands of enchanted and runed iron kept the gate from catching fire.

On all other sides of the city, jets of high-pressure steam began to blast out of vents every few feet around the base of the wall, killing some and wounding many of the soldiers at the walls. The shriek of the wounded and dying was incredible. Still, the imperial forces, seemingly inexhaustible, came forward through the orchards below. They began to amass on all sides except the south, which was now unapproachable.

"Dareth, go to the north wall. I shall go west, Erik to the east! Princess, stay here and ready your crusher. Let's hope another huge mass of dead will turn them away!" commanded Jase. Everyone took their positions on their walls.

To Erik's surprise, his son was there in vicious-looking armor, like a tyrant king of ancient lore. Three black horn-like spires rose from his grotesquely masked helmet. His armor, of grayish steel scales, was topped with gigantic horned spaulders leading down to heavily plated bracers and gauntlets, all ferociously covered in hardened steel spikes and black-enameled sigils. In truth, he looked more like a nightmarish monster than a young man.

"Son, be careful out here—you're half of everything I have in this world!" said Erik.

"A prince must defend his people!" answered Jetherion from under the mask of the helm.

"And a lord must protect his prince!" shouted Grimhold as he joined them atop the eastern wall. Grimhold was now in his ancient armor, with his hammers at his sides.

The surrounding armies finally had success in erecting ladders and throwing hooks up to the walls. The knights of Hillsbrand initially were equally successful in dislodging them and pushing them away with pole arms, but not for long.

Soon, fighting broke out on the north and then east and west walls. Trumpets sounded again throughout the hills. Gayle looked out and saw the imperial army advancing war machines and heavy infantry forward up the green path.

"Just a little closer, my little rams, to the slaughter!" said Gayle, readying her bow.

Jase withdrew a short double-ended spear from under his cloak. As he held it out, it extended to the length of a full spear and started resonating, and the metal spheres in the base of each spearhead began to spin.

Like a bolt of fiery shadow, Jase dashed from place to place atop the western wall, killing at will. Dareth and Jilian were doing well on the north wall, aided by the overhead fire from the women who were posted above the trades guild. However, the invaders were in greatest number on the east wall, and they were being dealt with swiftly.

Erik, by simply waving his hands here and there, was sending enemy after enemy falling to his death. Grimhold, even at a ripe age, bludgeoned to death any who set foot on the northern end of the east wall. The southern end was held by the sheer undeniable power of Jetherion, who was either completely pulverizing soldiers with a single punch or grabbing them and tearing limbs off, or even tossing them headfirst down into the city street with unbelievable force. The enemy soldiers began to shout warnings to each other. "Beware of the demon king who has risen on the east wall!" one was heard saying.

Erik suddenly heard Gayle's voice cry out and turned north to see a bright rainbow-like ring of enchantment rise into the air in the distance. It shot suddenly to the ground in the middle of the enemy siege engines that were preparing to fire. The blast was wholly incredible, aided by the explosive projectiles meant for the war machines. It obliterated everything in its path, all the way up to the city. The shock wave rattled the city gate but did no serious damage to it.

Gayle looked out in awe. Where there once had been a hill filled with approaching siege engines, there now was only a pit of scorched earth, ringed by hundreds of flattened trees. The orchards south of Hillsbrand were no more. Erik lowered his staff and felt his body grow weak. Protecting the city of Hillsbrand from the blast of Gayle's prismatic arrow had proved very draining. The feeling passed just in time for him to blast a few more invaders from the wall.

Gayle looked out into the distance and watched in disbelief as more imperial troops began to spill into the pit and advance.

Within moments, Jase had cleared the western wall, just before the shock wave from Gayle's arrow passed inexplicably around the city. He thought he could see movement of even more troops approaching in the west. When his vision cleared, he was sure of it. These troops were moving very fast, and as they came closer, the sound of a chorus of howls echoed over the hills.

The Hillmen had come. With Majick in the front of no less than a dozen war parties from different tribes, they came crashing into the eastern ranks of the imperials. The city knights took up a cheer, and the forces on the north wall abandoned their efforts, to keep the eastern forces from being annihilated.

Gayle, unblinking, reloaded her last few arrows when she heard a familiar sound. It was not the cry of wolves or the cheers of her knights—it was the whispering groan, the hissing howls, the wailing screeches of the dead.

As the imperials marched out of the pit and back up the green path, the dead rose from the ground and from under the fallen trees near the imperial army. The dead were everywhere among them, many armed with rusted blades and mail. Others came at the imperials with just their teeth and bony hands. Fear gripped the advancing ranks of the imperial forces, and they began to retreat.

The Hillmen attacking from the west proved as deadly in the field of battle as they were hunting in the hills. The soldiers of the empire, even in heavy armor, could not match the prowess of the Hillmen, who fought wearing only the hides of the beasts they had killed. Majick was unstoppable, killing the merged forces from the east and north in heaps, paralyzing them with her bestial roars and making them easy prey for the Hillmen she led.

In the south, the retreat of the empire was disastrous. In an effort to regroup, the commanders of the empire finally showed their presence atop a distant hill. Gayle's jeweled eye flashed as she looked closer to be sure.

There they were, on large armored horses, wearing what looked like parade armor, brightly polished and jeweled. One very large Vanguard man was surrounded by a dozen heavy cavalry. Beside him rode a short, fat-looking man in fancy clothing, and to his right was another large man wearing plated armor and a tall crested helm.

"Finally, the snake shows its head!" said Gayle, notching one of her last few arrows.

The commander of the advancing southern army managed to regroup his troops at the base of the hill and was preparing his men to take a charge from the slower-moving undead. Gayle looked out over the undead and at their head saw someone unmistakable at their lead—Dregor. The host of the undead stopped and formed ranks at Dregor's command. Though not nearly matching the number of the imperial army, they had the advantage of being fearless, and of course, already being dead, they were very hard to stop. Many of their enemies' weapons were still protruding from them.

"Seek!" commanded Gayle as she let her first arrow fly, killing the fat lord sitting on his horse in the distance. Before the general and his captain were able to find cover, they met the same end as their lord. Finally, at long last, a blast of horns rang out from the southern host, signaling the retreat. It was then that the undead charged, and despite being pierced by many flights of crossbow bolts, they advanced very quickly.

The retreat of the southern forces was en route. The forces to the west began to withdraw to the south but could not escape the war parties of the Hillmen and were cut down before they could make it to the orchards next to the green path.

The eastern imperial army managed a retreat into the east toward the delves. Jase, now standing on the eastern wall, laughed at the thought of their fate should they reach the delves.

Breathing a sigh of relief that the city was safe, Gayle gave the command to open the gate and let the Hillmen war parties inside the city. The knights hesitated to the point that Jetherion had to open the gate himself, manning the winch alone. The Hillmen war parties came in through the gate howling and yelling their cries of victory. At their head was Majick, covered with the spray of her enemies' blood and smiling ear to ear. Beside her was a man wearing a bear cowl and walking with a large bone spear in his hand. Erik, Jase, Gayle, and Grimhold all came down from their positions on the walls to greet them.

Majick bowed slightly and said, "May I introduce the war chief of the eastern tribes, Restavix the bear hunter, not to mention, the uncle of Fenrix the great dragon slayer."

The bear-masked Hillman said, "Hello, Princess Gayle. We have done good trading together these many years. It would be a shame to see you all enslaved to the empire. Their traders are little more than liars and thieves in our dealings with them."

"We are in your debt," said Gayle with a short bow.

"The dead are approaching!" yelled a knight posted on the southern wall.

"Do not bother with the gate. I will turn them if need be!" declared Erik.

Chapter 10

◇ ◇ ◇

As Evil Comes

Erik strode toward the pile of cooled molten metal and burnt remains at the gate. He could see a column of dead approaching, with Dregor at their lead. All the flesh was gone from his body, and Erik recognized him only by his unique armor. Though his head was now only a bare skull, he still seemed to smile, if possible, and looking at Erik, he readied his long sword. The column of undead began to veer to the right before reaching the gate and marched down the length of the western wall in single file. Erik only watched as many of the undead, whom he could still recognize, passed one by one.

When they all had passed, only Dregor remained. "Be ready, Erik, from the north they come! The servants of Dagoth," he whispered.

Erik's eyes grew wide with dread as he turned and hurried toward the square where everyone was gathered. There among the crowd, Restavix was telling Gayle about their villages being attacked by darbeck in the night and how their families were in hiding. Restavix was asking Gayle for asylum for his families until after winter when Erik interrupted.

"These darbeck that attacked you—did they come from the north?" asked Erik.

Restavix paused for a moment as though recalling an unpleasant memory

but answered, "They came in the night, only a few at a time to each village, then more each night after. We followed their scent north to the foot of the mountains, to the villages of the Mountainfolk, but they… were all gone. Something evil sleeps in those mountains," His voice was ominous.

Jilian, on the north wall, shouted down, "The dead are forming ranks along the face of the north slope!"

"I believe that whatever sleeps in the Northridge Mountains is now awake," said Jase.

Leaving a streak of shadowy black smoke in the air, Jase flew to the top of the north wall. There he saw the undead in ranks facing the north, standing cold and quiet. Jase's eyes narrowed as he scanned the distance for any sign of danger. There he saw small gray and black objects moving in mass, coming down the southern faces of the Northridge Mountains.

"Wizard!" shouted Jase, motioning for Erik to join him.

Gayle granted the Hillmen asylum and ordered the knights to shut the gate. Grimhold ordered the militia into the square, and they took up positions throughout the town while the wounded knights and Hillmen were sent to the hospital to rest. Gayle, with Jetherion, Restavix, and Majick, joined Jase and Erik on the north wall. Dareth began giving instructions for the militia in case of another siege.

Erik looked out over the Northridge Mountains. He too could see small objects moving quickly down the slopes. Then to confirm his fears, two red points of light flashed out from the mountaintop, painting the slopes the color of war. "Gargoyles—the eyes of Dagoth!" exclaimed Erik.

What at first looked like black clouds started to rise from the mountain. "Yes, indeed, and not just one Brooding in the dark. Two serving a purpose. Where eyes are, the hands follow," said Jase.

Gayle, looking north, could see clearly hundreds of adult darbeck. Too heavy to fly, they were running on all fours like great jungle cats. She could also see thousands of young darbeck swarming in the air in a great swirling mass, and with something else too small and quick for her to be sure.

"What the hell is this?" asked Gayle desperately.

"The host of a servant of Dagoth. Where the servant goes, so too does the host," answered Jase coldly.

"What do we do? How can we fight this?" implored Gayle.

Restavix hesitated and then answered, "This happened once in my grandfather's time. The tribes farther west were gone in one night. The rest took flight to the east."

"How do we fight them?" asked Gayle.

To that, all fell silent. At last, Jase said only, "The best we can."

Jase turned to the crowd gathering in the square and shouted in a deep, steely tone, "Warriors of the western tribes, citizens of Hillsbrand, the evil of the ancient world has been left unchecked for four hundred years. Now the servants of Dagoth are upon us. They come in the times you are the weakest. They do not show mercy. They do not know fear. The only thing you can do is set your steel to them and hope it is enough. You must fight now! Fight for everything that makes you do anything in this world. Fight for war, fight for peace. Fight for day and night, both love and hate. The good and the bad! Fight for friend and foe, anger and joy. Fight to the death so that maybe, just maybe, someone may live!"

The Hillmen in the square began to howl and scream, compelled by their lust for blood. The militia took longer to get excited but soon gave up a roar of their own.

"Our walls will be no use against that flying scourge. We will all be fighting in the streets. Damn, and I have no time to recover any arrows!" said Gayle.

"If the lines of the undead do not hold, the adult darbeck will scale our walls with little effort," added Jase grimly.

Jase began to groan and creak with the complaint of twisting metal, like some large machine heating up rapidly. Now audibly growling, he held his spear above his head and instantly became wrapped in a blanket of orange flame. The sky once again darkened with black swirling clouds. The clouds above the mountains twisted into two funnels and descended full of glowing embers, with bolts of lightning arching between them. The cyclones of elemental fury began to lick the face of the Northridge Mountains.

Erik saw the awesome power of Jase's enchantment and focused his mind to it. Drawing his dagger and raising his staff in the air, Erik cried out, "I give power to the mechanism!"

The black clouds began to rain down meteoric blasts of burning brimstone, and it seemed like the entire mountain range was being torn open with giant bolts of lightning. The swarms of darbeck and giant flying insects that were not sucked into the cyclones were catching fire and falling to the ground. The darbeck moving on the ground fared little better, being blasted with lightning or crushed by falling debris.

Finally, the enchantment gave way, and Erik and Jase both stumbled forward, leaning on their props. The advancing horde had been greatly lessened but not stopped, and soon the young darbeck began to fly into the city by the dozen. They were badly burnt and still disoriented and were easily dealt with.

The large wasp-like insects that came falling out of the sky, with wings burning, were another matter entirely. They were crawling on the ground like giant ants, as large as a man's boot, and they went unnoticed for the most part until the militia started to drop dead, one after another. A single sting was all it took; within seconds, the victims were dead.

The entire square became filled with men either swatting at large bat-like creatures in the air or stomping furiously at giant insects on the ground.

Jase mustered enough strength to keep the vermin off of himself but could do little more. At the same time, Erik could do little more than meditate a small enchantment around himself to keep the vermin away. Gayle, with a quiver full of used regular arrows, was doing her best to stay alive with her son, with Grimhold close by to protect her. Gayle glanced to the north and saw that the points of red light were now closer, and between them was a gigantic gray figure riding on a large, black cat-like drake, or so she thought.

"The eyes approach!" yelled Gayle.

Jase looked out from the wall to the north and saw what he knew of only from the tales that Kylratha had told him in his youth—an ogre, a servant of Dagoth. Jase said, "Behold, an ogre! If the cyclops-like gargoyles are Dagoth's eyes, the ogres are his hands. They are ancient immortals that came with Dagoth in the first days—powerful, cruel, and nearly unstoppable. The only account of their defeat I have heard of was at the hands of many elders."

The adult darbeck that survived the storm of fire and lightning had reached the front lines of the dead. They showed no interest in the dead, however. The first few darbeck were cut, bitten, and clawed down before they could make it past even the front lines, but more and more came. Soon, there were so many that several dozen had broken through the lines of the dead uncontested, and they began to scale the walls of the city.

Crawling up the stones like giant spiders, several bounded to the top of the wall at once. Jilian was the first to perish from the giant claws at the end of their winged arms. Dareth screamed a terrible cry of fury, amplifying his voice to its limit in a loathsome roar.

He chopped at the darbeck devouring his wife so powerfully that his claymore, after passing through his intended target, plunged deeply into his wife as well. After seeing what he had done, he went mad with anger and despair. He gave no care to defending his fellow man or thought toward his duty. All that mattered to Dareth was what he could kill next.

More adult darbeck came leaping over the wall and down into the city. The militia and Hillmen, mostly rid of the vermin, were now faced with the apish and bat-like creatures of the forgotten underworld. They did not fare well. The darbeck, being much larger and stronger than most men, simply overpowered them, forcing them to the ground and tearing them apart, mail included.

Jetherion and Majick saw the slaughter and dropped from the north wall down into the streets to help. Jetherion, crushing one under his feet as he landed, quickly ran around the corner to the square full of darbeck, to see only a few pockets of men withstanding them.

Majick heard the screams of the young women posted above the trades guild and scrambled up its side. When she got to the top, she gasped at the carnage. An adult darbeck had climbed to the top from the square, finding the young women of the city armed only with short bows and little training. It had slain them all to the last woman, and in the corner with a half-dozen arrows still protruding from its thick hide, it was gorging itself on their bodies. Majick, enraged, dashed forward, and wanting the pleasure of a close kill, she gave out a roar booming with the fury of the ancient scerpent of her totem. Tackling the darbeck and slinging it off its feet, she then proceeded to beat the darbeck to death with her bare hands. With Majick possessed with the fury of the serpent, the darbeck was powerless to stop her. In a few furious moments, the beast was little more than pulp under her fists.

Meanwhile, Jetherion was an unstoppable force in the battle for the square. Each swing of his fist was a killing blow, and even the darbeck began to flee once aware of his presence. However, he could not be everywhere in the square at once, and the militia was now all but gone. Only a small group, with Emry, remained in front of Grimhold's smithy. The knights of Hillsbrand and the Hillmen were still fighting well, but the darbeck continued to leap down into the square.

"Stop them at the damn wall!" shouted Jetherion.

His voice was lost in the chaos. The only one with ears sharp enough to hear him was Majick. As she looked down from the rooftop of the trades guild and saw the desperate situation in the square, she jumped down to help.

The situation outside the north wall was little better. The lines of the dead had broken, and now they were massed at the base of the city wall, trying desperately to keep the darbeck from climbing up. Despite the efforts of the dead, the darbeck were stopped only a few at a time.

Jase, barely able to move, could not kill a single one. Gayle, out of arrows, was scrambling out of the way of the melee, while Grimhold was doing the best he could against the oversized beasts.

Erik, looking out to the north and trying to gather himself, saw the eyes of Dagoth at the base of the hill, with their ogre general between them. The undead, seeing the arrival of the eyes, abandoned the wall and charged.

The eyes did not move, but the black reptilian creature on which the ogre rode punched through the dead and then jumped to the top of the wall. The ogre was wearing armor made from heavy plates of a dull gray metal, unadorned and simple. Its gray skin was barely distinguishable from its armor. It held a large steel mallet in its right hand, which it pointed at Erik while charging at him across the wall.

The galloping dragon knocked Grimhold from the wall and narrowly missed Gayle as it went by, charging at Erik. Erik, now panicked from seeing this large creature nearly crush his wife, summoned a blast of force that knocked the dragon and its rider over the corner of the trades guild and into the town square and out of Erik's sight.

Jase continued to survey the north field while slumped over his spear. The undead were being decimated by the eyes of Dagoth. The two colossal gargoyles were tearing through the dead with their claws like scythes through grass.

Erik grabbed Jase and shook him. "There is no time for sightseeing, brother—that demon and his dragon are in the square!"

"I know! Erik, you must stop them if you can. Now listen! This is important! They say the ancients can see thoughts. Use only what enchantments come naturally. Don't think about it—just act!" Jase then jumped down to the north slope and began to charge down the hill toward the eyes.

"Jase!" yelled Erik after him.

Gayle came running over to the eastern part of the north wall to see around the trades guild into the square. She passed Erik and shouted above the chaos and random noises, "I have only half a dozen arrows left and one runic, and I'm not sure what it does! You have to go help them!"

Dareth continued to rampage past them, just missing them both, wildly flailing his sword as he charged at two more darbeck on the north wall.

"Will you be all right, my love?" asked Erik, wiping his forehead off with the back of his fist.

"I'll be fine—now go!" commanded Gayle forcefully as she drew back another arrow.

Jetherion and Majick had nearly cleared the square of darbeck. One of the last was locked in combat with a few militia outside Grimhold's smithy. There, Jetherion saw Emry rush forward and smash it over the head with her smithing hammer as it lunged at her. It recoiled back only to be killed by Jetherion, sent flying onto the roof of the smithy by a single punch.

Jetherion looked down at Emry, who was breathing heavily but still managed smile, happy to see Jetherion alive.

"You shouldn't be out here! Go back to your smithy and lock yourself inside!" shouted Jetherion.

"I'm just—" was all Emry managed to say before she fell to the ground, grasping her right calf. She looked down and saw the wasp that had stung her. She smashed it with a crackle. She stood back up, looking angry, but almost immediately, all expression left her face. Dropping her hammer, she stumbled sleepily toward Jetherion. Jetherion took her up in his arms. She stared up at the cloudy sky and said only, "I wish—" before she closed her eyes.

Jetherion tried to call her name, but all his words stuck in his throat. The only thing that would come to the surface were the tears of anger that welled in his eyes as he carried her to the smithy. Laying her on a bench just inside the forge, he knew all life had left her. He could feel real, pure, uncontaminated fury building inside him. It came crawling up his spine like a geyser of lava. The Intense flow of his anger spread everywhere throughout his body, and he clenched his fists. He felt the metal of his gauntlets crumble in his own grip. In anger he tore away his gauntlets, bracers, and spaulders like foil, stripping his massive arms of any armor of any kind. Jetherion set his helmet down next to where Emry's head rested.

"I will kill my enemies with my own hands!" swore Jetherion in a rage. As he turned to the square, he felt the quake of two impact tremors shake the ground beneath him.

Majick too felt the ground beneath her feet shake and turned to see a gigantic man-like figure and a black, cat-like dragon crash into the square. The ogre stood and pointed its hammer toward the middle of the square and said something in a voice so deep that it was more felt than heard.

The dragon answered something in response in a growling series of barks and then breathed a blast of red flame onto a group of knights still fighting the darbeck. Majick roared thunderously, the cry of the ancient scerpent causing the dragon to cringe and then lock its gaze on her. It lunged forward, and opening its mouth to inhale in preparation of blasting fire, it instead forcibly swallowed the flying head of Majick's chain mace.

The dragon began to cough and spit small pools of burning fluid onto the bloodied ground but could not dislodge the weapon. Majick pressed the rune to take in the chain and dashed forward. Leaping through the air while being pulled by her weapon, Majick readied her sword. The dragon whipped its head to the side, trying to smash Majick into a nearby building. Majick instead went flying under the dragon's head and swung fully around the dragon's neck and up onto its back. Majick then pushed against its upper back with her legs, and as she pulled on her mace with her left hand, the chain tightened.

The dragon began to gasp and swat at Majick with its spiny tail, which Majick shortened more and more with each stroke of her sword. The dragon began to panic and rolled onto its back, trying to crush Majick, but Majick could not be stopped. Channeling all the spirits of her totem, she began to look as though she was rimmed in flame. Majick, at last driving the dragon headfirst into the new mausoleum, stunned the creature. Letting go of her chain mace, she drove her sword down into the back of its skull with both of her hands and a gut-wrenching roar. The dragon gurgled out a long exhale and died.

The Ogre looked up from its combat with the few Hillsbrand Knights and Hillmen still resisting it and began to growl at the sight of its fallen companion, but was interrupted by a spear thrown by Restavix. The spear struck the ogre in the neck but fell away harmlessly. Turning its attention momentarily, the ogre stomped forward, shaking the ground as it went, and with one swing of its hammer, the ogre reduced Restavix to a bloody and mangled corpse.

Restavix went flying like a rag doll through the air and collided with the walls of the hospital with so much force that his skull and ribcage shattered against the stones. The ogre then began to swipe at the Hillmen and knights in the square, all with much the same effect, laughing as it went.

Jetherion came forth from the smith just in time to see Majick kill the dragon with the chain of her mace around its neck. He next saw a gray-skinned giant stop right in front of him after launching one of the town guards through the air with its hammer.

Despite the red eyes looking down at Jetherion in wonder, this young mortal was not afraid or armed. He just stood tall, though a few feet shorter than the ogre, with his fists clenched at his sides.

The ogre drew its hammer back to swing but stopped as Jetherion said, "Hello, demon. I am Jetherion the demon prince!"

The ogre understood his words and began to laugh. But the ogre was hushed as Jetherion, with astonishing speed, hooked his left arm up at the ogre, smashing his fist into its jaw. After the punch landed with a sickening crunch, the ogre fell back into a sitting position.

Jetherion looked around the town square to see most of his city in ruins and his friends dead. He could feel his body begin to change, and as the ogre arose, Jetherion grasped its hand and hoisted its arm over his shoulder. Then turning his hips in toward the monster, he smashed the demon headfirst into the pavement of the square, causing a rolling tremor to shake the city. The ogre, still not badly wounded, quickly stood, only to be hit by another of Jetherion's crushing blows. The ogre's legs wobbled, and it fell forward to its knees, only to be met by Jetherion's right fist rocketing up into its chin. The sound as the ogre's head flew back resembled that of a cracking whip, and the uppercut sent the ogre tumbling uncontrollably across the ground and all the way through the square, to collide with the northwest wall.

Erik, as he levitated down to the street, saw the ogre fly past him and smash into the nearby wall. Jetherion appeared around the corner and advanced on the ogre. The creature was enraged, and with its left hand, it leaned forward and grabbed Jetherion around the throat. Jetherion, smiling, grabbed the ogre's wrist with his hands and began to squeeze it until the bones started to crackle.

"Get that thing away from my son, Erik!" screamed Gayle, looking down from the wall above in terror.

In a panic, Erik waved his staff, and in a flash of blue light, he disappeared with the ogre. Erik found himself at the top of the barren hill directly to the north of Hillsbrand, with the ogre standing back up on its feet and staring straight at him. "Oh no" said Erik to himself.

Gayle panicked upon witnessing her husband and the giant demon disappear together. She began to look all around and through the buildings in town. She saw the burning corpse of the dead dragon, and she saw Jetherion helping Grimhold to his feet. She saw Dareth with nothing left to kill, crying over the body of his dead wife. She looked onto the north slopes and saw the charred bodies of the eyes of Dagoth ringed by the undead, who were still tearing at their hides. She realized that with the captain of the host transported out of the city, the battle for the survival of Hillsbrand was coming to an end. She then saw Jase and Dregor running north to the top of a barren hill, where she could also see Erik standing alone with the ogre. Gayle reached into her quiver for the arrow that had the rune of Kylratha on it. "I don't know what you do, but do something great! Kylratha!" screamed Gayle as she loosened her arrow toward the hill.

Chapter 11

◈ ◈ ◈

The Counterbalance

Erik tried to push the ogre back, blasting it with shockwaves of force, but it only slowed its approach slightly. The ogre then advanced on Erik with its hammer pulled back, but it was met midair by a bold of shadowy fire that was Jase.

Twirling his spear masterfully, Jase began to rip at the ogre with little effect. With a swipe of his hammer, the ogre knocked Jase down the hill in a staggering sort of dance, despite Jase's having blocked the stroke. Dregor appeared suddenly out of a veil of passing mist and lurched forward., and grabbing the ogre around its left leg, he lifted the giant demon, drove it back up the hill, and slammed it into the dirt.

The ogre landed with a rumbling thud and then, rearing its leg back, kicked Dregor in the chest, sending him hurling down the hill. Erik's eyes were drawn upward as a ring of dark enchantment and energy erupted in the sky against the black clouds. The ogre stood back up, secured a firm grip on its hammer, and began to stomp its way toward Erik.

Something was different this time. The ogre had an enormous shadow behind him despite the dim light. An icy cold voice came echoing down from above, speaking some forgotten language. The ogre looked up in surprise just in time for a giant great sword to pass through its neck as

Kylratha descended. The ogre's head fell forward from its body with a spray of yellowish bile. Its body, still standing there shaking, was launched toward the northern mountains by the impact of Kylratha's backhanded gesture. The force from the strike shook the hilltop and left a strange coppery smell in the air. There stood Kylratha, the greatest citizen of Elvendom, looking down at Erik menacingly.

"A wondrous mess you have made, Erik. I would have found and slain this whelp nearly two decades ago if you had not interfered by killing one of its guardian eyes and alerting it to my presence," lectured Kylratha coldly.

Erik grabbed a handful of his own hair and leaned on his staff as he looked down, puffing up his cheeks, blowing out a deep breath of relief, and nearly falling forward.

Dregor approached and kneeled at the sight of Kylratha and would not move.

The silence was broken by the sound of Jase's voice. "Kylratha!" Jase screamed as he enveloped himself in red flame and rushed at Kylratha.

Kylratha flew into the air in a streak of dark violet fire, and there in the blackened sky, the two dark elf lords did battle. The cold, emotionless voice of Kylratha echoed out in contrast to the fiery chorus of screams with which Jase filled the blackened air with spells of death. It was more than a contest of skill and enchantment; this was a battle between master and pupil that streaked the blackened air, threatening to tear the skies in two.

Erik watched in awe, helpless and sad. Majick appeared like a flash out of nowhere, and looking up at the sky, she began to scream, "He's dying!"

"Who?" asked Erik as he looked back into the sky. He watched as the two bolts of fire collided in a great explosion and then came streaking back down to the hilltop. Kylratha, coming out of a flash of enchantment, stood unscathed, pointing his great sword with his left hand at Jase. Jase was standing with his head bowed and only half of his spear in his left hand. His right arm was missing, with blood spilling from his shoulder. Jase looked up at Kylratha with the light in his eyes wavering and took a knee, admitting defeat.

"You dare challenge me after I spared you all? You dare use the fire enchantments against me when it was I who stood before the throne of ages and crafted them with my own hands? You would dare use the King's speech against the most powerful warrior to ever live? I have given all fair warning in dreams not to further upset the counterbalance and here you are meddling with the counterbalance and it's master," scolded Kylratha.

"Against a villain!" shouted Majick as she lunged at Kylratha with a mighty swing. Kylratha blocked her strike and stared at her with his steely gaze. Majick drew back another blow and shouted, "You killed maidens and elflings and hung them to be eaten by vermin!"

After her next attack was blocked, she spun around, coiling her body like a serpent, and with a roar and a blast of enchantments from her blade, she drove Kylratha back on his heels. She shouted, "The children of Hillsbrand live in fear of the walking dead, too frightened to visit the graves over their ancestors because of you!"

As they separated, Erik could hear the unmistakable voice of Jetherion from further down the hill. A shadow appeared in the air above them. It was Jetherion, still consumed with madness over his lost love. He was now aloft in an impossible leap for any normal man of Grea'nock. Majick and Kylratha both narrowly escaped his landing. A plume of pulverized earth and rock erupted from underneath his fists and feet as he met the ground again.

As the dust settled, all those present could see the unsettling image of Jetherion in his madness, standing still and straight and softly laughing at Kylratha.

"One demon or another, it doesn't matter. You will all bow before me," said Jetherion as he rushed forward at Kylratha.

Jetherion's punch was stopped by the lightly outstretched palm of Kylratha's gauntlet, as though there was no force behind Jetherion's attack whatsoever.

"So this is the Kingsteel Reforged? It is just as before, the first one did not know me either," said Kylratha. Through the enchantments of shadow and smoke, Erik could see Kylratha smiling at his son.

Jetherion only screamed and threw another punch at Kylratha with his right hand. Kylratha did not attempt to stop his attack, but Jetherion's blow fell with so little force that it did not even make a sound as he fell forward into it. Catching Jetherion, Kylratha helped him to a seat and said, "You would not know that I am not your enemy, child."

"Nor would anyone!" shouted Majick. "You are a pitiful coward and slayer of children—a true enemy of the world and a servant of Dagoth!" As she shouted, she lunged forward with another attack.

Kylratha grew angry, and with one stroke, he knocked Majick down to her knees, shattering her sword. An echoing robotic laugh came from inside Jase's chest as a blast of steam came from his mask. "Go ahead, slay the granddaughter of Eltrinia and become a true servant of Dagoth!" taunted Jase.

Kylratha stepped back and paused. Thrusting his great sword into the hill, he asked, "Eltrinia had a granddaughter?" Kylratha put his head in his hands and said, "And I nearly spilled her precious blood? Have I fallen that far?"

Erik, seeing an opportunity, drove his staff into the ground and caused the silvery white blossoms of Ellhom to bloom everywhere around Kylratha. The sweet fragrance of the tree filled the air as Erik said, "There is always a chance to start anew."

"Indeed," said Kylratha as a radiant tear fell down his cheek and onto a blossom, setting it ablaze.

Kylratha walked slowly toward Majick, and reaching up to his neck, he removed a chain of shiny black metal, on which hung a single red jewel. As he took it off, the wisps of shadow hiding most of his body faded away. He handed the pendant to Majick, and she took it hesitantly.

Kylratha's full form could now be seen. He was a tall plated soldier, and his armor was covered in ancient writing that blazed with its own light. The Kylratha that Jase remembered from the fortress wars, the lord general, his old mentor, stood there now, silent and sad. Kylratha's steely eyes looked down to his hands, gloved with clawed gauntlets. He removed two large runic metal rings, one from each wrist, and dropped the rings at Majick's feet. The heavy plated armor encasing him slowly disappeared from sight. Only a simple white robe, shimmering in the dim light, remained.

Kylratha's eyes turned from murderous steel globes to glistening silvery jewels, deep wells of thoughtfulness and sorrow. His skin turned from ashen steel to a golden bronze, and his hair from gray to white. Now, instead of a dark lord, there stood an ancient elf, beautiful and solemn. Kylratha actually smiled as he stepped forward and held Majick.

"You are my granddaughter," he said softly. "I loved the Lady Eltrinia. We were mated in secret among the shadows within the root of the city of Ellhom. When she died giving birth to your mother Ellay I fled. I was too ashamed to face her. My love killed Eltrinia Scion of the Gnomare'! I did not wish for it to poison my beloved daughter as well."

He kissed Majick softly on the forehead, and with a flash, the faintly glowing rune of the Gnomare' on her brow was replaced by the violet glow of the rune of Kylvara'. It was hung in a field of shimmering stars. "Behold Majick, First Lady of the Kylvara', my granddaughter!" declared Kylratha, whose voice rolled over the hills like the blast of thousands of horns.

Majick dropped to her knees, feeling her heart give way, and cried.

"Be a lady of the counter balance as I was its lord, and remember it is sadness from which the counterbalance draws its strength," said Kylratha. He then turned away toward his sword.

Jase, seeing his opportunity, lunged at Kylratha and struck him in the neck with his broken spear. The head of the spear shattered as it struck Kylratha's neck, and Jase stumbled forward into Kylratha's embrace. Kylratha passed his hand over Jase's shoulder, and it stopped bleeding immediately. Jase felt all pain leave his body as the high lord held him.

Kylratha smiled and said, "If I had a son, my only wish for him would be that he would become as strong, dedicated, and cunning as you have been—as powerful as a Kylvara', as noble as the Eldare'. I am very proud of you. Now rest and find strength."

Kylratha's eyes flashed, and Jase went limp in his arms as he laid him down on the hillside beside Jetherion, who was still sitting with his head in his hands. Kylratha approached his sword, and gripping it in the middle of the blade, he withdrew it from the ground. He walked close to Erik and said, "Tell them to hasten to the shores of Nem. Only when you posses the might of full might and wealth of your house can you succeed.. Only then can this empire be checked."

"Will you not help then, eldest?" asked Erik.

The sky to the north went red as Kylratha turned to face the mountains. Erik could see several points of red lights that could only be many of the eyes of Dagoth. Kylratha smiled as the red beams painted the hill a murderous hue.

"I have a new mission now. I have seen a great evil rise in this world, and I must destroy it while I can still see it clearly," answered Kylratha ominously. Then, with his right hand, Kylratha plunged his great sword into his own chest, up to where his hand was holding the blade, and produced a guttural groan.

"No!" screamed Majick as she tried to cast life enchantments, but she was silenced. Kylratha reached forward to the crossbar of his sword and pulled the rest of the blade into his chest.

As he dropped to his knees, his eyes began to dart around in all directions, as he wondered why his spirit stayed despite so much pain. Kylratha then grabbed the handle sticking out of his chest and pulled it violently to the right. The motion caused the blade to slash out from the left side of his torso, abducting his left arm from his body as the sword came free. Kylratha screamed in pain as he held his sword aloft. His blood like burning metal began to devour the blossoms of Ellhom as it spilled from his hideous wounds.

Looking to the sky, Kylratha shouted, "Starblade, Kingsteel, Shames— Do you see these children? They shine with your stars," Baring his ferociously sharp teeth and grimacing in pain, he then said softly, "My father, my king. This is sorrow," He then tossed his great sword in front of Majick and fell forward, lifeless.

Majick, feeling her voice return, came forward despite the flame caused by Kylratha's blood and laid her body across his mighty shoulders. She wailed and pulled at her hair at the demise of her grandfather and the thought that she had played a part in it.

Erik began to chant, desperately trying to revive the ancient lord, but the air around them all became still and lifeless. As he looked up, he could see the red points of light on the Northridge Mountains disappear beyond the horizon.

Dregor, now standing close by, said in a hissing whisper, "We are all sinners, yet we do not all do good. Were his crimes so much greater than ours? Did he deserve this? He brought me back so that I could defend the ones I love. We attacked him with those that he loved and brought him shame and death. This is no victory."

Dregor turned and disappeared into the shadows, as did the host of the undead, on the north slope of Hillsbrand. Erik began to feel sick to his stomach but soon turned his thoughts to his friends and family. Telling Majick that he would take Jase to the hospital, he disappeared with a flash along with Jase and his son.

As Erik laid Jase on the bed and Jetherion on the floor in the trauma room, he said to himself, "Now, I feel like my heart's been ripped from my chest."

Chapter 12

◆ ◆ ◆

To What End?

The following days were grim indeed. Jase slept in the hospital while Majick took the relics of Kylratha and packed them away with Jase's things, preparing for her journey. The city militia had been killed to the last man. Of the knights, only Dareth remained, although he had become dark and distant. The young women of the town were all but wiped out, and Grimhold, learning of his daughter's death, would not leave his home. To everyone's curiosity, the bodies of the fallen who were not buried disappeared that very first night. Erik supposed that Dregor had gone recruiting and now marched at the head of a vast army.

After a week had passed, the refugees of the Hillman villages came, led by the last three Hillmen left standing after the battle. The seniors in the hospital were untouched. However, a wasp had found its way down to the basement of the training halls and stung several children to death before an adventurous toddler named William picked it up and pulled its head off.

Gayle, overcome with grief, spent most of the days crying in her bedroom while Erik ran the town the best he could.

A company of dwarfs from the eastern delves arrived The week following the Hillman people's arrival. with provisions and tools for reconstruction.

They had destroyed the forces that retreated east from Hillsbrand in a day, but gathering emergency provisions had proved difficult and was the reason for their tardiness.

The family dynamic in Hillsbrand was strange and sad. There were so many orphaned children that each family had to take at least one. Erik took William.

Each single man, there being now so few, was encouraged to take at least two, sometimes three, wives. Seeing as there were only three men of the eastern tribes left alive, there were plenty of widows. Even Dareth found comfort in the care of twin sisters, Danielle and Marie. Jetherion, however, refused to take any wives, saying that he preferred dwarf women.

At long last, Majick was ready to travel back to the tree. As a parting gift, she recovered many of Gayle's runic arrows, including the crusher and the one marked by Kylratha. With a sturdy covered wagon pulled by two large oxen she had bought from a widow, and with Erik's help, she laid Jase down with the rest of their belongings.

"Are you leaving so soon, Majick?" asked Erik with a sad look on his face.

"Yes, Jase needs the skills of Enock, Ellen, and perhaps the other elders to return to us. We will meet again. I promise," declared Majick as she led the oxen away.

Grimhold after his mourning came forth from his smithy and greeted the dwarfs from the delves in the square near at hand, and after speaking with them for a long while, he agreed to work again. Grimhold turned to Erik and said solemnly, "My Iron Cap brothers are so grateful to us for us driving off the empire that they have agreed to restore the city to its former glory just like it was."

Erik shook his head and shouted, "No! We will not cling to the past or worry about the world that was. We will instead labor to what it should be, and since nothing can ever be the same, we will do as we should and make all things new! This is only the beginning!"

Epilogue

◆ ◆ ◆

Of Dregor and Dareth

Dareth, only seven years of age, stood in the main road of Hillsborough coming into the town from the south gate. He spent his summer days there playing by himself, kicking a leather ball against the city wall. He didn't play with the other children. He was smaller than the others, very skinny, and was bullied daily for it. The other children would call him "Stick boy" and then, after pushing him around on the ground or in the mud, would call him "Dirty Dareth"

He kicked the ball in anger, smashing it against the wall as hard as he could. On this occasion, he was not concerned about the kids who always bullied him. Instead, he was upset that his parents had adopted another boy.

His name was Dregor; his parents had been killed by a drake in the hills north of the city. He was bloodied and wounded when he crawled up to the gate half-dead. Halagre, Dareth's father and the captain of the town guard, found him and took him in.

Why am I not enough for them? thought Dareth as he kicked the ball against the wall.

Dareth felt a sudden impact to the back of his head and fell to the ground stunned. "Oh, Dirty Dareth lost his ball!" said a voice from behind. Darth shook his head and looked up to see Stephan, the worst of his tormentors, holding his ball.

Dareth stood up and hung his head. "Give it back, Stephan!" said Dareth in a shaky voice. Stephan turned and threw the ball over the east wall.

"Go get it!" answered Stephan with a laugh.

Dareth turned slowly toward the south gate. As soon as he took a step, he was shoved to the ground by Stephan. "Not until you're good and filthy. You should crawl out the gate from here and make pig noises. That would suit you perfectly, Dirty Dareth!" taunted Stephan.

Dareth shook his head and began to get up but was shoved backward to the ground again, smacking his head on the cobblestones. Clutching his head, Dareth yelled up at Stephan, "If I was your size, you would be sorry!"

"I am his size, and he is about to be very sorry!" Dareth heard someone say. He looked up and saw that it was Dregor, standing straight up and looking Stephan in the eye. Ignoring the pain of his recent wounds, Dregor stood tall, holding his crutch in his right hand like a club.

"I think I can handle a cripple and a weakling just fine on my own," said Stephan defiantly, and he stepped back and brought up his clenched fists.

Dregor scowled and asked, "Do you know how I survived the drake that killed my parents?"

A deep, grumbling, bear-like growl began to emanate from Dregor's chest. Stephan began to say something but instead caught the end of Dregor's crutch in the mouth. Stephan fell to the ground, spitting blood and teeth out on the cobblestones. Dregor continued to beat Stephan mercilessly and refused to relent until he began to crawl and make pig noises at Dregor's bidding.

At last, the thrashing stopped, and Stephan rolled over and cried, "Why? He is not even your brother!"

Dregor growled back at Stephan, "For Hillmen, family is a choice. Halagre took me as a son. I take Dareth as a brother. I choose to love him and hate you, and as long as I'm around, you will not touch him!"

- - -

DARETH WOKE UP IN A cold sweat. He was not seven; he was thirty-five. He was not a skinny young boy, but the only surviving knight of

Hillsbrand. Getting out of his bed quietly, so as not to disturb his wives, he stood in the dark and stretched with a yawn.

Suddenly, he heard the murmur of a whispering voice from somewhere downstairs. Dareth could feel his hair stand on end as he left the room. He went to the weapon rack that he kept in the upstairs hall and took his runed claymore from it. Looking down the stairs of his home, he saw a pale lavender light coming from what must be his den. Raising his sword, he proceeded down his stairs carefully and quietly.

The whispering voice came through the house again. "Dareth," it said. Dareth rounded the corner at the bottom of the steps and crept into the den. There, Dareth came face to face with the sad truth. There Dareth saw the skeletal face of his beloved brother Dregor. Dregor stood there, arms folded across the battered breastplate of his dwarven armor. The enchantments within him illuminated his entire body with an unsettling aura.

"Dregor?" whispered Dareth ecstatically. Paying no mind that his brother was a skeleton encased in armor, he grabbed him and hugged him. Dregor gave out a faint laugh.

"Why are you here? How are you here? And more importantly, how long can you stay?" asked Dareth.

Dregor motioned toward the bench against the den wall and sat down. Dareth joined him on the bench and put his arm around Dregor's neck.

"Brother, I have missed you. Thank you so much for saving our skin in the war; we were completely over matched."

"From what I saw, there was a knight on the north wall worth the strength of a hundred imperials!" whispered Dregor.

"I was enraged. The world had ended, and nothing would have pleased me more than to be struck down to rise again at your side!" declared Dareth grimly.

Dregor turned his head slowly and whispered, "You were not the only one to say that. Into the field and into the graves I went, giving the fallen the same choice I was given by Kylratha. I have mustered a mighty army by giving them the choice either to pass away in peace or to walk the world again and keep the darkness that gathers in the void from spilling into this world."

"Kylratha raised the dead to terrorize this city, nothing more," argued Dareth.

"No, brother, he raised us to battle the imperials. The dead attacked only those who attacked them first. Kylratha did not anticipate the great power of the adventurous youths that arose in the night. It impressed him greatly and gave him hope for the future. Kylratha, in his eternity of service, indeed had become a danger even to those he loved. However, before his shame overcame him, and sorrow took his life, he gave his lordship of the fallen to me and gave me a new mission," hissed Dregor in his deathly voice.

"What mission is that, brother?" asked Dareth, his interest now truly piqued.

"Kylratha told me to march south," answered Dregor.

"Ah, to make war on the empire," stated Dareth.

"No! That is a matter for the living, brother. There lies, in the south, an ancient servant of Dagoth. She marshals an army of the half dead to her island necropolis. When her numbers are great enough, and her demon fleets are built, she will cover this world in death and sit at the head of all tables," whispered Dregor.

"So you're leading this army to defeat her. What's to stop your soldiers from joining her?" asked Dareth.

"Because they have made a choice and walk freely in the world under my banner. They would not become slaves to her will. Kylratha gave me his authority over the fallen; it cannot be countered. However, we don't go to open war. We will give them a choice first. The only one need be destroyed is her."

"Then why are you here, brother?" asked Dareth.

"We didn't want to leave without explaining first. We wanted to say goodbye," replied Dregor.

"We?" inquired Dareth curiously.

"As I said before, I gave many the same choice Kylratha gave me," answered Dregor.

Out of the darkness in the corner stepped Jilian. Dareth sprang from the bench. The words stolen from his mind, all he could squeak out was "Jil—"

Jilian, her eyes whitening with death, and her skin blue and drawn, stood still. She reached out and wiped the tears from Dareth's face with her cold fingers. Dareth spun around toward Dregor, a look of burning rage in his eyes and said, "What have you done?"

"I gave her a choice, if for nothing more than to see you again," replied Dregor.

"Kill me! Or I shall do it myself. We can all walk the mists of the world together!" begged Dareth desperately. Feeling Jilian's cold hand on his shoulder, Dareth turned to face her. Lacking the power of speech, she looked long into his eyes and then shook her head slowly in disapproval.

"She says that it would be a waste, for it is something that will happen eventually. She says that she will always love you, and she wants you to live happily with your new wives. She likes them very much. Then one day, you shall be reunited, and we will fight to keep the darkness at bay together," explained Dregor.

Jilian took Dareth's hand and kissed it. He immediately felt all the strength leave his body and fell asleep. He woke to the pale beams of daylight coming through his bedroom window and sat up suddenly.

"Bad dreams, husband?" asked Danielle, who was startled awake.

"No, sad dreams, my love. Sad, but good," said Dareth as he pulled the sheets over them both.

Of Gayle and William

Gayle had been a woman of high spirits all her life, but now she spent all her days crying. She was grieving the recent loss of most of her childhood friends in the war. She was angry at herself for being strong enough to survive the war but not powerful enough to save her friends. The loss of her parents, seventeen years ago, had been a hard-enough loss, as had been the loss of her brother, whom had died along side his parents in the square.

Back then, she found joy in her new marriage to the wizard Erik Ironrod, as well as healing with the birth of her son Jetherion. After the loss of her family, her duties as the newly appointed princess of Hillsbrand kept her mind distracted from her grief.

Now was a different story. Her husband, who was busy with the reconstruction of the city, was of little comfort. Her son, Jetherion, now seventeen years old, was mourning the loss of his lover.

Jetherion had become grim and short-tempered, and he seldom came home. He would not eat or sleep for days at a time, and he spent his days walking the streets, slowly talking to himself. This only added to Gayle's grief. She felt powerless as the princess and useless as a mother. She put her head against the wall of the den and clenched her teeth, fighting to hold back her lamentation.

As she began to cry again, despite her best efforts, she heard someone come through the front door. Gayle left the den, and there she saw her husband come through the door holding a small child in his arms. The child looked at Gayle and smiled. Barely a year old, he had a large round head and eyes equal parts blue and gold. Not all of his teeth grown in yet, giving his smile a comedic look.

Gayle shook her head and asked, "What do you have there, Erik?"

Erik smiled as he lifted the child, who began to giggle.

"An orphan of the war. His name is William, and he is ours now. He's special, I can tell," said Erik with a grin.

Erik walked up to Gayle and handed William to her, and the giggling child began to laugh and then slobber on her clothes. Gayle, caught in a combination of amusement, anger, and sadness, was speechless as she watched the child chew on her hair.

"I think he is hungry," said Erik as he walked past Gayle into the dining room.

As Gayle followed, she saw Erik touch his staff to a chair at the dinner table. The chair grew into a suitable highchair for a child William's size. Gayle let the child down, and William began to crawl away immediately.

Erik gave Gayle a hug and said, "It was agreed that every family must take a child, and I missed having a young one around. William seemed like a natural choice. I have some reading to do, so I'll let you two get acquainted."

Gayle looked unsure but said, "Well, he is the child of one of my cousins, I believe, so it makes sense, I guess."

Erik left for the den while Gayle went to the icebox and took out some milk and other food that a one-year-old could eat. Turning around, she yelped with alarm to see William in the highchair laughing and clapping.

"Is everything all right in there?" asked Erik from the other room.

"Just fine, prankster!" answered Gayle dismissively.

Gayle put a small plate of food in front of William, and he bean to eat and play with it. After a few minutes, William was covered in as much food as he had eaten. Gayle giggled at the sight; Jetherion would not have wasted a morsel of food. This baby seemed more interested in enjoying the food than devouring it like a starving animal.

Gayle was a good mother and knew what was coming next, so she went to look for the changing clothes she used to keep. When she returned with what she needed for a changing from the corner of a mostly unused cupboard, William had fallen asleep in the highchair. Gayle tried to approach quietly, but as soon as she tried to wipe the food off his face, he started to cry and reach for her. From the overpowering odor that resembled death and livestock, Gayle knew it was time for a changing.

After completing the least pleasant task of young parenthood, Gayle decided to give William a bath. The advantage of being the princess and having a wizard as a husband was that Gayle's plumbing had been the first to be restored.

She walked William upstairs while he continued to chew on her hair. Upon entering the washroom, she lit the lamp, shut the door, and let little William crawl on the floor while she ran warm water into a large copper bathtub lined in gold. Once the water was deep enough for a child to bathe, she shut the water off and turned around.

To Gayle's surprise, he wasn't on the floor, and she turned immediately back to the sound of laughter in the tub. There, she saw William sliding around on a tub of frozen water, laughing. He kicked off the side, sliding from one end to the other on his belly laughing, but soon he began to shiver.

Gayle pushed open the door and shouted Erik's name down toward the stairs.

"What?" came an annoyed voice from downstairs, as a spray of warm water splashed Gayle. She spun back around to see William splashing in a tub of warm steaming water. Gayle, now annoyed by Erik's old pranks, finished giving William a bath and drained the tub. She turned to grab a towel that she had brought, but it was not there. Gayle by this time was not surprised to see little William wrapped in the towel looking up at her wild-eyed from the bottom of the tub. She picked him up, squeezing a giggle out of him and then cradling him against her chest, and stormed downstairs.

Gayle entered the den to see Erik engrossed in a book of Feyara' runes. She walked up and smacked him on the back of the head.

"What was that for?" asked Erik, now a little angry.

"Because!" answered Gayle, looking down at William, now asleep with his head against her chest. William was smiling slightly and humming with each breath.

Gayle smiled and said softly, "This fits."

Jetherion's Passion

Jetherion spent the first days after Emry's burial in complete despair. The guilt he felt for being at hand when she was killed was overwhelming. He could no longer sleep, too troubled in his mind to relax, and every time he closed his eyes, the image of Emry dying continued to play over and over in his head. The pain in his heart was real both emotionally and physically. He could not eat. The pain of his heartache was so intense that the feeling of nausea wouldn't leave him.

"Why couldn't I save her?" he kept saying to himself.

Jetherion quickly became tired of those trying to offer him comfort or sympathy. He began to snap at people, even his own family. On one occasion, he did an enormous amount of damage to the east wall just because his mother tried to give him a hug. Jetherion was angry at himself, mostly for not being able to find any words to say to Grimhold and Ruby. Jetherion felt truly in love with Emry, but he had never really had a way to express himself other than holding and loving her. He felt so much regret over not having filled the awkward silences with Emry with meaningful words.

Jetherion began to walk outside the city walls to avoid other people, for hours at a time at first and then for days. He did not eat or sleep and drank only a few sips of water a day. He began to spend most of his time on the slopes north of Hillsbrand.

The slopes were where the host of dead had slain the eyes of Dagoth. They were considered a haunted place now, and few people would dare go there.

There on the northern slopes, after several days of wandering in dark thought and sleeping under the stars in the autumn air, he awoke hearing a whisper. He looked over the hills south, toward Hillsbrand, and to the slopes toward the mountains. He saw no one. The starlight bathed the hills in celestial light. The stones that littered the hillside were scintillated with the silver light of the heavenly lamps of the night sky.

Then another whisper came. "Jetherion," the voice said.

"Who is that?" answered Jetherion, spinning round and looking in every direction.

"My love—" The voice began to sound like Emry.

"Emry?" asked Jetherion suspiciously. "How do I know it's you?"

"My right name is really Emerald, daughter of Grimhold, of the clan called Iron Caps. My father started calling me Emry right away because I was an abrasive child, with a very loud cry. Ask my father this; he will tell you the truth," answered the voice.

"Why can I not see you then?" replied Jetherion, still looking around and trying to follow the sound of the voice.

"I have passed from life into death. You are still very much alive. Your eyes cannot see me yet. They are still filled with the living world. All we can do for now is talk."

Jetherion, still unsure of the voice, spent many hours walking slowly over the northern hills, asking every question he could think of. By the time the sun rose, Jetherion was somewhat convinced. He then spent days on end slowly treading the city streets, talking with Emry.

To all the onlookers who did not hear the voice, it seemed as though Jetherion was just talking to himself. However, for Jetherion, this was his chance to finally share all the tender words he somehow could not find while Emry was alive.

After days more had passed, Jetherion asked, "Why do you have so few words to comfort me with, Emry?"

"My love, I wish to show you that I do," Emry answered.

She gave instructions for Jetherion to visit the outdoor forge. Upon arriving, Jetherion looking around at the smithy and said, "Emry, we never exchanged kind words while you were working."

"Before I show you, you in turn must promise me something," said the voice.

"Anything, my darling dwarf," answered Jetherion with a smirk.

"After I give you my words, I must go to that next place. You must again find the strength to stay here. Return home. There is food set out for you where we shared our last meal together. I want you to eat and find comfort in my words that I left for you beneath the anvil," Emry said.

Jetherion, still unsure of whether the voice was real or his imagination running wild, lunged toward the anvil and knocked it off its stone base. There, carefully tucked away in a hollow of the base was a small leather book wrapped in Emry's dress sash. He held the sash to his face and inhaled its sweet perfume.

"Goodbye, my love," said the voice, now clearer than ever, from behind.

Jetherion spun around and beheld through the tears in his eyes the fading image of Emry sitting on the stone fence of the smithy, smiling and waving goodbye. Jetherion dove for the image of Emry, only to smash the fence to rubble with his head. He looked up, and she was gone.

Gripping the book in his hand and gritting his teeth, he stood and walked slowly toward his home. As he entered the house, he went as instructed to the dining room table. Gayle had set out a sandwich and some milk every day around this time, hoping Jetherion would come in and eat.

Paying no attention to the food, he opened the small book. It was Emry's journal. Looking at the last entry first, Jetherion started reading.

Now that I am truly in love with my prince, I no longer fear what is to come. I am as happy now as I will ever be, and as the Empire approaches, I know if I fall, and if my love lives on, then so shall I. He will live in my heart forever, and I in his.

—*E.G.*

Jetherion cried aloud. He sorrowed and lamented and wept some more. He did not have a reckoning of the time. For him, it was an endless baptism of sadness and loss. When his eyes finally cleared, he was staring down at the food. Eating and drinking for the first time in weeks, he began to read Emry's journal, filling his head with bittersweet memories.

On the high northern slopes, looking down onto the city of Hillsbrand, Dregor was hunched forward, leaning on his long sword. He whispered, "Very good, Jilian, you are proving most helpful already."

The air next to Dregor began to waver with a heat like mirage. Out of which the image of Emry appeared. As if the air itself painted a new woman in her place in a series of colorful strokes' The image of Emry was replace with that of Jilian's.

She bowed slightly and said, "Thank you, my lord. I believe everything is in order here. The relics and enchantments of Kylratha serve us well." "Yes. Yes, indeed," whispered Dregor.

The two undead then became cloaked in a shroud of mist and departed south through the hills and beyond, into the waiting empire.

Glossary

ANCIENT—In some cases, the eldest of elves are referred to as ancients. "Ancients" is a reference strictly to age, not knowledge or ability, although they usually go hand in hand in most cases. "Ancient" refers to elves who were considered elders as far back as the elves' arrival on Avalon. By the time Erik arrives in the tree, only two remain in the world of Grea'nock: Kylratha and Enock.

ARCH MAGE—The title given by the house of Gnomare' to someone considered to have the knowledge and abilities of a grand master in more than two types of enchantment.

AVALON—The world the elves came from before they arrived on Grea'nock.

AVALONIAN IRON—A black metal with an adamantine luster and a slightly red aventuresence. It is a metal originating from Avalon and appears in Grea'nock only on rare occasions and in small amounts. It is used to temper and strengthen steel objects to an almost indestructible level.

BURIAL MOUNDS—The graves of the kings of the ancient Hillmen nations. The Hillmen had kings as rulers for only a few hundred years before their kingdom fragmented from constant attacks by dragons. The Hillmen then began to live in small nomadic tribes and no longer used burial mounds.

CALENDAR—The Grea'nock year consists of exactly 400 twenty-six-hour days. The Grea'nock year breaks down into ten months of forty days. The months break up into different seasons depending on the geographical location of the people. For instance, the people of Hillsborough have an early and late spring (two months); early and late summer (two months); early, mid, and late fall (three months, perhaps due to wishful thinking around harvest time); and early and late winter (two months).

In contrast, the Vanguard people of Mason Prime, being farther south geographically, have a cooler climate. Instead, they recognize winter as having three months.

CHANGELING CHRYSOBERYRL—A very rare gemstone on Grea'nock that not only shows several colors at once but also shows different colors under different types of light.

CHANNELING—A form of enchantment used by Hillmen hunters to take on the attributes of their tribal totem.

CHANTING—A way for lesser spells to be cast; also a way for incredibly complex spells to be cast by powerful wizards or wielders of enchantment who are weak in their conjuring.

CONJURING—A term used to describe the level of focus and inner strength of a spell caster. Example: Erik was strong enough in his conjuring, or Jase was too weak in his conjuring.

CRAFTING ENCHANTMENT—A very powerful type of enchantment created to aid already-existing crafts by allowing the user to manipulate the nature of the material being worked. Also, these enchantments allow the user to imbue or endow objects with energy or enchantment they could not normally hold.

DAGOTH—An extremely powerful and immortal being that arrived in the ancient prehistory of Grea'nock. Also known as the first evil, he was first imprisoned by the elves and then later destroyed by a superhuman being called Kingsteel.

DARBECK—Originally a species of enchanted mammals from the great forested regions of Grea'nock. Once they were beautiful and iridescently pelted animals similar to the flying fox of Earth. They are now large and apish bat-like creatures enslaved to the will of the servants of Dagoth.

DEMON—Any creature or being that arrived in Grea'nock with Dagoth, as well as some creatures later manipulated into his service.

DWARFS—One of the indigenous races of Grea'nock. Although shorter than most men by a few feet, they are nearly as broad as they are tall and are incredibly strong. They are traditionally communal people who live in very large families and prefer to live and work in a subterranean environment. They are not immortal but live very long lives, averaging about 500 years of hard labor-filled life.

EDICT OF STARBLADE—The last command of the usurper King Morgan Starblade also known as the usurper king, requiring the four elven houses to go into hiding and not bother with the conflicts between men and dwarfs.

ELDARE'—The elves of the house of Eldare' are considered the lords of Elvendom. The Eldare' do not rule from birth like royalty, but rather as they become elders, they are set to govern different facets of elven society. This tradition was ended after the usurper King Morgan Starblade passed the Edict of Starblade and abdicated his rule of the elvish people. The house of Eldare' was the smallest in number among the four houses. Never being more than a few hundred strong, they also were also had the fewest elders.

ELDER—"Elder" refers to an adult elf. born on Avalon of the generation sired by the Scions.

ELF STONES—Jewels made synthetically through the flame fusion of chemicals. They are highly prized on Grea'nock because of their clarity and size, not often found in naturally occurring minerals. The elves do not often make jewels strictly for decoration, and instead they use minerals as a way of focusing light or enchantments, thus making elf stones truly rare.

ELLHOM—The Tree of Two Worlds, Ellhom, is Enock's supreme achievement in the field of life enchantments. Ellhom is the largest tree on Grea'nock and was first planted in the days after the destruction of Dagoth as a symbol of new beginnings. Enock alone constructed the city of the tree and grew Ellhom to its full maturity in only a matter of years. Later, after the Edict of Starblade, Enock opened his home to the rest of the House of Gnomare'.

ELTERION—An elder of the house of Gnomare' known as the Grand Master Bowyer of all Elvendom. He is also a grand master in the use of most of the melee weapons used in the elvish style of combat. However, ironically, he is not renowned for great skill with a bow.

ELTRINIA—The mother of Ellay and the onetime lover of the High Lord Kylratha. She was an ancient of the house of Gnomare' and a grand master engineer. After finishing her magnum opus (the construction of the deep forges), she felt the presence of Kylratha calling to her from the deeps of the caverns beneath the tree. There in the shadows, she and Kylratha conceived Ellay. Kylratha stayed hidden near the roots of the City of Ellhom during her pregnancy. However, he melted away into the shadows with despair after feeling the spirit of Eltrinia leave during the birth of his daughter Ellay.

ELVENDOM—Refers to the elves who inhabit both Avalon and Grea'nock. The immortals known as elves who exist elsewhere are not considered part of Elvendom.

ELWAYNE—The high master of the combat arts in the city of the tree. He is in fact the understudy of Elterion, who retired from training new students. Elwayne was formerly the captain of High Guard of the tree, but after seeing Kirin's awesome talent, he stepped down from the post.

EYE OF DAGOTH—A creation of Dagoth after he was blinded in the first wars with the four houses. The eyes of Dagoth were made from the mutilated corpses of giant darbeck and carry large crystal globes in their skulls. They were originally a means for Dagoth to see despite his injuries.

After the destruction of Dagoth, they began serving as the watchdogs of his most powerful servants.

FEYARA'—The elves of the house of Feyara' are considered the greatest artists and medics among the elves, as well as the clergy of the elvish people. The house of Feyara' is not without its warriors, and in the ancient days, it boasted the largest and most powerful armies of the four houses. After the Edict of Starblade, the house of Feyara' retreated to the hidden city of High Feyar constructed for them by the Gnomare'. There the house of Feyara' has since splintered into several factions that have kept an uneasy balance of power among the people.

FIRE ENCHANTMENTS—One of the many achievements of Kylratha during his role in the battle for the Sanctuary of Starts. Before this, it was not possible to manipulate fire by runes or enchantment.

FORTRESS WARS—A fifteen-year conflict between the Vanguard empire and their giant fortress cities and the dwarven kingdoms in their mountain halls. The war came to an uncertain end 400 years before the meeting of Jase and Erik Ironrod. The dwarven empire was winning the field against the last standing fortress city when word came of the largest of the delves being suddenly destroyed. Halting their advance and striking an uneasy truce with the remaining Vanguard, they turned their blame to the remaining elves still aiding the Vanguard.

GNOMARE'—The elves of the house of Gnomare' are considered to be the greatest scientists and engineers of Elvendom. The Gnomare' also have many powerful warriors and have devised many different types of weapons and warfare unique to their house. After the Edict of Starblade, the Gnomare' retreated to the city of the tree as well as High Feyar.

GREAT COLD DRAKE—The juvenile form of the giant flying dragons that inhabit the frozen regions of Grea'nock. These drakes are monstrously large from a very young age. As juveniles, they are as large as many fully grown dragons of other breeds. These drakes not only are prized for the beauty and rarity of their hides, but also their scales are the most durable among drakes. They are extremely difficult to hunt because they nest in the most inaccessible parts of mountain ranges and soar high above cloud cover, offering no target for would-be hunters.

HIGH FEYAR—The elves of Gnomare' and Feyara' both call this enchanted city home. It was originally constructed by the Gnomare' as an observation post to warn against dragon attacks. It was later expanded after the destruction of Dagoth. Later, the Feyara' constructed the cathedrals of power and colony houses of artisans in place of the Gnomare' observatories. Though some Gnomare' still call High Feyar home, they are fewer in number than in the ancient days. The house of Feyara' has grown and possesses strength of arms and enchantment unmatched among the elven houses.

HILLMEN—One of the indigenous races of Grea'nock, the Hillmen have existed since the beginnings of all written histories as a tribe of hunters. They consider the historical figure Shames the great to be their patron saint or father.

IRILIA, HALF-ELVEN—Irilia, half-elven of the house of Feyara', was one of the dozen half-elf children whom the young Jase brought to the logging camp, called Hillsborough, at the end of the fortress wars. Irilia was the only one to stay after reaching adolescence and took up employment as a medic in the local hospital. Irilia, in her four hundred years of service to Hillsborough, was unmatched in her ability to heal and became an irreplaceable facet within the community. Sadly, Irilia met her end at the hands of the Vanguard heavy infantry, sent to subjugate Hillsborough on the night that Erik returned from the city of the tree.

IRON CAP CLAN—One of the many clans of dwarfs that have enjoyed success even after the great fortress wars. The Iron Caps are especially well known for their metal craft and engineering.

KING'S SPEECH—The enchantment of powerful speech unique to the house of Eldare'. The originator of this enchantment is unknown. However, it has been the means by which the house of Eldare' has kept order in Elvendom since the arrival of the four houses in Avalon.

KINGSTEEL—The man known as Kingsteel was born Drake Trollsbane of Scythesdale, the son of a blacksmith who lived in the plains region east of the great forest of Grenerret. Kingsteel is the greatest hero in the lore of Grea'nock. In the final battle with Dagoth at his fortress called Ironsheol, Kingsteel, with the aid of Morgan Starblade, Kylratha, and many other heroes of ancient legend, succeeded in destroying Dagoth where all others had failed.

KYLVARA'—The house of Kylvara' has, from the beginning of the immortals, been set apart from the other houses. The Kylvara' are like other elves in name only. They differ not only in the forms they inhabit but also in the very nature of their essence. Little is known about where they came from before their arrival on Avalon, beyond the fact that Kylratha was their lord, and his authority was without equal, even above the King's speech. The Kylvara' reluctantly lived and worked alongside of their cousins while on Avalon. After the arrival of the four houses on Grea'nock, the Kylvara' separated themselves from their cousins. The Kylvara' then divided their efforts between pursuing Dagoth and his minions and strengthening the societies of men and dwarfs against Dagoth's presence in the world. They eventually withdrew from their lives among men and dwarfs after the fortress wars. They have remained in the shadows of Grea'nock, on the hunt for Dagoth's servants, ever since.

LAND DRAKE—The juvenile form of the land-walking dragons that inhabit the temperate regions of Grea'nock. Large crocodile like creatures from birth, they are lethal from the moment they hatch. They become truly enormous over several hundred years. Once they become too large to hunt prey inland, they migrate to the sea in order to reach adulthood and become aware.

LAYLA—A young maiden skilled in the pleasure arts in the city of the tree. Layla, from an early age, has been known as a challenging and fearless spirit. She has openly spoken out against the Edict of Starblade on many occasions.

LIFE ENCHANTMENTS—The life enchantments were first a creation of the house of Feyara' as a means of medicine after their arrival on

Grea'nock. The life enchantments have since been applied in a wide variety of circumstances, from agriculture to warfare.

MOUNTAINFOLK—One of the indigenous races of Grea'nock. They are the largest of the races of men and in some cases tower over their cousins by several feet. Being a peaceful race of mostly loggers and trappers, only a few throughout the histories of Grea'nock have achieved great renown, one of them being Jetherion Trollsbane, the father of the warrior smith called Kingsteel.

OGRE—Sometimes called the fists of Dagoth, ogres were the foot soldiers of Dagoth from the beginning. Little is known about these ancient demons except that they arrived out of the void with Dagoth as his loyal servants. Immortal and with a might unmatched by the peoples of Grea'nock, they advanced across the land without opposition until the arrival of the four houses.

ORIGINAL SEED-The generation of elves that first arrived on Avalon. This generation was for the most part younger than the guardian saints of the houses. Some where in fact sire from the saints them selves. The Original Seed are sometimes referred to as the lost generation having sacrificed themselves early in the war against Dagoth to ensure a save decent in to underworld.

QUADRIAN—The Quadrian are the true outcasts of Grea'nock. A Quadrian is a being born from a human and a half-elf. Most Quadrians were born in the days before the fortress wars. Quadrian elves are immortal, yet many have perished as a result of their spirits becoming too powerful for their bodies to contain.

RUNES—Runes are the written form of elven enchantment. Runes serve as conduits in time and space, from the fire and energy of Avalon to the world of Grea'nock. The style and intensity of the rune determines the form of the energy it assumes in the world of Grea'nock.

RUNIC ARCHERY—One of the supreme achievements of elven warfare on Grea'nock. It allows a rune to travel at great speed through Grea'nock, multiplying the intensity of the rune many times over. The bow is merely the means of delivery, and only the sharpest elvish minds have ever mastered it.

RUNIC MASTERY—Runic mastery is a field of enchantment that allows the wielder to change the nature of a rune at any time, depending on the strength and focus of the master.

SAINTS—There were upon the elves arrival on Avalon four saints one to protect and teach each house. The saint were the wielders of mighty weapons that later became the symbol of each house. Two of the saints perished within the underworld of Ironsheol in combat against Dagoth. The weapons the Saints wielded were then passed the the eldest or most worthy elf of that house. That elf became known as a sword saint but even with the sword of sainthood was only a remnant of the ancient power wielded by the true saint.

SCERPENT—Scerpents are the enchanted and immortal creatures that used to rule the skies of ancient Grea'nock. Dagoth, jealous of their power and grace, devoted many ages to the capture and corruption of them, giving birth to dragons and many other leviathan-like creatures.

SCIONS—The generation of elves born on Avalon sire from the generation know as the original seed. Scions are refereed to as such because they came to their full maturity on Avalon and inherited the fullness of their parents strength and knowledge the same can not be said for any other generation of elves afterward.

SHAMES THE GREAT—One of the legendary companions of Kingsteel and a friend to Morgan Starblade. Shames was the first to unite and rule over the scattered tribes of Hillmen throughout ancient Grea'nock.

SIGILS—The written form of dwarven or dwarvish enchantment. Sigils change the energy inside a given substance without actually adding any enchantment of their own, thus making sigils very useful in crafting with enchanted or energetic materials and in enhancing items that may already hold enchantments.

THRONE OF AGES—The most sacred of places in elvish lore. It was where the first of all elves were brought together throughout the cosmos to receive their orders from the King of All Immortals.

VANGUARD—The Vanguard are the blend of the now-extinct plains tribes mingled with the blood of Hillmen and Mountainfolk. The Vanguard have named themselves so because they have seen themselves as ahead of what they call their savage brethren.